THE
SOUTHERN
VINEYARD

PETER O'MAHONEY

The Southern Vineyard: An Epic Legal Thriller
Joe Hennessy Legal Thrillers Book 6

Peter O'Mahoney

ALSO BY PETER O'MAHONEY

In the Joe Hennessy Legal Thriller series:

THE SOUTHERN LAWYER
THE SOUTHERN CRIMINAL
THE SOUTHERN KILLER
THE SOUTHERN TRIAL
THE SOUTHERN FRAUD

*****

In the Tex Hunter Legal Thriller series:

POWER AND JUSTICE
FAITH AND JUSTICE
CORRUPT JUSTICE
DEADLY JUSTICE
SAVING JUSTICE
NATURAL JUSTICE
FREEDOM AND JUSTICE
LOSING JUSTICE
FAILING JUSTICE
FINAL JUSTICE

THE SOUTHERN VINEYARD

JOE HENNESSY LEGAL THRILLER BOOK 6

PETER O'MAHONEY

CHAPTER 1

"If you want to get rich from crime, become a defense lawyer."

Criminal defense attorney Joe Hennessy recognized the voice that called out to him. He hadn't heard that long Southern drawl for many years, but he didn't miss it. He stopped outside his office, turning on the sidewalk to face the man waiting for him.

"Bernard Palin," Hennessy said as he wiped the sweat from his brow. A storm brewed over Charleston, South Carolina, and the city was drenched in jungle-like humidity. "I don't have time for you. Take your lies somewhere else."

"I have a lot of cash, Joe," Bernard Palin stated as he stepped away from his black sedan. Palin was a solid man with a round face, pale skin, and a double chin. His hair was gray and wispy, his eyelids drooped, and his nose was too large for his face. He wore a suit without a tie, with brown leather shoes, and a brown leather belt. "And I have enough cash to save your precious vineyard."

Hennessy didn't respond. For five years, he'd poured his heart and soul into saving his vineyard from the banks. During the weekdays, he worked as a defense lawyer in Charleston, trying to scrape together enough money to prevent a default on his loans.

"I thought that'd get your attention." Palin stepped forward, looking up at Hennessy's towering figure. "You're looking good, Joe. Even in your late fifties, you're still fit and strong. What's your secret?"

Again, Hennessy didn't respond. He had no interest in conversation with his old college classmate.

"Sure, I get it." Palin waved his non-response away. "It's been years since you and I sat down to chat. It'd be good to catch up as old friends."

"We're not friends. We never were."

Palin shrugged. "That's ok. I won't take any offense to that. We'll keep our relationship professional. And I like that attitude—don't get too close to your clients." Palin pulled a tissue from his pocket and dabbed the sweat from his brow. "Let's go somewhere quieter to speak. I have a sensitive matter I need you to work on."

"I've heard about your case, and you already have a lawyer."

"But he's not a very good one. He says the only option I have is to take a deal and spend some time in prison. I don't want to do that." Palin shrugged. "His attitude has made me realize I need the best lawyer on this case, and everyone around town is talking about you. And I'm willing to gamble a hundred-thousand-dollar retainer that says you can win my case."

As a man full of integrity, Hennessy hated that money had such a rule over him.

Without another word, Hennessy turned toward his office, opened the door, and entered. He strode up the steps, two at a time, and marched through the reception area. His assistant Jacinta was already there, working early so she could leave in the afternoon to volunteer at her child's school. Hennessy greeted Jacinta but didn't introduce Palin to her. He led Palin into his separate office, placed his briefcase down, and indicated toward the seat in front of his hefty mahogany desk.

"You have five minutes," Hennessy said as he sat down. "Start talking."

"This is a lovely office." Palin rolled his tongue around his mouth as he entered, looking over the bookshelf to the left of the room before he sat down. He leaned back in his chair, taking a long moment to get comfortable. "Life has a funny way of doing things, doesn't it? Here we are again, decades after we last talked. Our lives have taken very different paths, Joe. I remember when we were in our twenties, studying at college, young men with lots of energy and bright hopes for the future. They were good times, weren't they? The days when we could drink all night and still go to class the next day. Remember those times?"

Hennessy didn't answer, leaning back in his chair and crossing his arms.

"And I've heard about your vineyard Upstate. Outside Greenville, isn't it?" Palin continued. "And I've heard how a few bad seasons of droughts meant you had to return to Charleston to earn enough money to keep it. That's tough, but still, it must've been nice to raise your daughters around the vineyard. That's the dream. How's your family? Wendy was your wife's name, wasn't it?"

"My family is none of your business."

"And what was your boy's name? The one who was murdered in a botched kidnapping. Luca, wasn't it?"

Hennessy stood. The chair was pushed back behind him.

Palin flinched and raised his hands in surrender. "I didn't mean any offense. Please sit down. I don't want to fight with you."

Hennessy glared at Palin and then eased himself back into the chair. "Get to the point."

Palin dabbed his brow with a tissue again. "As you may have heard on the news, I've been hit with several felony fraud charges, but I was set up. My current lawyer is certain we won't win at trial and wants me to take a deal for fifteen years in prison, but I'm too old for that nonsense. If I listened to him, I'd die behind bars. I don't want that. That's why I need your skills. I need you to keep me out of prison."

"Why don't you run? You've got the money."

"I had the money, but it was frozen by the cops. If I ran, I'd be running with nothing, and after the life I've led, that'd be just as bad as prison. And then there's the ankle monitor. They gave me this thing after I got bail, and it's been a pain ever since. They put the thing on too tight, and it rubs against my skin all day and all night. Trust me, I've looked at ways to get rid of it, but nothing seems like it would work." Palin scratched his right ankle and then groaned. "After a tip-off, my accounting firm was the target of a fraud investigation, and they charged me with embezzling a million dollars from a charity foundation, but none of it is true. I was set up. Someone within my firm embezzled the money and made it look like I did it."

"You've been corrupt your entire life, and it's caught up with you. That's karma."

"I'll admit that parts of my past haven't been on the straight and narrow, but I didn't do this crime. Isn't that what the law is for? Justice shouldn't apply when it's convenient, it should apply at all times. I'm innocent of this crime and shouldn't be convicted."

Hennessy hated that Palin was right. "I've heard you're involved with a motorcycle gang that runs drugs through the state."

"My involvement with the Rebel Sons is legitimate. Several years ago, they invested in a construction company, Stanwell Construction, and I do their accounting. I don't do anything outside the law for them."

"The construction company is a front for money laundering."

"You're getting off-topic, Joe. Whoever set me up has got a vendetta against me. I'm well-connected, but someone went above my connections and set me up. Berkley was helping me, but someone went above him."

"Clarence Berkley?"

"That's right." A slight grin spread across Palin's face. "Your old friend and a former judge in this county."

"And a man who was disgraced from the bench after many allegations of sexual assault."

"None of which were ever proven. But again, we're getting off-topic," Palin said. "I have a lot of connections, and I'm sure I can get away from this case without prison time if I have the right lawyer. You're that lawyer, Joe. I've heard about your cases. The whole of Charleston has been talking about your clients. We've all seen you on the news. I need you in my corner."

"I don't trust that you'd pay me. You have a reputation for not paying your debts."

"That's why I'll transfer the hundred-thousand-dollar retainer as soon as you sign on. And it gets better—if you keep me out of prison, I'll pay you a two hundred-and-fifty-thousand-dollar bonus. That's enough to ride off into the sunset and retire to your vineyard Upstate."

"You mentioned your accounts have been frozen. You don't have the money to pay the retainer."

"Don't worry about the cash. I have connections that will help me out. I'll have the retainer in your bank account by the end of the week." When Hennessy didn't respond, Palin stood and began buttoning his jacket. "Good. I'm glad we've got a deal. I'll transfer half now, and when the money hits your bank account, we can go to the judge and tell them I've changed lawyers. Then I'll transfer you the other half, and you can start working on keeping me out of prison."

Palin gave Hennessy a sly wink before leaving the office.

Hennessy sat frozen, staring at the open office door. Defending Palin would mean trouble—the kind that had a way of sticking around long after the case was finalized. But then there was the vineyard, the loan, and the memory of his son etched into every vine.

As he leaned back in his chair, the leather creaking under the strain, a single thought troubled him: how much was he willing to risk to save the vineyard?

CHAPTER 2

Joe Hennessy's life had been a symphony of emotions, marked by the devastating lows of grief and heartache, and the soaring highs of love and joy.

More than twenty years earlier, he had become lost in a pit of sorrow after his ten-year-old son, Luca, was murdered. He suffered the torture of not knowing his son's killer for more than two decades. There was relief when the truth was uncovered, but the anguish remained. That grief, that terrible heartache, had defined much of his adult life, a feeling that was always there, lingering just over his shoulder, ready to confront him at unexpected times. It broke his heart when he thought of Luca—his beautiful smile, his buoyant energy, his sunny personality—but Hennessy accepted that grief was a part of his life.

With Wendy, his wife, he had escaped the pain and grief of Charleston and purchased a vineyard Upstate, raising two daughters amongst the vines. After several bad seasons on the vineyard, the Hennessys struggled to keep up with the loan payments. When the pressure from the banks became too much, Hennessy returned to Charleston to practice criminal law, earning enough money to keep the banks off their backs. But returning to Charleston had been fraught with danger. He had defended some of the city's worst people, and experienced shootings, beatings, and attempted stabbings. Through it all, he had remained steely focused. He was there for a reason, and his dream would become a reality if he could win Palin's case.

As Hennessy passed through the security scanner in the Charleston County Judicial Center courthouse foyer, he saw a familiar face behind him. Hennessy waited for the man as he had his briefcase scanned.

"Mr. Joe Hennessy." Assistant Solicitor Aaron Garrett was a youthful black man, still learning the political ropes of the Ninth Circuit Solicitor's Office, but a competent lawyer whose reputation was growing. In his early thirties, Garrett had a charming smile, a quick wit, and a powerful voice, perfect for a future in politics. "Good to see you."

"Mr. Garrett," Hennessy said as they shook hands

solidly. Hennessy respected a solid handshake. "Always a pleasure."

"Might we have a chat in private?"

Hennessy nodded, and Garrett led him through the foyer, and into one of the conference rooms on the first floor. Garrett held the door open for Hennessy and stepped inside. The windowless meeting room was small, and the oak conference table took up much of the space. Five new office chairs, with barely a mark on them, sat around the outside. A musty smell hung heavy in the air.

"I must say I was surprised when I saw your name on the Substitution of Counsel order for Bernard Palin's case," Garrett noted as he sat down. He drummed his hands on the edge of the table and leaned back. "Do you know what you're getting yourself in for?"

"I've read the case file."

"And you know the reputation of the defendant?"

Hennessy nodded. "I've known Bernard Palin for years."

"When I first read the charges, I couldn't believe it. I didn't think there could be a more despicable act. Palin was the accountant for the Wolfgang Berger

Foundation for half a decade, and he stole from them every year he worked for them. Based on the evidence, he was about to jump on a plane, fly to Costa Rica, and never return. And the more I looked at the evidence, the more furious I became that he would steal from vulnerable children. I'm sure any jury is going to feel the same. I can't understand how anyone could steal from sick and vulnerable children, but even more confusing is why you want to be associated with this case."

"Bernard Palin deserves a fair trial."

"The money was supposed to help struggling families. Families with sick kids and no money, or orphaned kids with health issues, or immigrant children with no other place to go. That's heartbreaking stuff. You and I both know the emotional component of this crime will influence any jury's decision. And the public, well, they're going to have so much hate for Palin."

"What's your point?"

"I'm saying that, as always, that hate will rub off on the defense lawyer. You'll do your best to defend your client, you'll do your job, and the public will hate you for it. They'll ask you, 'How could he defend someone who stole from sick children?' Is that what you want? To be hated by an entire city?"

"Any insinuation that the charges are more serious because of the victim's circumstance is prejudicial."

"Prejudicial?" Garrett smiled and shook his head. He leaned back in his chair, stretching one arm out wide to rest on the back of the chair next to him. "This crime is despicable. The lowest of the low. We've got the media reports prepared, and it doesn't look good for him. Bernard Palin is not likable. The media will eat him alive, and I'm surprised you'll stand next to him. Everyone that sees you with him will come to the same conclusion—that you approve of his actions."

"You can't allow this case to be a trial by media." Hennessy leaned forward, resting his elbows on the table. "This is a court case, not a popularity contest. If public opinion decided criminal trials, we'd be no better than a lynch mob."

"Don't give me that spin," Garrett scoffed. He leaned forward and pressed his index finger into the table. "I'll make it clear for you so there's no misunderstanding—this will be a very public court case. There's an election next year, and this trial will be a very easy way for our office to score points with the public. The jury won't even spend an hour deciding on Palin's guilt. You'll look like a fool, and the public will congratulate my office for such an amazing job."

"You need to win first."

"There's next to zero chance that we don't win. Have you even looked at the case file? This is open, shut, wrapped up, sealed, and sent to the records department."

"He claims he was set up."

"Of course, he would. That's his only excuse, and he's only saying that because he doesn't want to go to prison. I'd wish you luck for the case, but you'll need a lot more than that."

Garrett stood, tapped his hand on the table twice, offered Hennessy a half smile, and then left the room.

Hennessy remained seated, taking a moment to consider the conversation. The case was going to attract a lot of media attention. That worried him. And Garrett was right—Bernard Palin wasn't a likable man in any way, and the charges were despicable. The jury wouldn't warm to him, and with a convincing media release from the Circuit Solicitor's Office, the public would despise him.

After a minute of quiet consideration, Hennessy grunted, tapped his fist on the wooden table, and left the conference room. He walked into Courtroom 105 moments later, where he was met with the strong scent of pine cleaning products. Brown and cream were the dominant colors in the room. The chairs were dark brown, their polished surfaces gleaming under the overhead lights, and the walls were painted in a dull cream color. The carpet was brown, the curtains were brown, and the ceiling was cream. The colors were bland and deliberately so. This wasn't a place for fun—this was a room where killers, thieves, and vile criminals had their fate decided.

Hennessy sat in the back row of the courtroom, greeting Palin and his current defense lawyer, David Jones—a middle-aged man in an ill-fitting gray suit. When they spoke on the phone, Jones had seemed eager to be rid of Palin, though he lamented the loss of the retainer.

Judge Andrew Clayton ran a tight courtroom, moving through pretrial motions at pace and delivering his decisions with little emotion. A fit man in his fifties, he was well-groomed, with a neat and trimmed brown beard and short-cropped hair. He had been a judge for just over a year and had earned a reputation for being smart, intelligent, and quick-witted.

As soon as one decision was made, Judge Clayton waved the lawyers away, and the bailiff moved on to the next case, calling out the case number.

"Criminal Case 25-CR-6575." The bailiff called out, rising above the murmur of lawyers conferring, organizing, and wading through paperwork in the gallery.

Garrett walked to the front of the courtroom, striding through the gate with confidence. Once at the prosecutor's table, he opened his laptop and typed several lines. Hennessy led Palin and Jones to the defense table.

Judge Clayton welcomed them to the court and shook his head as he read the file. He confirmed Palin's name and then asked the lawyers to identify themselves. They did so, and Judge Clayton looked at Jones.

"I see we have a motion for a Substitution of Counsel. Please explain, Mr. Jones."

"Thank you, Your Honor," Jones stood. He

placed his legal pad on the table and fumbled through the pages, looking for the correct page. When he found it, he stared at the sheet of paper with only five lines of handwritten notes. "Uh, yes. Here. The defendant wishes to change counsel for personal reasons, and I have no objection to passing the case to Mr. Hennessy, the new lawyer seated here."

"Mr. Palin," Judge Clayton looked at the defendant. "Do you understand that you're applying to change lawyers, and thus, Mr. Jones will no longer be involved in your case?"

Palin stood. "I do, Your Honor."

"Good." Judge Clayton looked at Garrett, expecting the motion to be routine. "Any objection from the State to the Substitution of Counsel order?"

"The State requests that the substitution is denied." Garrett's response was fast. Judge Clayton raised his eyebrows. Garrett didn't miss a beat, continuing with his objection. "Mr. Palin is charged with a devious and cunning crime, and the overwhelming evidence is against him. The State believes this motion is nothing more than a delay tactic by the defense team. As we raised in the bail hearing, we believe the defendant is a flight risk and we don't want to allow him the extra time to organize the chance to flee the country."

"Your Honor." Hennessy stood. He stared at Garrett for a long moment and then turned to the judge. "This motion has not been accompanied by a request to delay the trial, and there's no need for any delaying tactics. This case is in its early phases, and the files I have received are complete."

"The State also wishes to raise issues with the new attorney's suitability for the case." Garrett remained standing but didn't look in Hennessy's direction. "While we acknowledge Mr. Hennessy has expertise in handling criminal cases, he has no experience in handling felony fraud or felony breach of trust cases, and we believe it isn't in the court's interest to allow an inexperienced lawyer to substitute for an experienced one. In fact, we believe the integrity of any future trial could be called into question by the approval of this motion."

"Your Honor, this is outrageous," Hennessy argued. "I'm prepared for this trial and have handled a fraud misdemeanor charge in the last year. I've served this court as a criminal defense attorney for almost five years and have ten years of experience in the Circuit Solicitor's Office. I assure the court that I'm prepared for this case, these charges, and any future trial."

"Anything further?" Judge Clayton looked at Garrett.

"Nothing further, Your Honor, however, we repeat that we believe the integrity of this court is paramount, and approving someone with no experience in felony fraud charges may call into question the integrity of this trial."

Judge Clayton looked at Hennessy, but Hennessy's stare remained on Garrett.

"Mr. Hennessy?" Judge Clayton pressed.

"Nothing further from the defense, Your Honor."

"Then I believe that Mr. Hennessy is experienced enough in criminal cases to handle this trial, and I see no reason why Mr. Hennessy would apply for a delay of trial this early in the process. The Substitution of Counsel motion is granted."

Garrett offered no response as Judge Clayton turned to the bailiff, who called the next case number.

Hennessy packed up his notes and talked to Palin and Jones for a moment. Both expressed their surprise at Garrett's arguments. Hennessy agreed.

Once his briefcase was closed, Hennessy strode out of the courtroom's doors. In the hallway, Hennessy spotted Garrett. He called out to him. "That was a cheap shot."

Garrett smiled and walked toward Hennessy. "You can't blame a man for trying. I'd much rather face Jones than you." He lowered his tone and leaned in close. "And let it serve as a warning—I need to win this case, and I'm going to do everything to make sure that happens."

CHAPTER 3

The early morning church bells rang out over Charleston, their rhythmic chimes a familiar part of Sunday mornings in the Holy City.

Every fifteen minutes, another church added its tune to the medley. Mixed with the chirping of seagulls, the sound created the perfect backdrop for the historic city. For Joe Hennessy, the bells were more than just a melody; they were a part of his childhood, a constant in the streets of the peninsula, and the soundtrack to his youth.

Joe walked in quiet reflection, one hand in his pocket and the other holding his wife Wendy's. Together, they strolled around Colonial Lake, basking in the warmth of the morning sun that lit up Charleston in a soft, golden glow. Away from the tourist hubs, Colonial Lake offered a peaceful oasis near the Ashley River, framed by mature trees, manicured bushes, and lush green grass. The air carried the sweet scent of wisteria while birds chirped and ducks waddled by. Locals, enjoying the calm morning, exchanged friendly smiles. In such serene surroundings, it was almost impossible not to smile.

"It's a lot of money, Joe," Wendy said as she held onto her husband's hand. "It's enough to clear the arrears on the bank loan, and it'd put us in front of the payments. We'd be comfortable on the vineyard, and with a few great seasons, we might even own it outright one day."

Wendy Hennessy came from a great South Carolina family, one that had been in the state since her forefathers first arrived in 1795. While Joe worked in Charleston, she ran the operations at the vineyard, a two-hour drive away. She always enjoyed returning to her home city, spending time with her husband, and catching up with old friends over coffee.

"Before we can even start thinking about the money, I need to win the case first."

"Even the retainer would clear the arrears and put us in front of the loan."

"It's going to get messy. Palin has dangerous connections, and if I lose, it could cost more than the vineyard." He squeezed Wendy's hand and gave her a reassuring smile. "But I don't plan on losing."

"Stay safe," Wendy said, her voice warm but with a flicker of concern. She tilted her head, studying Joe as if memorizing the moment. "You're not twenty-five anymore. You're much too old for trouble. The loans aren't worth your life."

"I was speaking to a friend who recently took out a loan for an exorcism." Joe tried not to smile, but his dimples gave him away. "She was told if she doesn't repay the loan, she'll get repossessed."

"That's a terrible joke," Wendy grinned. "Do you remember when we first signed the loan, and we asked the lender what the costs would be? He said, 'our sanity.' And how right he was. We've been fortunate to have the vineyard for twenty years and raise our daughters there, but it's ok if the dream is over."

"I'm not willing to give up on it yet," Joe changed the conversation. "Have you heard from Casey?"

"Every day," Wendy smiled. "I love getting her calls in the mornings."

"She's been sending me a message every day as well. We've talked a few evenings, and she seems to be settling in."

Only a month earlier, Casey had moved out of the family home at the vineyard to attend Clemson University. She was studying Agriculture Sciences on-campus, and while it was exciting for her to spread her wings away from home, she was missing time with her mother. The drive to Clemson was only an hour from the vineyard, just enough for her to feel free but still have the safety of home nearby.

"Can you believe she's at college, and Ellie is about to finish her undergraduate degree?" Wendy smiled. "They've grown up so fast. Our girls are now young women."

"One is studying law, and the other is studying agriculture with an interest in vineyards. We've certainly inspired them," Joe smiled. "I'm so proud of them."

"As am I," Wendy sighed a little. "But it feels strange. The whole empty nest thing. It'd be nice if you were there. It's like having someone in your house for almost two decades, and then, with a snap of the fingers, they're gone. I'm so proud of our girls but I miss them so much."

Joe hated he wasn't there for Wendy as their daughters left home. While he made the drive Upstate most weekends, he hated he wasn't there for the day-to-day transition to the empty nest. He wanted to be there for Wendy, support her, and love her through the difficult times. "I'll be there soon," Joe reassured her. "And then we can build the next chapter of our lives."

"Which, hopefully, involves grandchildren at some point."

"Think Ellie will come back to South Carolina?"

"Absolutely." Wendy gripped his hand tighter. "She always wanted to spread her wings and explore the world, and her years in New York have given her that. But while there are parts of the city she likes, the hustle and bustle of big city life is too much for her. Our girls are Southern girls. They love the open air, the mountains, and the slower pace of life. They've spent their entire lives here, and they're starting to realize how lucky they are."

A young woman walking five dogs passed them, scrolling on her cell phone, the leads attached to her waist. Wendy stopped to pat one of the dogs, and Joe patted another. They chatted with the young woman, who explained she was a dog walker for some of the locals nearby. They talked about the dogs, about the beautiful morning, and about the beautiful smells in the air before they wished each other a good day.

"What are the chances of winning the case?" Wendy's smile was broad, lifted by her interaction with the happy dogs.

"The State has a strong case. From an accounting point of view, Palin was caught with his hand deep inside the cookie jar. Our strongest hopes would be to either find a hole in the charges or suggest someone else had the opportunity and motive to do it."

"And if he's guilty of stealing money from a children's charity foundation?"

Joe took a few moments to answer. "My job isn't to defend the innocent. My job is to defend everyone's constitutional right to a fair trial."

"Joseph Hennessy, don't you dare spin me a media line." Wendy's tone was firm. "My question was, how would you feel if he admitted he stole from a children's charity foundation?"

"I'd feel terrible," Joe conceded.

"And you don't think Palin's connections will save him?"

"For decades, Palin did the accounting for some of

the most influential people in this town, and he knows more secrets than most, but his influence has waned as most of those powerful people have retired, passed away, or moved on. His connections didn't stop the prosecution from charging him. That shows how little influence he has now."

"If a man like Palin is going down, he'll go down swinging hard."

Joe nodded. He knew Wendy was right—there would be danger ahead. But if he wanted to save the vineyard from the banks, if he wanted to retire from law, it was the path he had to take.

CHAPTER 4

On the fifth floor of a prominent downtown building, the glass doors to Palin Accounting displayed a sign that looked straight out of the nineties—complete with shadow effects, purple and teal accents, and outdated graphics.

Hennessy opened the door and stepped into a forlorn, almost abandoned foyer. There was no receptionist, no one near the front door, and no sound coming from within the office. An old computer monitor sat on the empty receptionist's desk, the only hint of activity, but even that seemed lifeless—no papers, files, or calendars surrounded it. There wasn't even a keyboard attached.

"Hello," Hennessy called out. "Anyone here?"

"Through the doors," Palin called back, his voice echoing through the unoccupied space.

Hennessy walked through the reception area and into a space with five office cubicles on each side of the room. But again, none had any signs of life—no photos, no pens, nothing. Hennessy continued to the separate office at the rear of the space, stepping through the open door where he found Palin hunched over a paper file.

"Joe Hennessy," Palin said as Hennessy entered the room. He sat up and spread his arms wide. "Welcome to Palin Accounting."

Palin had the first two buttons of his white shirt open, exposing his hairy chest. His thin gray hair was slicked back, his skin appeared greasy, and he smelled of cheap aftershave.

"The place is empty." Hennessy unbuttoned his suit jacket, placed his briefcase on the floor, and sat down. The chair was firm and there was no comfort to it. "Where is everyone?"

"That's none of your business."

"If you want me to win this case, then it has to be my business."

"You'll do as I tell you to do," Palin snapped, pointing his finger in Hennessy's face. "You need to remember that you work for me, which makes me your boss."

"Unless you want that finger broken, you'll put it

down."

Palin curled his finger, cowering under Hennessy's stare.

"I can see we're not going to be friends, Joe. But that's ok. I'm paying you to do a job, and that's all I need from you."

"We don't have to be friends to win this case, but you need to answer all of my questions," Hennessy said. He had spent the weekend conducting a preliminary check on his former college associate. Hennessy called his contacts, sent emails to others, and searched Palin's name online. Nobody spoke positively about Palin. Several people commented they wouldn't trust him, several more stated that he was not to be believed at any cost, and some called him corrupt and evil. Palin had made enemies over the years, that much was clear. "What happened to the staff in the office?"

Palin grunted. "A mass walkout. All ten staff quit on the same day. It came as a shock to me, and they left me in the lurch."

"What was the reason for the walkout?"

"I'm not a very nice boss, apparently. They each wrote me a resignation letter about it. Ten letters were sitting on their desks when I came in. I read the first letter but didn't read the rest of them. I don't care about them." Palin sniffed and pulled a tissue from a nearby container. He blew hard into the tissue and then coughed. "Some of them went to a rival accounting firm and others retired. The staff orchestrated it behind my back and left me here with another year on the lease of this building."

"What did your clients think of that?"

"I didn't tell them. After the staff left, I employed some contractors in India to do the work. It worked out to be less than half the price, and I didn't have to worry about personal issues. I wished I'd done it years ago. It would've saved all the effort of managing those idiots I had for staff members."

"Half the price, but half the quality?"

"They made mistakes," Palin shrugged. "And so, I lost a few clients, but that doesn't worry me. Since my wife left five years ago, I've been working toward retirement. I was just about to retire to a beachfront apartment in Costa Rica when these charges came in. I would've left the country, but they've frozen my bank accounts and taken my passport."

"How do I know you won't run to Costa Rica if I

beat the charges for you?"

"You don't think I'll pay?" He chuckled. "I guess that's understandable, but you'll just have to trust me. I mean, as soon as they cut this stupid ankle monitor off me, I won't stay in South Carolina." He reached into his desk drawer and removed a check. He stared at it for a long moment before he passed it over to Hennessy. "That's the other half of the retainer, now that the judge has approved your involvement."

Hennessy reached forward and took the check. He looked at it, studied it, and ensured it was legitimate. When he was sure it was real, he picked up his briefcase, opened it, and pulled out five sheets of paper. "I need you to sign these. It states that I can use your house for collateral if we win and you refuse to pay the rest of the legal fees."

"What?" Palin grinned. "You really don't trust me, do you, Joe?"

Hennessy didn't respond. He would be surprised if anyone trusted Palin.

Palin reached forward and snatched the forms from Hennessy. He licked his finger as he turned each sheet, then took a pen from his pocket and signed his name on the bottom of each page.

"If you could convince the judge to unfreeze some of my assets, that would help me greatly."

"The judge intentionally made the order very broad." Hennessy removed another piece of paper from his briefcase and read over it. The order to freeze your assets applied to 'The term 'assets' encompasses, but is not limited to, all forms of property, rights, and interests, including transferred assets, promissory notes, intellectual property, rental income, leases, options, bonds, annuities, contract rights, creditor rights, future interests, beneficial interests, inherited property, real estate, mortgages, easements, interests in limited liability companies and similar entities, partnership interests, stocks, securities, livestock, chattel, mineral rights, and all rights to names, images, or likenesses. It also includes any rights or interests that can be monetized, whether known or unknown, whether presently owned, held, or controlled, previously owned, held, or controlled, or to be owned, held, or controlled in the future. This applies to actual or contingent ownership, direct or indirect control, and partial or whole interests. For clarity, 'assets' also includes any property or interests that have been transferred, concealed, hidden, sold, encumbered, or otherwise disposed of, and that were previously owned, held, or controlled by you, either directly or indirectly, in full or in part.' That's the most complete order I've ever seen a judge deliver."

"That sounds like it covers absolutely everything. So, no chance it can be changed?"

"It's very unlikely."

"That's what David Jones said as well," Palin grunted. "I would've kept him, but the man was a fool. I felt like he was working for the Solicitor's Office. It seemed like he was getting kickbacks from them. He was so desperate for me to strike a deal, do some years in prison, and pay a massive fine. He wouldn't even consider taking the case to trial. He got me bail, but that was just dumb luck. At one hearing, he showed up with the wrong case file. How was I going to win with that fool?"

"He knew you weren't going to win at trial." Hennessy kept his eyes on Palin. "The State has hit you with five charges, including breach of trust, fraud, forgery, money laundering, and tax evasion. All the charges are felony charges. They've stated you set up a transfer of more than a million dollars from a charity foundation into your bank accounts. The State claims you set up false accounts, created false invoices, and made false claims in the accounting documentation."

"I didn't do it."

"Is that your defense?"

"It had to be someone else in the office. I have my suspicions about who it was. Don't you think it's a coincidence that they all got up and left at the same time, and then these charges come in only weeks later? I'm not saying I'm squeaky clean because I'm not, but I didn't do this. Someone else funneled the money out of the Foundation. They either did it to set me up, or they planned on stealing all the money to keep for themselves."

"That doesn't sound believable."

"I get it, Joe. I know why you don't believe me, but trust me, I wouldn't steal money from a children's charity foundation. You need to beat the charges for me."

"At first glance, we should be able to get two of the charges dropped. The State has loaded the charges in the hope that you'll plead guilty to at least one of them, but they don't have enough evidence to continue with the felony money laundering or tax evasion charges. They've added those charges as a negotiation tactic."

"And the other charges?"

"With the other charges—the felony breach of trust, fraud, and forgery charges—there are several defenses we can work on. One—we can claim you didn't know about the transfers, and this was all one big numbers error, or two—we can claim that others in your organization had access to those files and those accounts. As the money wasn't withdrawn from the bank account, the State will struggle to prove that you had the intent to withdraw the money. Intent is an important aspect of the charges and the weakest part of the prosecution's case."

Palin's mouth hung open a little. "I knew you'd be great at this."

"We have one major issue," Hennessy read over the notes on his legal pad. "It doesn't look like we'll win at trial. If this was a set up, then they've done well. They've made it look like you, and only you, could've done this. Where would we look if we were to build a defense that you were framed?"

"John Tilly." Palin brushed the tip of his nose. "He was the Senior Accountant and had access to everything I had access to. He was the one who could've set up the bank transfer, made the fake invoices, and changed the reports. He was also the one who led the exodus out of here."

Hennessy knew not to believe a word that came out of the man's mouth. From their early adult years together, Hennessy remembered Palin as immoral, selfish, and narcissistic—and those were his best qualities.

"That's a lot of effort to set you up. Why would John Tilly go to those lengths to do this to you?"

"When I was much younger, almost twenty years ago, I slept with his wife. They weren't married yet, but they were dating. John didn't know about it until five years ago. I was drunk and I told him about it at one of the office Christmas parties. He was shocked, because he had no idea, but I told him it happened decades ago. His relationship with his wife fell apart after that, but he wouldn't leave her until their kids had moved out of home."

"You're a terrible person."

"But I had a good time," Palin chuckled, and when Hennessy didn't laugh as well, his face lost all emotion. "The past is the past. I can't do anything about it now. He held a grudge against me, but I didn't think he was brave enough to do anything about it. It looks like I was wrong."

"Five witnesses have requested that their names be redacted from their statements until the trial. Do you think John Tilly is one of the redacted witnesses?"

"I'm sure of it."

"And the other four redacted names?"

"Probably all former employees, as well."

"I need a list of all your former employees, dating back over the last five years."

"I can send that to your office."

"I also need a list of all your clients over the past five years. The prosecution has all the details connected to the Foundation and your bank accounts, but I need to look over everything you've done."

"That's not going to happen."

Hennessy squinted. "If we're going to have any chance at winning this case, I need you to provide me with the information to win. That's the only way you'll stay out of prison."

"No, I'll stay out of prison because you want my money. Some things are more important than this trial."

"You're looking at fifteen years behind bars. What could be more important than that?"

"My safety. There are things that happen in these books that can't be exposed to law enforcement. Some of my clients have nothing to do with this case and they need to be left out of it."

Hennessy's jaw clenched. "I need the information on all your clients."

"Like I said, my other clients have nothing to do with this case. You'll win this case with the information I give you. That's your job. I was framed. If you want my money, you need to win this in court. I'm innocent."

"You're not innocent. You may have been framed here, but the list of accusations against you goes on for a very long time."

"If you can get me a deal without prison time, I'll take it. I'm too old to do any prison time." He conceded, scrunched his face up, and then relaxed. "You should talk to Clarence Berkley. I ran his accounting for years, and he owes me a lot of favors. He'll help us. He still has enough connections in the justice system to manipulate the case and get the win. I'm sure he can talk to the Circuit Solicitor and get us a deal with no prison time. Berkley should also be able to help us with the names of the redacted witnesses."

"I'll talk to him." Hennessy collected the signed forms, placed them inside his briefcase and snapped it shut. "And I'll talk to everyone involved in this case. I need all the information about your clients over the last five years. You need to send those details through to my office. We can't have any surprises in the courtroom."

"Things aren't that straightforward, Joe." Palin leaned forward, taking the time to choose his next words carefully. "I run the accounting for several businesses that may or may not be involved in some unsavory behavior. They have nothing to do with this case, and they won't like it if you dig into their business records."

"And if I do?"

"Then I could imagine those people will get very angry."

CHAPTER 5

Clarence Berkley's antebellum mansion was a monument to the Southern affluence of a time past.

The stately two-story building overlooked the river, standing proudly behind two tall palmetto trees. The front porch's white columns were strong and prominent, and behind the white railings was a collection of wicker furniture. The cast iron gates creaked as Hennessy opened them, leading into a well-manicured garden. A warm breeze blew off the nearby Ashley River, bringing with it the salty smells of the pluff mud, and the temperature was pushing past eighty-five as the sun reached its highest point in the sky.

Hennessy admired the garden as he walked toward the top step of the front porch and rang the doorbell, listening to the chime echoing through the grand home. He had been to the mansion before, more than two decades earlier, when he was working in the prosecutor's office and Clarence Berkley was a respected judge. Berkley had always been an entertainer, and his annual law parties in the sprawling yard were locally famous.

It took several minutes before the thick door creaked open.

"Never thought I'd see you at my home again," Berkley scoffed as he looked up at Hennessy's tall figure. "But life has a way of surprising us all, doesn't it?"

"Judge Clarence Berkley."

Berkley was well past his prime, and it showed. His gray hair was almost all gone, his once athletic frame was slumped forward, and his once solid arms were bone thin. He had been a dominant force in the courtroom for decades, using his booming voice to exercise power over lawyers and their clients, but his dominance was a thing of the past.

"I'd say it's good to see you, Joe, but that would be a lie."

"You haven't changed a bit."

"I'm too old to change." He wiped his bony finger under his nose. "There are a lot of rumors going around town about you. One rumor even said that you're taking on the defense of Palin's case."

"They're not rumors."

"Why would you do that? He's a terrible, terrible man."

"He's not the one with a long line of sexual assault accusations."

"And none have ever stuck to me, if you remember." Berkley shook his head, looking over his shoulder back inside the house. "What do you want, Joe?"

"Palin said I should talk to you."

"Palin said that?" The comment had caught Berkley off-guard. He squinted as he looked at Hennessy, stepped further inside, and closed the door until it was only just open. "Wait here."

Hennessy heard voices from inside the home. Berkley opened the door again a few moments later. He pointed toward the gardens at the side of the house and began to walk that way.

"My wife is with the nurse," Berkley said as he held his hands behind his back. "The nurse comes daily to check on things and ensure everything is ok with her. It's dementia. Some days, Valeria is good; others, not so much. Some days, she doesn't remember who I am, and other days, she doesn't remember who she is."

"I'm sorry to hear that," Joe followed a step behind. "That must be hard."

"Ah." Berkley shrugged as if it was nothing. They stepped off the porch and onto the path at the edge of the yard.

The path led around the right side of the house, bringing them to the enormous rear yard. Greenery was abundant. Tall hedges lined the perimeter, another pathway led to a decorative fountain in the middle of the space, and hibiscus flowers blossomed in an array of pinks and yellows. Several large oaks stood at the rear of the yard, complete with Spanish moss gently blowing in the breeze. The yard was a showpiece, a testament to the wealth Berkley had inherited and later built upon.

Berkley stopped to admire the flowers for a moment, touching one of the leaves and rubbing it between his index finger and thumb before slowly walking with his hands behind his back.

"When you were in the prosecutor's office all those years ago, you were so righteous and firm in your belief of right and wrong. What happened? Why are your morals now for sale?"

"Palin is entitled to a defense."

"Yes, yes, of course." He gripped his hands behind his back and stopped before the fountain. "We all know the rules of the game, but that doesn't explain why you took the case. What could a man like Palin have on you? What's he blackmailing you with?"

"Money."

"Ah." Berkley smiled. "Never thought you'd be the one to chase a dollar at the expense of your morals."

"The money will afford me the chance to give all this away," Hennessy conceded. "And then I can return to the vineyard."

"The precious vineyard. Upstate, isn't it? I remember when you left Charleston twenty years ago after your son's death, and you bought that vineyard. Everyone understood why you left. We all would've done the same thing. It was too much to bear and then to hear that your old colleague Richard Longhouse was behind Luca's death. Well, that was as much a surprise to me as it was to anyone." Hennessy didn't respond, not wishing to be drawn into a discussion about old times with his former associate.

Berkley continued to wander with his hands behind his back, letting the silence sit between them. He stopped at the yard's edge and sat on a wooden bench. "How much do you know about Palin's case? Have you seen the full witness list yet?"

Hennessy sat next to Berkley, looking back toward the mansion. "The witness list is long. Five of the main witness names are currently redacted to protect them from threats of violence, but I'm not sure knowing the names would make any difference. The state has an almost perfect case against your friend."

"He's not my friend. Never was."

"Then why would he tell me to come here?"

Berkley grunted. "Because I've helped him in the past. He had evidence against me that I couldn't risk getting out, and he used that as blackmail. That's how he operated. He'd offer to do your accounting at a reduced rate, discover your secrets, and then blackmail you into doing favors for him. He'd overcharge for the accounting, sometimes more than double what it should've been, but that was the price he charged for keeping secrets. He did that to so many people. I have friends who were blackmailed by him right up until their deaths. That man has no morals."

"What did he have on you?"

"He did my accounting for many years, and let's say, in some of those years, I spent a certain amount of money on women who weren't my wife. He threatened to tell Valeria unless I did several favors for him. I couldn't let those secrets be made public, and I couldn't let my wife find out. So, I helped him by encouraging law enforcement to investigate two of his rival accounting firms. Palin was also in the pocket of some members of law enforcement, and I encouraged them to use some questionable charges of fraud. I approved the warrants and law enforcement did the rest. The rival firms must've known what was happening because they both shut down within weeks. Anytime a new firm tried to muscle into Palin's ground, the same thing happened. He was so well-connected that new accounting firms learned to avoid Charleston."

"And if you didn't help him, he would tell your wife about your extra-marital affairs."

"That's what he threatened me with, but that doesn't matter now. I'm no longer employed as a judge, and my wife has dementia. There's nothing he can do to me now."

"Palin thinks you can convince Judge Clayton to release the redacted witness list early. He also thinks you've still got contacts to help us strike a deal that would mean no prison time."

"I can't help you with any of that. I was asked to leave to the bench, remember? A disgraced judge isn't welcome back into the courtroom, Joe. My connections left me a long time ago."

"Then why did Palin tell me to come to you?"

Berkley groaned and shook his head. "Before he was charged, he came to me for legal advice, off the books, and I talked to him. He talked to me about transferring a certain amount of money to Costa Rica without it attracting attention, and I advised him on the best way to do it. I have some connections in Costa Rica, and he wanted to leverage that network."

"But?"

"But he was caught before he transferred the money. They closed the surrounding net faster than I thought they would."

"Did you know about the children's charity foundation?"

"I knew he was ripping someone off. Why else was

he about to run off to Costa Rica? It was clear that he had been involved in something illegal and wanted to escape it. I didn't ask how he got the money because I didn't want to know. I have no desire to involve myself in any more legal cases like that. I've left that life behind."

"Palin says one of his employees framed him."

"And maybe, for this instance, he's telling the truth. Maybe he was framed. It is a coincidence that they all quit on the same day. I don't know the truth. All I know is that the past catches up with all of us. Palin has managed so much corruption in his life that he wouldn't even know right and wrong anymore. When he had influence and money, he had a lot of friends and powerful allies, but times have changed. The people he was connected to have long retired, passed away or left the game, and now, he's finding out that he has no powerful friends left. The only people left on his side are that thug motorcycle gang."

"The Rebel Sons."

"I'd heard rumors about Palin doing work for them, and I have no interest in involving myself in their dramas."

"Would you testify as a character witness for

Palin?"

Berkley laughed, his voice carrying around the spacious yard. "No, Joe. I'm not going to testify on Palin's behalf. He's spent his life dealing in manipulation and threats. He's blackmailed law enforcement, politicians, business owners, and me. And he's ripped off more people than you and I could ever imagine. He's going to get what's been coming to him for decades. It's time he paid for all the hurt and pain he's caused so many people."

"So, you won't help him?"

"There's no chance I'll testify on his behalf," Berkley stood and began to walk back toward the home. "And as an old colleague, I'll give you a piece of advice—Palin is a sinking ship. And when he goes down, he's going to take everyone else down with him."

CHAPTER 6

"Joe, this is bad." Assistant Jacinta Templeton tapped her fingers on the file resting on the boardroom table. "Palin has a long list of accusations, but nothing has ever stuck. So many allegations— rumors of fraud, rumors of corruption, and so many claims of criminal behavior."

"He used to have a lot of contacts." Hennessy sat at the head of the table, one long leg crossed over the other. "He used to know all the right people to keep him out of prison, but they've mostly moved on. When he had connections, he could do whatever he wanted. But now, he's discovering how the law works for most people."

The Joe Hennessy Law Office boardroom was cool, thanks to an overworked air conditioner. A large painting of Folly Beach hung on the wall at the left of the room, and a whiteboard filled with scribbles was to the right. The table was cluttered with files, neatly organized by Jacinta: case notes in one pile, discovery files in another, and background information on Palin next to notes from the original lawyer.

"Sounds like his past has caught up to him," Barry Lockett, Hennessy's investigator, added. Lockett's intimidating presence—tattooed arms, scarred knuckles, and a strong jawline—often alarmed people, but his cheeky smile and Australian accent put them at ease. Dressed in his usual black t-shirt and jeans, he leaned forward. "What are your thoughts, Joe?"

"That he did it."

"Defense?"

"That someone else did it."

"I love it when you dumb all that legal jargon down for me," Lockett laughed. "Do you have any candidates?"

"The first place to look is one of his staff members. All ten quit on the same day, just weeks before the charges were laid. Palin said when he came in one Monday morning, there was a resignation letter on each desk. Five staff members went to a rival accounting firm, three to a financial services company, and two retired, even though they were only in their early fifties. They had to have been involved or, at the very least, tipped off about the arrest. The timing's too coincidental."

"Sounds like they knew about it," Lockett commented. "Any idea which of the staff members would be involved?"

"The two people who retired will be our starting point. The senior accountant was John Tilly, and the office manager was Debra Fisher. Fisher has a background in HR, but Tilly's the main candidate. He had access to all the reports Palin did. While the accounts were in Palin's name, Tilly was a signatory. Barry, can you look into their lives and see if there are any connections between Fisher and Tilly?"

"On it," Barry said, making several notes on his cell phone. "You're saying that he transferred the money to the accounts and then set up Palin?"

"We could argue that Tilly had access to the bank accounts and was planning to take the money. We can claim he was the person who was embezzling money from the Foundation. He was waiting for the right time to transfer it but didn't touch the accounts once Palin was charged."

"I like it," Lockett agreed. "What's he like?"

"I'm not sure yet, but Palin also mentioned that

Tilly had a grudge against him. Tilly could've been building a retirement fund before he was found out. We need to discover everything about him and anything that could point to fraudulent behavior."

"I'll see what I can dig up," Jacinta said. "Do you think he's one of the redacted witnesses?"

"A lot of the witness statements are redacted, and we won't see the full statements until a week before the trial. Of the parts that aren't redacted, we can see that three of the witnesses have made statements about working for Palin, and it would make sense that the two most senior people in the office would make those statements. The redacted witness statements refer to how Palin often fudged the accounting for several businesses. They claim Palin created fake invoices, altered the timesheets, and overcharged his clients. When the staff members investigated the money trail, they found he was ripping people off. He made the paper trail long and complicated, but it always returned to the business."

"But that's not what he's charged with?"

"No, but their statements create a clear pattern of behavior." Hennessy shook his head. "Palin has been charged with diverting money from the Wolfgang

Berger Foundation. The foundation makes two payments per year to the MUSC Shawn Jenkin's Children's Hospital. Every year for five years, one payment went to the hospital, and the other payment was diverted into one of Palin's bank accounts."

"And the money came into an account that Tilly was a signatory on," Jacinta added.

"If either Fisher or Tilly knew about the withdrawals, they must be accomplices, right?" Lockett questioned.

"I imagine the prosecution struck a deal with them for their testimonies. Testify against Palin, and they will walk away without a charge. We won't talk to Tilly yet. We don't want to spook him. Once we have a clearer picture of the whole scenario, we'll set up a meeting and see how it plays out." Hennessy looked over a file in front of him, flicking through several pages. "The previous lawyer didn't even dispute the redacted witness names. I've looked at the file, and he hasn't even requested their names from the prosecution."

"What can you do about it?"

"We'll go to court and apply to the judge for further information on the redacted witnesses. I don't imagine the judge will allow it, but we're sending a message to the prosecution that this will be a fight. They'll start working on a better deal as soon as they receive the notice that we're applying for further information."

"There's something I don't understand," Jacinta said. "Why keep the money in the account for five years? If this was a deliberate transfer, why not take the money out of the account and use it?"

"The prosecution claims that Palin was putting the money aside for retirement. The money was transferred to a high-interest account and earned around one hundred and fifty thousand in interest over the five years."

"Seems strange to leave it in the account. It'd increase the chances of getting caught."

"The prosecution's theory is that Palin was going to use the funds to buy an apartment in Costa Rica and live a happy retirement. They claim he left the money in the account because he didn't think anyone else would discover the transfer."

"And could he claim it was an accounting error if anyone discovered it?"

"Possibly, but the prosecution is convinced that

his intention was to use the money. They must have another piece of evidence we haven't seen yet." Hennessy stood and walked to the whiteboard, staring at Palin's name written in the middle of it. Around the board were numerous names and companies that were connected to Palin Accounting. Hennessy tapped on one name at the side of the board. "What do we know about the Foundation that Palin allegedly stole from?"

"The Wolfgang Berger Foundation. Run by Michelle Stevenson, the daughter of Wolfgang Berger." Jacinta said as she flicked a page over in the file in front of her. "After Mr. Wolfgang Berger's death, he left every cent of his estate to establish the Foundation. Mr. Berger was a wealthy man when he died and left none of his estate to his only surviving family member, Michelle. However, the will did state that she was to be in control of the Foundation and paid an income of one-hundred-and-fifty thousand per year, which was to be increased in line with inflation."

"Did she dispute the will?"

Jacinta read a few more lines. "She did. The will states several times that the money is only left to the

Foundation if Michelle serves and is paid as CEO. While five people are serving on the board for the Foundation, they know that if they fire her, there will be legal challenges about the estate. While the Foundation may still exist, its primary source of funding, the estate, will be withdrawn. So, while the charity board is independent of Mrs. Stevenson, they know withdrawing support for her as CEO would mean withdrawing the main source of income for the Foundation."

"Effectively meaning that she's untouchable in the position of CEO."

"Maybe she wanted all the money for herself," Lockett stated. "John Tilly may not be the only option for the third-party culpability."

"It could be an option," Hennessy said. "We need to speak with Michelle Stevenson."

CHAPTER 7

The Wolfgang Berger Foundation's office was on East Bay Street in Downtown Charleston, overlooking the Old Exchange Building. The area was filled with tourists, wandering through the historic city, taking photos of everything at every opportunity, and filling the air with joy. Tourists were a constant of life on the peninsula, and the locals accepted them as a part of living in such a historic and picturesque city.

Hennessy and Lockett entered the building, walked up several flights of stairs, and entered the only office on the top floor. The reception area of the Foundation was bathed in prestige. Gold trim circled the door, framed paintings of the Civil War hung on the walls, and the smell of fresh roses filled the air. The reception desk was large and appeared new, the carpet was plush, and there wasn't a mark on the white walls.

The receptionist introduced herself as Maxine

Summers. Her smile was easy, her eyes were kind, and her tone was warm and welcoming. She wore a nice woolen sweater, a black skirt, and hooped earrings.

"Please, have a seat," she directed them to the waiting area next to her reception desk. "Ms. Stevenson is on her way in now."

"She doesn't work from the office?" Hennessy questioned.

"No." Maxine pondered her words carefully. "Ms. Stevenson works mostly from home. She doesn't come into the office much, maybe once a week."

"I take it by your tone that you do most of the work?" Lockett questioned.

Maxine shrugged. "I do... a lot, yes."

"And what does Mrs. Stevenson's role include?"

"Honestly, I don't know." Maxine shrugged as she went to sit behind the receptionist's desk again. "I started in this role five years ago, just after the Foundation started, and in that time, I haven't seen her do much. Ms. Stevenson originally told me it was her role to gather more funding for the Foundation, but the only funding we get is from her family's estate."

"She hasn't brought in any more funding?"

"Never." She shook her head. "But the Foundation does a lot of good for a lot of children. Lives are changed because of the donations made by her family's estate. The charity foundation mostly supports hospitals throughout South Carolina but also donates to other causes, such as education and school events."

"And you're paid less than her?"

She stared at Hennessy and nodded. "I earn a lot less than her."

"Even though you do most of the work?"

"All of the work," she quipped and then provided them with a small smile. She had said enough. "You must excuse me. I need to get back to doing these spreadsheets. Since we lost our accountant, my workload has doubled."

When Maxine turned back to her computer, Hennessy and Lockett exchanged a nod.

Fifteen minutes passed before Michelle Stevenson, Wolfgang Berger's only daughter, entered the office.

Michelle was a contrast to Maxine. There was nothing easy about her. Not the way she stood, not the expression on her face, not the look in her eyes. Everything about her was hard. Her black suit jacket sat square on her shoulders, and her black trousers were fitted to her muscular legs. Veins were visible in her hands, and her jaw was clenched. Her blonde hair was pulled back tightly, not a strand out of place, and her eyebrows were thin and almost straight.

"Mrs. Stevenson," Hennessy greeted her. "My name is Joe Hennessy, and this is Mr. Barry Lockett. We spoke on the phone earlier."

"Yes, yes," she was dismissive of his introduction. "And it's Ms., not Mrs. I divorced my prick of a husband when I found out he was sleeping with his colleague."

"My apologies," Hennessy said and held out his hand.

She shook it lightly and then indicated to the door to her separate office. "Hurry up," she snapped. "I don't have all day."

Hennessy nodded and led Lockett inside. The office was wide and spacious. There was abstract art on the wall. A leather couch in the corner. A large and expensive mahogany desk. The room smelled of lavender, and the tall windows looked over the beautiful architecture of Charleston.

Hennessy and Lockett sat down on the leather

couch, and while Michelle waded through pleasantries, it was clear she had little interest in the conversation. Yes, it was hot. Looking forward to the cooler weather, she agreed. Yes, it was a lovely building that housed the office of the Foundation. Charleston had the nicest architecture in the country, she said.

"But you want to talk about what that accountant did to my father's money, don't you?" She glared at Hennessy after five minutes of small talk. There was no warmth, or any emotion, in her voice.

"We'd like to talk about the Foundation," Hennessy said. "How long have you been CEO?"

"Five years. Ever since my stupid father died." She glanced at the men and then shook her head. "I'm sorry. I shouldn't speak about him like that. He immigrated from Germany and brought his family here just after I was born. My mother missed home, but my father saw this place as a way to succeed. He started as a car salesman before he opened a chain of dealerships across the east coast. He made tens of millions, not that anyone would know it. He pinched money so hard it would squeal. Wouldn't spend a cent on anyone. One of my earliest childhood memories was I remember him complaining about my mother buying a bottle of ketchup when the other one wasn't empty yet. This guy was worth millions of dollars and was arguing over money spent on a ketchup bottle."

"He left the money to a worthy cause," Lockett said. "That's honorable."

"And not a cent of his estate was left to me," she scoffed. "Not a cent. He even wrote in his will that his house had to be sold, and the profits would go into the Foundation. The only thing the stupid old man left me was this job. He wrote in his will that I had to run the Foundation, and I got the 'privilege' of earning a decent wage. And he knew what he was doing. He didn't want me to have a cent of 'his' money. He wanted me to work for it."

"That may be true in the beginning, but the board of directors has kept you on."

"Because they know there'll be legal challenges if they don't. My father's will directly states that I'm to be CEO of the Foundation and earn this wage. If not, the estate can withdraw their funding, and the money will go to another cause."

"And who would choose that different cause?"

"The executor of the will."

"Which, I assume, is you?"

"Correct."

Hennessy glanced at Lockett. Their silent exchange was heavy with understanding. "When did you discover that some of the funds were missing?"

"When the police called me and said they were investigating Palin Accounting for fraud."

"You didn't notice it before then?"

"No!" she snapped. "Why would I? That's what I employed the accounting firm for. They even told me how much to pay and where to transfer it. I never had a reason not to trust them. I signed the checks, gave the money away, and moved on to the next thing. I didn't have the time to waste on numbers and spreadsheets."

The tension in the room was palpable, but Hennessy figured that was par for the course whenever Melissa was around. "Are you involved in the day-to-day activities of helping the children?"

"No. My job is to distribute the money to the children's charities. I have nothing to do with them. I had one son who ended up being a drug addict, and that was enough dealing with children for me. My assistant, Maxine, deals with the day-to-day activities around here. She's lovely but much too emotional."

"And you don't interact with the families or the children?"

"No."

Hennessy looked at Lockett. They exchanged a nod.

"Thank you for your time, Ms. Stevenson. You've been very helpful." Hennessy stood and shook her hand again. As he reached for the door, he turned back to her. "If you could receive more money from your father's estate, would you claim that money?"

"Of course." She glared at Hennessy. "These little brats are getting my inheritance."

CHAPTER 8

"Mr. Hennessy." Aaron Garrett greeted Hennessy with a solid handshake and a slight nod. "Thank you for making time before our motion hearing."

"You said you wanted to discuss a deal." Hennessy opened the door to the conference room on the first floor of the courthouse. "Any decent lawyer would take time out of their schedule to discuss an early end to the case."

Garrett stepped inside the conference room and sat at the head of the rectangular wooden table. Hennessy closed the door and sat to Garrett's left. The room was filled with natural light, streaming through the window at the far end and cooled by the hum of the air-conditioner. The smell was musty in the windowless room.

"I saw your motion for discovery about the redacted witness information, and along with my superiors, we gave some thought to a better deal for

Mr. Palin. We all want an early end to this case," Garrett said as he leaned back in his chair. "What we would like is that your client pleads guilty to the fraud charges, makes a statement of apology, and then serves some time in prison."

"What are you offering?"

"Five years prison, the rest of the sentence suspended."

"With offers like that, he should take his chance in court."

"He needs to consider it," Garrett implored. "If he takes this to trial and loses, he's looking at fifteen years plus behind bars. If he doesn't take this deal, he'll spend the rest of his life locked up."

"I'll take it to him, but he wants to walk away without any prison time."

"You and I both know that can't happen after what he did." Garrett sighed. "He stole money from sick children, Joe. The public thinks it's a disgraceful action, and we agree. He needs to do some prison time. Work with us. Convince him to do some time and then live the rest of his life."

"I expected a better offer, but I'll take this one to him." Hennessy nodded, picked up his briefcase, and exited the room.

A few moments later, he was in courtroom 105, sitting in the gallery, waiting for his case to be called. Garrett entered the courtroom after a few minutes, carrying a steamy coffee in a to-go cup. He removed the lid, blew steam off the hot drink, and sipped it. He leaned close to Hennessy and whispered, "Did you call Palin?"

"I'll call him this afternoon." Hennessy shook his head. "He's busy today."

"Is he walking around the hospital asking sick children for money?"

Hennessy ignored the jibe, and a moment later, the court clerk read their case number. The clerk's voice boomed across the courtroom, and the lawyers took their places at their respective tables. Judge Clayton had to move through five cases that morning, and he needed each hearing to be quick. He had no time to waste on lawyer games. Hennessy walked through the bar, with Garrett a step behind him. Garrett appeared confident—his chin was up, his shoulders were back, and a smug smile was on his face.

Judge Clayton groaned as he read the file. "I see we're back again, gentlemen." Judge Clayton was still reading the brief as he waved at the lawyers. "A Motion to Compel Discovery for the list of witness names?"

"Thank you, Your Honor," Hennessy began. "We've lodged a motion to compel discovery under South Carolina Rule of Criminal Procedure Rule 5. We've been forced to file this motion to receive discovery information that the prosecution is determined to withhold from the defense."

Judge Clayton responded and turned to Garrett. "Care to explain, Mr. Garrett?"

"Certainly, Your Honor," Garrett stated. "The State has adhered to all the requests for discovery, including all the evidence, the witness statements, depositions, and forensic accounting required in this case. However, five witnesses feared for their safety and wished to keep their names redacted in the witness statements until the trial date."

"Which severely reduces the defense's ability to prepare for trial," Hennessy interrupted. "It's a constitutional right for the accused to confront their accuser, and the prosecution is denying that right."

"Your Honor," Garrett snapped. "The safety of the witnesses needs to be paramount. This is not a decision that we took lightly. In fact, we went through several options until we decided this was the right course of action. The prosecution has adhered to discovery rules in this case with the defense; however, we're concerned about the safety of these five witnesses. More than a hundred witnesses are listed in the discovery material, but five witnesses have expressed safety concerns."

"And what are those concerns?

"The defendant, Mr. Palin, made direct threats on the lives of all five of these witnesses."

"And how did he make those threats?"

"Via email, Your Honor. He made the threats to their lives directly to their personal emails. He told these witnesses that if they ever testified against him, they or their families would be punished. As he reportedly made the same threat to many people, we believe he currently doesn't know the names of the witnesses, and for their safety, we would like to keep their names suppressed for the next five weeks while we arrange for their protection."

Garrett passed a folder to the bailiff, who passed it to the judge. He read over the emails and then sighed. "That's hard to argue with. Are you applying for the reversal of bail?"

"Not at this stage, Your Honor. We would like to note that the court can deny this motion to compel if there's a substantial risk to the witness that outweighs the usefulness of the disclosure."

"I'm aware of the rules." Judge Clayton grunted. "And this hasn't been raised previously?"

"Not that I'm aware of, Your Honor," Hennessy responded. "My client's previous lawyer, Mr. David Jones, did not request these details from the State."

"Very well," Judge Clayton said. "And we're set to start this trial in five weeks?"

"We are," Garrett replied. "And the State requests the suppression of the witnesses' names to continue until the trial. The witnesses' lives are at stake, and we need to keep them safe, as is their right. Justice shouldn't run from threats of violence."

"That's inflammatory, Your Honor," Hennessy argued. "The lack of information weakens the defense's ability to prepare for trial. The entire first two pages of Witness One's statement has been redacted."

"It's been redacted for the witnesses' safety," Garrett argued. "It contains identifying information."

"And it's no coincidence that the five redacted testimonies are the five most important testimonies in this case," Hennessy continued. "The lack of information about these witnesses disadvantages the defense. We need to research the witnesses to assess their credibility."

"But you have the redacted witnesses' statements, Mr. Hennessy?"

"The statements are missing vital information."

"Your Honor, we've redacted any identifying information from the witness statements, and we have not redacted any vital part of their testimonies, as Mr. Hennessy suggests," Garrett argued. "We're currently arranging for protection for these witnesses, but they live complicated lives, and the process takes time. And we have a limited budget to work with. The State is asking for the identifying information in the witness statements to continue to be redacted until the ability to protect these witnesses is put in place. This is a standard procedure in this situation."

"And when do you intend to release the witness names to the defense?" Judge Clayton asked.

"A week before the trial. That should be enough time for the defense to prepare."

Judge Clayton nodded. "Anything further, Mr. Hennessy?"

"Your Honor, the defense has the right to investigate the credibility of these five key witnesses. That right is defined in the Constitution."

"I agree, Mr. Hennessy. However, the safety of the witnesses must be paramount. Given the very real threats against the witnesses, I understand the prosecution's concerns. Considering that the defense has the witness statements available and can conduct depositions via email, I don't believe the defense is unfairly disadvantaged. In the interest of a fair trial, the names of these five witnesses will be withheld until one week before the trial. The motion to compel discovery is denied."

"Thank you, Your Honor." The lawyers stated in unison.

The clerk called the next case number, and the lawyers packed up their briefcases, quickly replaced at the tables by the following case. Garrett couldn't wipe the smile off his face as they exited the courtroom.

"The deal for five years is still on the table, Joe," Garrett stated once they were in the hallway. "I suggest Palin accepts it because if he takes this to court, we're going to throw all our resources at it, and we'll make sure that man never walks free again."

CHAPTER 9

After several stressful weeks, Joe drove home to Luca's Vineyard for a weekend break.

On the three-hour drive back to the vineyard, he called several clients of Palin Accounting. Most were reluctant to talk. As one of Palin's largest clients, Joe called Stanwell Construction and asked for a time to meet the owner, Tony Stanwell. The receptionist was very reluctant to discuss anything or even acknowledge that Tony Stanwell owned the business. When Joe mentioned a deposition in front of lawyers, the receptionist advised that she would take the message to her boss. When the call finished, Joe made a conscious decision not to think about the case for the rest of the weekend.

He arrived at the vineyard at midday on Friday. He kissed Wendy, and they shared a coffee, talking about their days ahead. The harvest was going to be large, Wendy said. Joe agreed, and they discussed timeframes and bringing in seasonal staff to help. There were always college students looking to pick up extra work, and there wasn't a better place to work outside. They agreed to put an advertisement out over the coming days.

Wendy said that Casey would be home from college for the weekend. Joe smiled. He loved that his youngest child was now an adult, growing into the world, but he missed having her at home. In his heart, he wanted her to remain an innocent five-year-old forever, but he had learned to let go and allow her to become her own woman.

Set on fifty-five acres in Upstate South Carolina, Luca's Vineyard had a chateau to the east of the property, which featured a café, a store for direct sales, and a dining space for events. The Hennessy homestead was at the west of the property, sitting at the top of a hill above the rows and rows of vines. Twenty-five minutes outside of Greenville, the vineyard employed ten staff, who were treated like family.

Wendy and Joe spent the afternoon walking amongst the vines. As they walked, Joe could feel his lungs fill with clean air. The fresh air seemed to reach deep into his body, refreshing his soul. Wendy talked about her optimism for the harvest, and how the sugar levels, acidity, and tannin development were all being closely monitored. It could be one of their best years, she said.

They stopped at the main shed and checked on their equipment. It all looked in good working order. The tractors, two beautiful old John Deere's, were running well. The irrigation lines were flowing without a problem. The pruning equipment was in good order.

After a break for an afternoon snack, Joe spent some time on the riding mower, clearing the weeds between the vines. Joe loved the land. He loved working, getting dirty, being out in nature, and creating something others could enjoy.

Before his son's death, his world had been law and justice. Most of his time was spent in the office, some weeks putting in over seventy-five hours under the ambiance of artificial light. In his younger years, he worked so hard for justice. He worked so hard for the people of Charleston. In the year after Luca's murder, he questioned everyone and everything, until it drove him to the edge of insanity. He left Charleston without knowing who murdered his son, and the lands became his place to heal. He found serenity among the vines, where he could let go for a few moments at a time. Eventually, he buried his grief deep under a wall of stoicism and focused on the grapes.

Casey arrived in the late afternoon and spent the last daylight hours helping her father. They pruned the older vines, delicately handling the mature plants. Casey talked about her studies at Clemson and everything she learned in agricultural studies. Joe was surprised by some of the things she'd learned. Casey explained there was so much science in agriculture, and even artificial intelligence was being used to replace some processes. Joe listened, nodded in the right places, and then told her nothing could replace a farmer's intuition. It's the reason why doctors still use stethoscopes, Joe said. All the technology in the world can't replace intuition.

As the sun set on their Friday, Casey and Joe returned to the five-bedroom brick home and were greeted by the wonderful smells of fried chicken. Casey couldn't contain her excitement. After a week of eating college dorm food, the idea of her mother's home-cooked fried chicken was like a gift from heaven.

"Are there any boys in the picture?" Wendy asked Casey when they all sat down at the table to eat. "Anyone we should know about?"

Joe's hand gripped his knife firmly.

"Not yet," Casey said, and Joe's hand eased from around the knife. "But there are some very handsome young men in my class."

"As long as they treat you well," Joe said. "And if they don't, you need to call me straight away."

"I'm ok, Dad," Casey said. "I'm an adult now. I can handle these little boys."

Joe smiled, proud of his strong and capable daughter. They ate dinner, played cards, and laughed together for the rest of the evening. On Saturday, they all rose early and worked the lands. Joe set up the smoker in the yard and began the long process of making what he claimed was the best brisket in the state. At midday, Wendy and Casey spent some time in the shop, talking to interested tourists and locals alike.

By 5 p.m., they had all returned home, exhausted but happy after a full day. Joe poured two glasses of

Merlot and went to the chairs outside their home, handing one glass to Wendy. They sat silently for a few moments, enjoying the views of the nearby lower lands. Joe felt a sense of relaxation he hadn't felt in weeks.

When the brisket was ready, Joe set up the table on the back porch, and they ate dinner overlooking the vineyard. They called Ellie, who was studying in New York, and kept her on speakerphone so she could join in their dinner conversations. As the sun set on another day, the family talked about everything and nothing—Ellie talked about New York and the craziness of the big city. Casey talked about Clemson and how she had made so many new friends already. The daughters compared notes on studying, and Ellie gave her younger sister several tips. Wendy talked about the vineyard and the upcoming harvest. Joe talked about his brisket and how much precision was required to get the taste just right. Wendy and Casey complimented him on the flavor, and Ellie complimented him on the idea of it. Together, they ate, told stories of their busy lives, and laughed. It was a night of nothing but love and family.

Once dinner was cleaned up, Joe returned to the

back porch, a glass of Merlot in his hand, looking over the valley. A tinge of sadness washed over him when he thought about the drive back to Charleston the next day.

Away from the pressure of the law, everything seemed quieter. The tension disappeared from his muscles. His mind was clearer. This was home, and he knew it in his heart. This was where he was supposed to be.

If he could win the case, if he could secure payment from Palin, he could leave his life in Charleston behind.

He just had to survive until then.

CHAPTER 10

On Monday evening, after another day scouring through evidence, Hennessy walked into Ted's Butcherblock, his favorite butcher in Charleston, and purchased a thick cut of beautifully marbled boneless ribeye.

He chatted with the butcher about the week, the weather, and the recent controversies around town. There was always something going on, and the butcher, a hub for the community, knew everyone and everything. There were disputes between business groups, politicians not delivering on promises, potential professional sports stars in high school, and always trouble with flooding.

As they chatted, a woman and her daughter entered the store. Hennessy recognized the face as an old high school friend of Wendy's. They hadn't seen each other for more than ten years. They greeted each other with surprise and then a hug. Hennessy told her she hadn't aged a day, and she said he was still the charming Joe Hennessy she remembered. She introduced her teenage daughter, and Hennessy couldn't believe how tall she was. Time goes by so fast, they agreed. He asked about her husband, work, and other children. She asked about Wendy, his daughters, and the vineyard. He told her they were well, and his daughters had flown the nest. They laughed about the passage of time again before he wished her a good night. She would call Wendy, she said, and Joe said she was welcome at the vineyard anytime.

As he stepped out of the butcher, a smile on his face, Hennessy noticed the black Range Rover SUV waiting on the opposite side of the road. He knew that car. He grunted, stood still for a moment, and then stepped toward the car. He walked up beside the driver's side window, leaned his tall frame against the door, and looked in the window. The driver didn't react, keeping his eyes facing out.

"Nice evening for a drive," Roger East stated. "Not too hot."

East was dressed in a white shirt, without a tie, with the shirt sleeves rolled up to his elbows. He was solid, muscular, and clean-cut. His face was weathered by the sun, and a heavy scent of Old Spice surrounded him.

"Are you following me?"

"Not following." East turned to look at Hennessy. "But keeping an eye on you. We need to talk. Get in."

Hennessy eyed the man and then looked around the area. He looked at the street that led to his home and groaned. He didn't want to talk—he was looking forward to cooking his steak—but he knew men like East didn't present many opportunities. East was connected to some of the most powerful people in the city of Charleston and sold his negotiation services to the highest bidder. If anyone wanted something done off the books, they contacted Roger East to organize it.

Hennessy walked around the SUV, opened the passenger door, and sat in the seat, squeezing his long legs into the car. He pushed the seat back and waited for East to start talking.

East began, "I heard you were representing Bernard Palin."

When Hennessy didn't respond, East drew a long breath.

"Let me give you a background on that man—he's had a lifetime of corruption and good favors, but it's all run out. Palin's connections have either died, retired, or moved on. There's nobody left to protect him. He's going down, and when a man like that goes down, he goes down swinging."

Again, Hennessy didn't respond.

"Come on, Hennessy. I'm here to help you."

"Why?"

"Because…" East looked around and shifted in his seat. "While Palin's connections to the rich and powerful have faded, he recently got into bed with another group—Stanwell Construction. I'm sure you're aware that they're a front for the not-so-legal activities of the Rebel Sons."

"Money laundering."

"Call it whatever you like," East stated. "Tony Stanwell, the owner, linked up with the Rebel Sons a few years ago, and they've been good partners ever since. It's a reciprocal arrangement. Money is put into the business and paid to bikers who 'work' there, and Tony takes a nice little slice of the pie. He also gets protection for free. So I advise avoiding their activities and not digging into their books. I told

David Jones the same thing, and like a good boy, he listened to me. I suggest you do the same. Stay well away from Stanwell Construction. Don't bring them into this case."

"What's your involvement in this?"

"I'm protecting the interests of people concerned about disrupted business activities by this court case. That might include people who could be exposed to illegal activities if you involve them. Nobody wants that."

Hennessy stared at him.

The cars beside them were moving at a snail's pace. It was high tide, which meant flooding in the low-lying parts of the city. Despite efforts to pump water away, the flooding was getting worse. Too many new buildings, some said. Too little planning, others complained. Flooding was a part of life in Charleston, even on a clear, sunny day.

"You're working for Stanwell Construction?"

"Not working for, just helping out. They said you were hounding them for a meeting, and you wouldn't take no for an answer."

"I need to talk with them."

"No, you don't. They've got nothing to do with

this case. Law enforcement didn't look at them, the prosecution isn't looking at them, and you don't need to look at them."

"I need an edge. I need something that raises a reasonable doubt in the courtroom. And if you don't want me looking into their business, you'd better tell me where to look."

"Sounds like a fair deal. I've been watching the case, and I know a few things. I'll give two names—John Tilly and Debra Fisher."

"I know the names. They're former employees of Palin Accounting."

"And I'm sure you've figured out that they're two of the redacted witnesses." When Hennessy didn't respond, East continued. "But here's the kicker—they've been having a five-year-long affair."

"An affair?"

"And if you look into their activities, you'll find neither has gone into further employment. They've both retired. And if you look even deeper, you'll see that both have older children who have left home for college. They were the two most senior staff in Palin Accounting and encouraged everyone to quit a week before the arrest. Coincidence? I think not." East tapped his hand on the steering wheel. "They were planning on running away together, and a million dollars would help them start a new life."

Hennessy nodded and reached for the door.

"Before you go," East held his hand out as a sign to stop. "I need to warn you that those connected to Stanwell Construction don't mess around. You made the wrong phone call, and that's why I'm here. And they won't hesitate to put a defense lawyer in hospital."

"I'll do what I need to do to win." Hennessy eyed East for a long moment and then exited the SUV. He swung the door shut, took out his cell, and called his investigator.

"Barry," Hennessy said. "We need to talk to John Tilly and Debra Fisher."

CHAPTER 11

Barry Lockett quickly built a file on Witness Two, Debra Fisher.

She had married her high school boyfriend, had two children who were now adults and had worked at Palin Accounting for fifteen years before she resigned. Her husband had several charges of drunk driving and public disorderly conduct. There were also several reports of domestic violence at their home, but no charges were ever laid. Both of their children had left for college in another state. It didn't appear to be a happy domestic situation.

When digging deeper, Lockett found that Fisher and her colleague, John Tilly, had been on many work trips together, and there were photos on social media of their joint attendance at many conferences. It didn't take much to connect the dots.

When Hennessy called Debra Fisher, she found an excuse to end the phone call almost as soon as he said his name. Hennessy warned her that her private information could be exposed to the world if she didn't agree to meet, but still, she ended the call. She called back an hour later, agreeing to meet if her sister, a family law attorney, could also be in attendance. Hennessy agreed.

The square two-story white building in Mount Pleasant was hidden behind a row of thick oak trees, blocking out the view from the street. Hennessy parked his red pickup near the front door and exited his car into a thick wall of humid air. He wiped his brow and stepped inside the cold building. The air conditioner was pumping above the door, providing a blast of cold relief from the humid conditions. He greeted the receptionist, and she led him down the wide hallway to a spacious meeting room. The meeting room was the same as the rest of the building—devoid of life, flair, or interest. Plain white walls and a wooden table. No artwork, no potted plants, and no signs of any character at all. The black leather office chairs were new, but their style didn't match the much older table. Hennessy sat at the end of the room, and a minute later, Debra Fisher entered. She was followed by her sister, attorney

Georgie Green.

Hennessy stood, and they shook hands.

The two women were clearly sisters—the same short height, the same full body shape, and the same shuffling walk. They had the same flat nose, green eyes, and chin. Debra's hair was shorter and darker, and she looked like the younger sister. The women also dressed alike—black skirts, white shirts, but different colored jackets. Once the pleasantries were completed, Green sat at the head of the table, and Fisher next to her.

"First, I'm not sure why we're having this meeting." Green leaned her elbows on the table and clasped her fingers together. "Debra is not listed as a witness on any court documents in Mr. Palin's criminal trial. And while I might be in family law, I know the procedures for criminal law. You have five redacted witness names for a reason."

"Mrs. Fisher is a former employee of my client," Hennessy said. "That's why I would like to talk to her. That's all. I'm not inferring that she's one of the redacted witnesses."

It wasn't the truth, and everyone in the room knew it.

"Do you think I'm one of the redacted witnesses?" Fisher asked. Her voice was soft, but her facial expression was cold.

"I'm not here to talk about whether or not you are a redacted witness." Hennessy shook his head. "I would like to discuss your employment with Palin Accounting. You were employed by the firm for fifteen years, and I would like to know what you saw during that time. I'm talking with all the former employees, and that's why I requested to speak with you."

"And what specifically would you like to talk about?" Green asked.

"Mrs. Fisher, I'd like to know about your relationship with Mr. John Tilly."

Debra sat back, shocked by the question.

When she didn't answer, Green answered for her, "They worked together."

"Is that all?"

"We were…" Fisher crossed her arms over her chest. "We were close friends. We'd worked together for five years, and when you work with someone that closely, you get to know them well. We had to travel to several conferences together, but that was normal work behavior for two senior people in the firm."

"I must warn you, Mrs. Fisher, that any relationships you had in that firm will be talked about in open court. The information stated during the trial will be publicly available, and there will be questions about your relationships with all the staff at Palin Accounting. It will be essential to the case that we examine the depth of those relationships."

Debra looked at her sister. Green nodded. "Mr. Hennessy, we agreed to this meeting in good faith. We didn't come here to be threatened about exposing personal relationships that have nothing to do with the corrupt behavior of Mr. Palin."

"Relationships have everything to do with this case. Two staff members had access to all the reports of Palin Accounting, and both quit on the same day. If those staff members were also in a close personal relationship, their behavior needs to be put under a microscope. That's the process, and that's how trials are conducted."

Fisher's mouth hung open. "But I didn't do anything."

"Are you implying that Debra was complicit with Mr. Palin's corrupt actions?" Green's tone was firm.

She was in attack mode—shoulders tightened, eyes narrowed, fists clenched. "Because if you are, this meeting is over."

"I'm not implying anything. I'm asking questions to get to the truth."

"You have the truth," Green snapped. "Mr. Palin stole money from the Foundation to fund his retirement. You know that, and I know that. The evidence against him is overwhelming and any suggestion that Debra had anything to do with it is fanciful, and quite frankly, it's a cheap move. I expected better than that from a lawyer of your experience."

Hennessy had hit the right buttons. Green could throw all the insults she wanted. It didn't matter to Hennessy. The meeting was having its desired effect. He could see the shock on Debra's face. When he let the pause sit in the room, she started biting her fingernails, staring at the table in front of her.

"Debra, do you have anything that you want to tell me?" Hennessy softened his tone. "It's best to put this information on the table early."

"Don't say anything," Green cautioned her, but it didn't work. "You don't have to talk."

"It was all Bernard," Fisher whispered as she bit her fingernails. "Always was. We discovered his crimes when he left for a conference earlier this year, and he asked me—" Green held out her hand to stop her sister. "I mean… one of the staff members, to update some information in one of the files. That staff member looked at the file and saw that what he was running wasn't legitimate. It was clear he was transferring money from the Foundation and keeping it in Palin Accounting. When looking deeper, it was clear nobody in the Foundation knew about his actions."

"That's enough. You've said more than enough for this meeting," Green stopped her sister from going into any more detail. "If you wish to have a deposition with Mrs. Fisher, you'll need to do it through the proper channels. I believe the judge has said you can depose the redacted witnesses via email. We came to this meeting in good faith, and all you've done is throw ridiculous allegations our way. This meeting is over."

Green stood and then directed Fisher to do the same. Fisher moved slowly, overwhelmed by the allegation that she might be involved. Before she reached the door, she turned back to Hennessy.

"Bernard Palin is a terrible man. He deserves whatever is coming to him."

CHAPTER 12

An hour after the meeting with Debra Fisher, Hennessy parked outside a Brazilian Jujitsu Club at the back of a Gold's Gym in the same suburb of Mount Pleasant. Lockett had found that John Tilly was a regular at the martial arts club, earning himself a brown belt after several years of training.

Unlike Fisher, Tilly refused to answer any of Hennessy's attempts at contact via calls or emails. Based on the details in the witness statement, Hennessy assumed he was Witness Three.

Hennessy waited in the parking lot, standing in front of his old pickup as several members of the martial arts class exited the building. They were jovial, happy, having exhausted themselves with hours of physical contact and training. The group leaving the building were of varying ages, sizes, and ethnic backgrounds. It was a club that welcomed one and all.

Ten minutes after most of the class had left, John

Tilly walked out in his Gi with a sports bag slung over his shoulder.

"John Tilly," Hennessy stated as he approached.

Tilly stopped and looked at Hennessy. Tilly was a solid man—five-ten, with broad shoulders and big hands. In his fifties, he had retained his strength and power. His black hair was grayed at the sides, and his skin was healthy and tanned. A smell of Brut deodorant followed him.

"You're the new lawyer for Palin." Tilly eyed Hennessy and then turned to his new black Mercedes sedan. He opened the back door, threw the bag inside, and shut the door. "You're persistent, aren't you?"

"I need to talk to you."

Tilly pursed his lips, tucked his hands behind his lower back, and leaned against his car door. "Debra said that she spoke to you earlier today. She wasn't very happy with what you suggested."

"I didn't suggest anything. All I did was discuss the impact of Mr. Palin's upcoming trial on the people involved. I'd like to talk to you about the trial as well, but you haven't returned my calls."

"I didn't return your calls because I didn't want to

talk to you."

"You're a part of this trial, whether you like it or not. You were employed as the senior accountant at Palin Accounting for five years, and that means you have inside knowledge of his processes and procedures. When this case goes to trial, you'll be called as a witness, whether by me or the prosecution."

"Stop beating around the bush." He scoffed. "I'm sure you're smart enough to work out that I'm one of the redacted witnesses. It's obvious from my statement. I didn't even request to have my name redacted. The prosecution did that, but I didn't complain. And I've spoken to a lawyer. Because my witness statement is redacted, it means I don't have to talk to you. If you want to ask me questions about the case, you need to do it via email."

Hennessy stepped closer. "When were you planning to run off with Mrs. Fisher?"

His mouth hung open for a long moment before he smiled and shook his head.

"You've had a five-year-long affair with Mrs. Fisher," Hennessy stated. "Now that all your children have gone to college, it'd be the perfect time to leave.

And a million dollars would help you start a new life."

"You're wrong." Tilly shook his head several times. "That's not what happened. We had nothing to do with it. It was all that stupid old prick. We saw him stealing from the Foundation, and we all wanted out. That's why we arranged the walkout. And before you ask, we didn't report it to the police because we were all scared of Palin. Nobody wanted to mess with him."

"Before this case makes it to trial, I'm going to dig deep into the backgrounds of everyone involved. That includes your activities with Mrs. Fisher. And once this trial begins, all that knowledge will be put on the public record. We already have evidence of you sharing a room on a work trip to Florida. According to the work claims, you and Mrs. Fisher drove to Jacksonville for a conference, and while you claimed two hotel rooms, you only paid for one."

"If you keep digging, you won't like what you find," Tilly scoffed again and looked around the parking lot. "If you look too far into Palin's business dealings, you'll only find more evidence of Palin's corruption. He's a terrible man with no morals. And if you want to talk any more to me, you'll have to do it through the proper channels." He turned toward his car and reached for the doorhandle. He paused before he opened the door, turning back to Hennessy. "I'm not sure you know what you've got yourself in for, so I'll warn you—don't dig too deep into the books at Palin Accounting."

"What are you scared we'll find out about you?"

"It's not about me or Debra." Tilly looked around the parking lot before he continued. "Palin ran the books for some companies that appeared to be fronts for drug-running operations. If they're exposed… well, I don't want anything to do with it. I never did."

"Stanwell Construction. What about them?"

Tilly looked around the parking lot and bit his lip. "I think they were in on it. There were links between Stanwell Construction and the Wolfgang Berger Foundation in the accounting. They knew about the money being embezzled. If you want more information, you need to talk to them."

CHAPTER 13

"Are you sure this is a good idea?"

Lockett checked his handgun as he sat in the passenger seat of Hennessy's pickup truck. Parked outside a construction site for a new housing development, the two men watched as a procession of work trucks rolled out of the front entrance.

Hennessy checked his Glock and then looked at Lockett. "This is a terrible idea."

"Then remind me why we're doing it."

"Because everyone is telling me not to do it."

"That seems like a legitimate reason," Lockett smiled. "You're the guy who pushes the big red button when told not to do it."

"You know me too well." Hennessy said. "We need to talk with Tony Stanwell because I'm not getting any information from Palin. We can't be surprised at the trial by these guys. And you can guarantee that Garrett is putting together an angle to get these guys in court. But if we push them now, Palin will see how serious we are, and he'll give us the information we need. We need to know what happens in this business."

"I can tell you that—they run drugs here."

"And how is Palin involved?"

"I would suggest he makes the books dodgy so they can cover their tracks."

"That's what I need him to tell me. How does he cover their tracks? What accounting does he change? Where does the money go? I need to know it all. Once I know that, I can stop the prosecution from surprising us at trial."

"It would be easier if Palin just told you."

"He's not playing nicely. He won't talk to me about Stanwell Construction. And if I don't know the truth about what happens here, it opens us up to exposure in court. Garrett could call several law enforcement witnesses to testify about this place, and I wouldn't even see it coming. To win the trial, I need to know what happens here."

Tony Stanwell was a hard man to meet with. Hennessy had tried to meet with him several times but never received a response. The only way

Hennessy could convince him was to threaten him with a subpoena, which would mean an appearance in court, something that Stanwell was desperate to avoid. After Stanwell had discussed the situation with his lawyers, he agreed to meet at his location, at a time convenient to him—5 p.m., at the site of a new housing development outside North Charleston.

"Fifty new homes will be built behind that fence." Lockett pointed to the tall chain-link fence blocking the public from the construction site. "Let's not be the first people to be buried there."

"Agreed," Hennessy said. "And we're just going to talk. That's all. Nothing more. We're not making threats, we're not pushing the boundaries, and we're not digging too deep. We're feeling this man out."

Lockett nodded and stepped out of the truck, tucking his weapon into his belt and hiding it under his jacket. Hennessy did the same. Together, the two tall men strode through the gate at the start of the development and toward the site office—a temporary building at the far left side of the lot.

As they walked toward the building, Hennessy wondered what the neighborhood would look like in ten years. Stanwell Construction had a reputation for cutting corners and doing things cheaply. Their previous developments were all experiencing problems—flooding, sewer constraints, cracks in the walls of the cheaply made homes. Stanwell Construction avoided the blame by bribing the right people and keeping the pockets of those in power full. Despite the history of sub-par developments, Stanwell Construction kept winning bids from the city council to develop new neighborhoods. Hennessy knew how that worked.

As they approached the building site office, two burly construction workers stood outside the entrance, both as tall as Hennessy and Lockett. The men could've passed for bodybuilders, and Hennessy had no doubt that steroids were involved. Both men had neck tattoos, and one had a face tattoo.

As Hennessy approached, they stepped toward each other, blocking the entrance to the site office. Hennessy held eye contact with them for a long moment before he said, "We're here to see Mr. Tony Stanwell."

The men didn't move for a moment, until the broader man stepped back. The second man followed his lead.

"The boss said he wants to talk to you inside." The first one grunted. "It's not safe out here, being a construction site. We wouldn't want you to hurt yourself with all this dangerous equipment around."

Hennessy led the way inside, and Lockett followed a step behind.

Inside, the site office was a mess. Papers were everywhere, empty soda cans were on the floor, and trash was overflowing from the trash can. The place smelled like cigarettes, whiskey, and male body odor.

Tony Stanwell sat behind the desk at the far end of the room with his expensive leather shoes resting on the plastic tabletop. His relaxed and expansive pose presented the appearance that he was in charge.

Stanwell's Italian heritage was evident. He had tanned skin, thick black hair, and the top of his hairy chest was exposed by a white polo shirt. A gold chain hung around his neck, and several rings clung to his fingers.

"Mr. Stanwell. Thank you for meeting with us," Hennessy stated. "We understand you're a busy man."

"You didn't give me much of a choice." Stanwell waved the comment away, feet still up on the desk. His voice was loud and croaky. "Sit down, boys."

Hennessy folded his tall frame into the office chair, his body barely fitting between the arms of the plastic chair. Lockett did the same next to him and the chair almost crumbled under his weight.

The two burly men from outside entered the room and stood at the room's rear without a word to each other.

"Were you aware of any illegal activities involving Palin Accounting?" Hennessy wasted no time in feeling out Stanwell.

"Ha ha!" Stanwell sat up straight, taking his feet off the table. "This is a legitimate business."

"I didn't say it wasn't."

Stanwell scoffed and then laughed again. He waved his finger at Hennessy. "Palin said you weren't one to take a backward step, and I guess he was right. But I fail to see what my legitimate business activities have to do with Palin's fraud case."

"It's all connected." Hennessy leaned forward. "And like I told you over the phone, you can answer my questions here or in court. I'm going to know the truth either way. How we do it is your choice."

"You're either very courageous or very stupid, Mr. Hennessy. You've walked into a construction site where concrete foundations are still being laid, and you're making threats. Concrete covers most things, and nobody will knock down a new building to search for a body."

"You can talk to me about Palin here, or we can do it in court," Hennessy repeated.

"Palin, Palin, Palin. I hate the guy, but he knows too much to be abandoned." Stanwell rolled his tongue around his mouth as he considered the name. "We don't like that Palin has been charged with a fraud that has nothing to do with us. If the allegations are true, we hate it. Stealing from sick kids? That's terrible. But it has nothing to do with us."

"One of the prosecution's witnesses suggested it might."

Stanwell squinted, surprised by the comment. "Who?"

"One of the redacted witnesses who will testify for the prosecution has said they found links between Stanwell Construction and the Wolfgang Berger Foundation in the accounting files."

Stanwell stood and leaned his hands on the table. "That's a lie. We would never steal from sick children, and we want nothing to do with it. Who said that

116

there were links to us?"

"I can't tell you that."

"You're bluffing. There are no witnesses who would be brave enough to say that."

"That's why their statement is redacted until a week before the trial. The prosecution is going to link you to Palin's crimes. One of the redacted witnesses is going to point the finger at you. I need to be prepared so I can stop them. If I know what's coming, I can lodge pretrial motions to keep your business name out of the courtroom."

Stanwell pulled out a piece of gum from a packet on his desk. He threw a piece in his mouth and chewed it aggressively. He walked to the window at the side of the room. "That's not good. We can't have that."

"If it comes out in court that you're involved, it could destroy the reputation of the entire business. No council is going to want to approve a development with an organization that steals money from sick children."

"That's enough. It's time for you to go. I don't want to listen to this anymore." Stanwell waved them away. "Watch your step on the way out. This is a worksite, and I would hate it if you fell over and hurt yourself."

Hennessy looked at Lockett. Lockett nodded. It was time to go. The two men stood and walked toward the exit. The two construction workers were waiting by the door. That wasn't a good sign.

Hennessy turned back to Stanwell. Stanwell glared at Hennessy before he nodded to the men.

The two men looked at each other and then stepped aside. Hennessy and Lockett strode through the exit, not looking back at the building site.

They had escaped without trouble, but Hennessy was sure danger was to follow them.

CHAPTER 14

Hennessy spent the following day in his office, reviewing the file for Palin's case.

He had several other cases on his desk—DUIs, a petit larceny, and several traffic violations. Nothing that could sustain him for long and nothing that would stop the banks from taking his vineyard. His focus had to be on winning Palin's case.

The case against John Tilly was building nicely. He didn't need to hand the jury a smoking gun. All he had to do was plant the seed of doubt—show them the cracks in the story, the shadows where the truth could hide. Opportunity and motive, that was his play. If he could make the jurors believe Tilly had both, if he could convince the jury there was reasonable doubt that Palin was guilty, he could retire to the vineyard.

Stanwell Construction was a problem. Hennessy assumed Garrett would work them into the case to discredit Palin's character. Hennessy knew little about the construction company, and while the discovery material had access to some of Palin's accounting for them, it appeared nothing more than advice via a few emails and filing several hundred invoices. There was little indication that the company was a money laundering business.

After their meeting the day before, Hennessy expected Stanwell to react. Stanwell wasn't the sort of man who would stand by while his livelihood was threatened.

As the time ticked past 10 p.m., Hennessy locked his office, checked the street, and walked to the parking lot at the rear of his building. Hennessy's pickup truck was parked at the rear of the lot, in the furthest corner away from the building. It was dark, and only the single light next to the fence provided any illumination. He noticed the movement in the shadows as he approached.

Two men. Both tall. Both broad shouldered.

"Can I help you?" Hennessy called out.

The two men stepped out of the shadows and into the light. They were the same two men from the work site the day before. "You sure can help us, pal."

Hennessy tightened his grip on his briefcase. He calmed his breath as he gauged the distance to his truck. Fifteen feet.

"What do you want?"

"To convince you not to dig into areas you shouldn't."

The men were within striking distance. Hennessy had always loved boxing. It had been his passion for decades, a way to release the emotions he was too scared to talk about.

"And how would you convince me to do that?"

"With our fists."

The first swinging fist came from the left. Hennessy saw it coming, and leaned to his right, allowing the punch to whizz past in thin air. The second fist came from the second man. It was a wild hook. Hennessy leaned back, stepping out of range.

Both men looked at each other. "You move well for an old man."

Hennessy responded with a quick left jab to the man's nose, followed by a solid right hook to the chin. It was his favorite combination, the one he'd practiced thousands of times over and over again in the boxing gym. The first man fell to the ground.

The second man lunged, swinging hard. Hennessy slipped to his right and smashed his left fist into the man's open ribs. The man doubled over, gasping for air.

The first man rose to his feet. He lifted his shirt to show the Glock tucked into his jeans. He removed it and held it in front of him.

Hennessy stepped back.

"Not so tough now, are ya?"

Hennessy resisted the urge to point out the irony of the statement. He didn't think the man would understand. As much as he enjoyed fighting, as skillful as he was at boxing, he couldn't dodge a bullet.

The second man stood up straight, holding his hand on his ribs. He stood next to Hennessy and leaned close. "I'm going to punch you in the ribs, and you're not going to move."

Hennessy took a step back.

"Or we can sort it out another way." The first man wiped the blood from his mouth and waved the gun. "Your choice, old man."

The Glock remained steady in the man's hands. It was clear it wasn't the first time he pointed a gun at a man.

While Hennessy's attention was on the weapon, the second man delivered a brutal punch to his ribs. Pain shot through Hennessy as he collapsed to his knees. A boot followed, slamming into his stomach and robbing him of air. Hennessy gasped, clutching his midsection as another kick sent him sprawling to the ground.

Another boot connected with his stomach. Hennessy sucked in deep.

"This is the only time we ask—do not dig into Stanwell Construction's business dealings." The first man leaned down close to Hennessy's ear. "Because we won't be as nice if we need to return and ask you again."

CHAPTER 15

Barry Lockett handed Hennessy a beer.

They sat on two camping chairs in Lockett's yard, enjoying the weekend sunshine. His yard was big, edged by tall trees, and with the perfect lawn. The grass was so green it almost looked painted. It was a source of pride for Lockett. He had erected four posts at the back of the yard, two tall ones in the middle and two smaller ones on the outside, determined to teach his son to play his beloved sport of Australian Rules Football. He wasn't having much luck. Like most of the boys in his class, his son was inspired by the NFL.

Hennessy grimaced as he moved to his left.

"You'll be sore for a week," Lockett said, pointing to Hennessy's ribs. "With a bruise like that, I'm surprised they're not broken."

Hennessy nodded. After the assault, he got behind the wheel, drove himself to the hospital, and let them slide him under the cold glare of an X-ray machine. There were no breaks, the doctors told him, but he'd be sore for a while. When they asked him what happened, he said he fell down the stairs. They didn't believe him, but that didn't matter. Hennessy wasn't going to go after the thugs of Stanwell Construction.

Two days later, he was on a diet of Advil and beer, sitting in Lockett's yard, enjoying the sunshine.

"Need me to stick around the office?" Lockett offered. "Provide some protection?"

"No, I'm good. They won't come back unless I do something stupid."

"I wouldn't put it past you."

"I might be courageous, but I'm not dumb," Hennessy responded and pointed to the large yard. "You won't have time to do it anyway. You've got to look after this beautiful lawn. I don't think I've seen a lawn as nice as this in someone's yard. This is good enough to play golf on."

"I love having a green lawn," Lockett said as he pointed to the large patch of grass. "In Queensland, Australia, where I grew up, you could only have a lawn if we weren't going through a drought. If there was a drought, you couldn't water your lawn. It's too much of a waste of water. So, for most of my childhood, my family's lawn was just a patch of dusty, dry grass. But when the drought broke, and we could have a lawn again, you felt so privileged, like a higher power was working in your favor." Lockett admired his lawn for a moment and smiled. "I love that my kids get the privilege of having a nice lawn."

"We love to give our kids what we didn't have," Hennessy said as Lockett's youngest child ran around with a football, passing it to one of his friends. They screamed with delight when one of the kids threw a perfect spiral. "Your kids are growing up. They're going to be young adults before you know it."

"My eldest is a senior high school student next year, and the youngest is in his last year of middle school. They've got their mother's genes when it comes to intelligence. The two of them are smarter than I ever was. My daughter was doing her math homework last night, and I looked at it, and it made my head spin. X equals Y, and B equals A, and C equals D. Man, I can't keep up. So, I said to her, 'Do you know what's odd about math?' She didn't know, so I told her, 'Every other number.'"

"Ha," Hennessy chuckled. "I like it."

"Yeah. She didn't laugh."

"You should ask her why you should never argue with a ninety-degree angle—it's because they're always right."

"That's worse than mine, and she'll hate that, so I'll definitely tell her that one." Lockett laughed. He sipped on his beer as a gentle breeze blew through the yard. "How's the vineyard? Good crop this year?"

"It's looking like one of our best years. We've had a warm growing season with lots of sunlight. We've had enough rain, but not too much, and there's been no signs of black rot. It's shaping up as our best ever year."

"Good to hear." Lockett paused and leaned forward, resting his elbows on his knees. "And if you win this case? Is that it in Charleston?"

Hennessy nodded. "That was always the goal. Earn enough to get in front of the bank loans and then move back to the vineyard. That was the only reason I came back to practice law. And if we win this case, I can move back Upstate."

"And the firm?"

"It would be the end of it."

"If it comes to that, then I just want to say—"

"Save it," Hennessy smiled. "We haven't won the case yet. Don't jinx us."

"I was going to say, 'If it comes to that, and you close the firm, then I want you to know that you've been the worst boss I've ever had,' but sure, I'll save it until we've won the case," Lockett laughed.

Hennessy laughed with him. "A part of me will miss all this. The intensity of a trial, the investigation, uncovering new angles. There's always been something about the law that fascinates me. I love the courtroom."

"And you really think you can win it? The evidence against Palin is solid."

"The evidence is good, but there's hope. Debra Fisher and John Tilly are our best chances to convince a jury that someone else could've done this. They had access to the files, they had access to the accounts, and they had the motive to steal the money." Hennessy sipped his beer. "If we can get them on the stand and expose their affair, then there's a good chance they'll crumble under the pressure."

"Think the jury would buy it?"

"Tilly and Fisher both come from marriages where the children have left home. Tilly had access to the bank accounts, and both Fisher and Tilly had access to the reports. They could've worked together to plan the transfers. And their affair makes them look morally questionable. If it weren't for the tip-off that said Palin was the guilty party, the police would've gone after them first."

Hennessy's cell rang. He looked at the number, nodded to Barry, and answered the call. "Aaron Garrett. It's a Sunday afternoon. I wouldn't have expected you to be working."

"I wish this call was under better circumstances," Garrett said. "I've just received news about the Palin case, and I feel it's best that you hear it from me."

"What is it?"

"We've a police report that states Witness Two and Witness Three have been reported as missing persons."

CHAPTER 16

At 9 a.m. Monday morning, Hennessy strode through the front door of Palin Accounting's desolate office, almost pushing the doors off the hinges. Palin was sitting behind his desk, staring at his laptop screen, coffee mug on one side, and a smoking ashtray on the other.

"What happened to them?" Hennessy stood over Palin's desk.

"Who?" Palin squinted as he looked up at Hennessy.

"Don't play the fool with me. What happened to Debra Fisher and John Tilly?"

Palin shrugged. "How would I know?"

"Where are they?"

Palin clucked his tongue several times and leaned back in his chair. He looked at his smoldering cigarette and smiled. "You know, the best thing about not having anyone else in the office is that I can go back to the old ways, and I don't have to worry about breaking any workplace laws. I can smoke in the office, I can swear, and I can do all the crazy things that are against workplace laws now. I guess all I need is a cute little secretary to slap on the bottom every now and again, and it'd be just like the good old days. They were good times, Joe. Remember those days?"

Hennessy ignored his comment. "You didn't answer my question. What happened to Fisher and Tilly?"

Palin sighed and looked around. He avoided eye contact with Hennessy. "They were told to move along."

"Is that all?"

"I'm not sure how much convincing they needed, but you can imagine that the request from Tony Stanwell wasn't polite."

"Are they safe?"

"I think so, but I'm not sure."

"They're important to your defense. We were building a case against them. If we tricked them on the stand, we could've thrown reasonable doubt over your charges."

"But they were going to suggest that Stanwell

Construction was involved in this case."

"How do you know that?"

"After Tony's chat with you, he called Roger East. East put two and two together, and assumed you talked to Tilly and Fisher. So, East went and had a quiet chat with them, suggesting they move along before the trial." Palin sighed and leaned forward, resting his heavy arms on the table. "As soon as they brought Tony's name into the scenario, there was nothing else I could do. Obviously, Tony doesn't want his business name exposed in the case. It would be bad for his business."

"Is he involved?"

"In what?"

"The embezzlement of funds from the Foundation. John Tilly told me there were a lot of links between Stanwell Construction and the Foundation. He said there were links in your files that connected Stanwell Construction and the Wolfgang Berger Foundation."

"I don't think Stanwell Construction is involved, but like I've told you so many times, I don't know. I didn't take those funds, and I don't know who did."

Palin picked up his cigarette, had a long drag, and then tapped it in the ashtray. "Why did you go and talk to Tony anyway? Didn't I tell you not to do that?"

"I talked to Tony because you didn't give me the information I needed." Hennessy sat down. "I need to know how you change the records for Stanwell Construction. I need to know what accounting is not legitimate. If we're going to win, we need to be prepared. We can't be surprised by the link in court."

"Everything I do for that company is legitimate. There isn't a piece of accounting that isn't correct. If the company informs me they've received money from certain places, then I record it as income." Palin took another long drag on his cigarette and then conceded the truth. "But Stanwell Construction also does smaller jobs. Jobs that cost around nine-thousand dollars each."

"Which is under the Currency Transaction Report threshold. The Bank Secrecy Act requires banks to notify the Financial Crimes Enforcement Network of any cash transactions that exceed ten thousand dollars."

"Very clever, Joe. There, it didn't take you long to

work it out. If Stanwell Construction goes to a house and fixes the drywall, or the plumbing, or a broken fence, then that may cost between five thousand and nine thousand dollars each time. Now, this happens in a lot of new building developments—a hole in a wall here, a crack in the concrete slab there, or even a broken window. Of course, the owner of the new house pays in cash, and the money is deposited into a bank account. Do ten of those a day by five staff members, and you're cleaning fifty-thousand dollars in cold, hard cash."

"Except there never was a problem with the drywall, or the plumbing, or the broken fence."

"But nobody can prove there was or there wasn't. If someone went to that home and looked at the drywall, they'd see the problem has been fixed."

"You could've told me that earlier. It would've saved a lot of problems."

"Where's the fun in that?" He smirked. "Honestly, I didn't think you'd be that determined. I'm glad I've got you in my corner, Joe. You're like a very tall pit bull." Palin put his feet on the desk and leaned back in his chair. "But do you know what I think, Joe? I think Tilly played you. He sent you to Stanwell

Construction because he knew what would happen. He was setting you up to get hurt." Palin glanced at Hennessy's ribs. "And he was right."

Hennessy's fist clenched. "Did you know about it?"

"Not before. Only afterward." Palin avoided eye contact. "Tony called me and said two of his boys went to chat with you and that you might have sore ribs next time we spoke. He also said that his boys were impressed with the way you moved. They said they didn't hurt you too much because they respected your fighting ability. You did well." Palin reached for his cigarette again and sucked hard on the little white stick. He tapped it on the ashtray before he continued. "And John Tilly was dumb. Always was. He had no common sense. He's good with numbers, but common sense was never his thing. By suggesting that Stanwell Construction was involved, he placed himself in the thick of it. And Tony doesn't like people who throw his name around like it's a plaything."

"Will they still testify?"

"Does it matter?"

Hennessy drew a long breath and exhaled heavily.

He tapped his thumb on the armrest of his chair. "Right now, we're building a case against Tilly. We can proceed whether they testify or not, but I need to know where they stand. Our case shows they had access to the files, bank accounts, and systems that generated the invoices. The accounting records confirm the fraudulent transactions came from a specific login at Palin Accounting. Only two people had access to those credentials—you and your senior accountant, Tilly. Another login was used to alter the reports presented to the Foundation's board, and five people, including Debra Fisher, had access to it. Given that Tilly and Fisher also had an affair, it doesn't paint a pretty picture for them."

A sly grin spread across Palin's face. "I like it when you talk like that. It makes me sound innocent."

"Nothing could make you sound innocent," Hennessy stated. "However, given the situation, there's enough evidence to suggest there's reasonable doubt that you were involved."

"So, our case is stronger if they don't testify?"

"Given that their statements point the finger squarely at you, then yes, our case is stronger without their testimonies."

Palin chuckled to himself. "Sounds like I might win this thing."

Hennessy shook his head, disappointed more with himself than Palin. Every time he saw Palin's sly smile and heard Palin talk about the case, he wondered how much he had sold his morals for.

"Witness One is our biggest problem," Hennessy said. "That's the witness who provided the tipoff. It looks like it's someone else you previously employed, but the first two pages of their statement is redacted. Any idea who it is?"

"No idea. We had a high staff turnover rate. Lots of people didn't last five months with us." Palin shrugged. "I spoke with Clarence Berkley again yesterday, and he said he's going to get me the list of all the redacted witness names. I told him it was Witness One who ratted me out. He said he would look into it for me."

"The last time I spoke to him, he told me he wanted nothing to do with you."

"Well, let's just say that I used my knowledge of his history to convince him otherwise." Another sly grin spread across Palin's face. "There were several allegations against Berkley that were swept under the carpet, including one allegation that involved an underage girl. After I suggested I have evidence of that, Berkley's tone changed."

"If you have evidence of criminal activity, you need to give it to law enforcement. There's no statute of limitations on Criminal Sexual Conduct with a minor. That's a matter for the police."

"Maybe I have evidence, maybe I don't. Maybe there were only rumors about it. Berkley doesn't know the difference." Palin grinned. "And right now, I can guarantee that Berkley is working hard for me, and he's going to expose the identity of Witness One shortly."

CHAPTER 17

The Gibbes Museum of Art was housed in a historic Beaux-Arts building off Meeting Street in downtown Charleston. Opened in 1905, the museum's art collection reflected Charleston's rich artistic heritage, spanning Gullah art, classical works, and modern pieces. Renovated in 2016, the building also featured several artist studios on the ground floor, an impressive rear garden, and a striking glass dome surrounded by architectural details such as pedimented windows and elegant Doric columns.

Hennessy moved through the well-dressed crowd, who were mingling with glasses of champagne in hand. Rumors whispered from one socialite to another at the opening of the museum's latest exhibition. The rich and powerful were happy to mingle—another event on their calendars to network, leverage, or gossip. The room smelled of fine perfume and expensive champagne. Hennessy made his way to the rear of the room, toward the man he needed to speak with.

Deep in conversation with another retired judge, Clarence Berkley looked up, took a second glance, and then sighed. Berkley was dressed in a fitted blue suit with a red bowtie and black thin-rimmed glasses. He said something to the other judge and then turned to the beautiful younger woman beside him. He leaned in close, whispered in her ear, and then looked back at Hennessy. Berkley grunted and then walked through the door to the left. Hennessy followed.

Berkley entered the hallway that led to the stairwell and stopped at the end, well away from the ears of the socialite crowd. He leaned against the wall and folded his arms. "Why'd you confront me here? You could've called me and arranged to meet."

"I called you. You didn't return my calls."

"True." Berkley shrugged. "What do you want? I'm in the middle of something."

"With a woman who isn't your wife."

"That's your problem?" Berkley groaned. "My wife has dementia and can barely remember who I am anymore. What am I supposed to do all day? Hold her hand and reminisce? No thanks. She has a nurse to look after her, and I still need to live my life."

"Did you pay the woman?"

"Oh, come on, Joe." Berkley shook his head. "Why do you think a beautiful woman like that would be on my arm? She's not an escort but now owns one of my wife's old diamond necklaces."

"You haven't changed."

"Why would I? I'm too old to change my ways now. A man has to have fun."

Hennessy shook his head in disgust. "Do you know what happened to Witness Two and Three in Palin's case?"

Berkley hesitated, went to open his mouth, and then closed it again. He shook his head and leaned his back against the wall. "What happened to them?"

"They're missing."

"That's no surprise," Berkley said. "I assume you knew who they were."

"John Tilly and Debra Fisher. Former employees of Palin."

"And it's no surprise they were former employees either. Given what Palin has told me about their witness statements, I would assume all five of them are former employees." Berkley squinted and leaned forward. "Are you suggesting I had something to do with their disappearance?"

"Palin said you were working behind the scenes to expose the names of all the witnesses. He said you were leveraging your contacts and talking to people in law enforcement. He thinks you're working hard to expose the name of Witness One as soon as possible."

"I told you I wouldn't help him."

"He's convinced you will."

"That's because he's an idiot. I've been trying to get him off my back for years, but he keeps hounding me like I owe him something. I owe him nothing. He used me, blackmailed me, and now he thinks we're friends? He's delusional."

"Then why do you answer his calls?"

"What am I supposed to do? Ignore him. That's not how things work in the South, Joe. You know that." Berkley nodded slowly, his expression shifting as thoughts rolled through his mind. "And I suggest you haven't investigated as much as you should have."

"I don't buy it. Your fingers are reaching into this somehow, and Palin is convinced you're helping him."

"He's an idiot. I want nothing to do with him. He keeps coming to me, threatening he's going to tell my wife about my affairs, but it doesn't matter. He could tell her about every single one of the women I've slept with, and it wouldn't matter. I'm not helping him anymore."

Hennessy leaned forward. "As a former judge, I'm sure you remember that there's no statute of limitations on criminal sexual conduct with a minor."

Berkley's mouth hung open for a few moments before he groaned. "He told you about that?"

Hennessy nodded.

"Alright. Alright. Tell him not to panic. You can tell Palin that I'm working hard to get the names of the redacted witnesses. I should have them over the next week or so. There are people here who are still connected to the justice system who can help me, and I will try to leverage them."

"I don't believe a single word coming out of your mouth." Hennessy studied Berkley. He was shifty under Hennessy's gaze. "And you know something that you're not telling me?"

"This isn't as simple as you want it to be, Joe. The

world you're stepping into has many links, many connections, and many people have been affected by Palin's actions. We've got to unravel the links before we can help him. I can't be tied to this at all, so I need to use intermediaries to get the information. The problem is that most people think he's guilty and want nothing to do with it. It was a despicable crime."

"You need to tell me if you know something that can clear Palin."

"Palin has a long history of corruption. There's no doubt about what he's done." Berkley threw his hands in the air and walked back toward the doors out of the hallway. "Now, let me get back to networking and see if I can convince someone to help him."

Hennessy lingered in the hallway, his gaze fixed on the doors swinging shut behind Berkley. The faint echo of footsteps faded into the crowd's din, leaving him cloaked in an uneasy silence.

The deeper Hennessy dug, the more complicated the case became.

CHAPTER 18

In the weeks leading up to the trial, Joe made frequent trips to the vineyard, savoring every moment among the vines. He knew he wouldn't see the vines for weeks once the trial began. He would be tied to his desk, working early and late, and everything in between.

As he drove into Luca's Vineyard one Friday evening, he stopped at the entrance sign on the left side of the property. The entrance was for the events held on the grassed area outside the chateau, where loved ones were married, milestones were celebrated, and where families enjoyed a Sunday afternoon picnic.

The shop was closed, the workers had gone home, and the area was empty. Wendy had messaged him earlier and stated she had forgotten to close the gate and asked if he could do it on his way in. As he swung the gate closed, he paused and looked up at the vineyard's name.

Joe always ensured the painting on Luca's name was touched up every year. A faded sign felt like a faded memory, and he couldn't bear that—not for Luca.

Standing under the sign, the memories of Luca came flooding back. They were always there, crammed deep inside of him, waiting for the smallest crack to pour out. As soon as one memory surfaced, the rest followed—a stream of moments, a world of memories, hopes, and dreams.

The waves came, rolling in and easing out.

He thought of Luca's birthdays, his paintings, his broad smiles when swimming. He thought of the moments when they threw the baseball together, when they spent a week building a soapbox cart, and when they played football in the pouring rain because Luca refused to go inside. The times when Luca presented work at school, when he was learning the guitar, and when he proudly gave Joe a Christmas present.

Joe remembered the eulogy he gave at Luca's funeral, barely able to deliver the words over his tears. Being a stoic man, he was embarrassed to cry, but time had taught him that emotions matter and shouldn't be hidden from the world. Joe remembered the church, the photos of Luca that were displayed, and the faces of those in attendance. Most of the day was a blur, but he remembered the eulogy clearly.

Standing under the sign for Luca's Vineyard, he softly repeated the final lines of that eulogy, as if speaking them aloud could bring him closer to his son, "Love means there's no end. Not today, not tomorrow, and not a single breath I take, will be without love for you. In the stars, in the oceans, and in the woods, you will find my love. I've had the opportunity to love you, to feel deeply, and there is no end to that love. To my beautiful Luca, I will love you always. Rest in peace."

He placed his hand on the wooden post holding the sign and stood silently.

Death was not the end of Luca.

Luca still lived strong in the minds of his father, his mother, and even the sisters he never met.

Over his decades of struggle, a truth had settled with Joe. There would always be sorrow in his soul.

He accepted it now. He acknowledged it. Through that pain, through that sense of melancholy, he could find happiness. Happiness that he was allowed to share ten years with Luca. Happiness that they had so many great memories together. Happiness that he would see Luca again one day.

Despite Joe's reluctance to return to church, he still believed in an afterlife. He still believed he would see his son again.

And that meant the world to him.

CHAPTER 19

The weeks passed quickly and without further violence.

Hennessy spent much of his time in the office, studying the witness statements line by line, tracking every number in the financial analysis of the accounting, and picking apart every fraudulent invoice.

Berkley hadn't come good on his promise to help. It didn't surprise Hennessy. He expected Berkley wanted to distance himself from Palin, and Hennessy didn't blame him.

On the last Monday before the trial, Hennessy walked to his office, wandering through the streets of Charleston, a to-go coffee in his hand. The morning sun streamed through the thin clouds, and the shine reflected off the beautiful buildings.

Hennessy loved his home city of Charleston. The beauty was everywhere in downtown, presenting a city full of grace and grit, opulence and affluence, a seamless blend of its terrible history and weathered resilience. Grand antebellum homes lined the streets, their facades cracked and chipped by centuries of hurricanes and humidity, alleys paved in cobblestones whispered secrets of merchants and smugglers, and pastel row houses with steep gabled roofs hugged one another tightly. The streets were a testament to Charleston's enduring character—a city haunted by the past yet proud of its heritage.

As he walked, he took in the delights of his home city. Old sports cars were parked outside large colonial-styled buildings, gardeners were busy pruning back the ever-growing trees, and locals greeted each other loudly with handshakes for men, and kisses on the cheek for women.

Embracing the gentle breeze, his thoughts turned to Palin's case.

The trial was due to start in a week, and Tilly and Fisher still hadn't been found. It was a problem for both the prosecution and the defense. Hennessy's entire case was focused on using them as his third-party culpability targets, and the prosecution's case was angling toward them as their major witnesses.

Their testimonies pointed the finger at Palin. For the prosecution, they were the crucial link that unified the overwhelming array of evidence.

Nobody had heard from them. Not the spouses nor their friends. Both sets of children refused to talk to the police. Were they killed and their bodies dumped somewhere, or did they run off together, escaping the pressure of the trial and their failing marriages? Would they return for the trial? Would they surprise everyone with an appearance?

Hennessy didn't know. The uncertainty gnawed at him, leaving him with headaches he couldn't shake. Advil didn't help. Neither did shoulder massages. A glass of whiskey seemed to be the best remedy.

He had spent weeks preparing for the trial, staring at the evidence, trawling through information on Palin and his corrupt behavior. If one thing was clear, it was that Palin didn't have many friends left.

The prosecution had dropped two charges—Tax Fraud and Money Laundering. They never had much of a chance at winning those, but the charges had been included to pressure Palin into a plea. It hadn't worked.

Hennessy had spent time investigating Maxine

Summers and Melissa Stevenson. They were both squeaky clean. They volunteered at their respective churches, never had as much as a speeding ticket, and both had many people willing to testify about their good characters. Melissa Stevenson may have had a cold personality but was good to people. Maxine appeared to be a saint. Hennessy crossed them off the list of potential targets for third-party culpability.

The remaining redacted witnesses were an issue. He would get them a week before the trial, but he had a good idea of who they could be.

Witness One knew a lot of inside information about Palin's business and was likely another employee. As the person who provided the initial tip-off, Witness One was one of the strongest witnesses for the prosecution. Hennessy requested a deposition, and Judge Clayton approved it being conducted via email. The deposition revealed some details but left much unanswered.

Witness One's statement testified that Palin had told them about his activities, how he was about to move to Costa Rica, and how much money he had stolen. Palin denied everything, but if Witness One appeared reliable on the stand, it would be a serious problem.

Lockett had searched the details of all the other employees, checking every lead, scanning every document, and investigating every idea. Lockett had searched through a mountain of paperwork and listened to a long list of interviews and depositions. There wasn't much to go on. Apart from Tilly and Fisher, the other employees were squeaky-clean accountants who had never strayed beyond the confines of balance sheets and tax codes.

Witness Four was likely to be another business owner Palin had defrauded, and Witness Five seemed like another employee. The redacted statements from Witness Five offered little to the case, and Hennessy suspected they were a distraction.

The remaining prosecution witnesses were mostly experts in their respective fields. From data analysts to financial accountants to money specialists, they could all talk the talk.

Palin's appearance was going to be a problem in court. There was nothing about him that appeared likable or trustworthy. Even in his best suit, he still looked like a creep. The jury would see that. They would see his shifty eyes, the snarl on his face, and sense his lack of morals from across the room.

Palin hadn't been easy to deal with. Hennessy dreaded every phone call, every meeting, and every email. Palin had made it clear that Hennessy was working for him, and he tried to drain every minute of his time. Hennessy didn't trust him, and doubted anyone could. But the more he investigated, the less convinced he was that Palin had transferred the funds.

Did Palin set up the accounts in preparation for an escape? Or was it the affair couple who were looking to the future? Hennessy didn't know the answer but knew Palin was guilty of so much more. He had a history of crime and a history of inappropriate behavior. Life, karma, and perhaps even justice had caught up to him.

Jacinta's knock on his office door caught him by surprise. "Assistant Solicitor Aaron Garrett is here for his ten o'clock." She stepped in the door of Hennessy's office. She looked over her shoulder and stepped further into the room, gently shutting the door behind her. When she approached the desk, she whispered, "And a heads up, he looks nervous."

CHAPTER 20

"Five years." Aaron Garrett stated as soon as he stepped into the room. He was dressed well in a black fitted suit, with a blue tie lying straight down the middle of his crisp white shirt. "Early guilty plea, and he serves five years. That deal is still on the table, and I suggest your client takes it."

Hennessy closed his laptop, turned over the file on his desk, and invited Garrett to sit. "He won't even consider it."

"Will you at least encourage him to take it?"

"I presented it to him, but he doesn't want to do a day in prison. He says he's too old for prison and doesn't like the idea of dying back there. It doesn't matter if it's one year or fifteen; he's not going to survive behind bars."

Garrett placed his briefcase beside him and sat down, leaning back in his chair, trying to present an image of confidence. But it was fake confidence, trying to mask the nerves he was feeling. His movements were twitchy, and he couldn't find a comfortable position in the chair. He avoided eye contact with Hennessy. "He could survive five years. If he keeps his head down and doesn't make any trouble, he could be out before he knows it. Then, he has a chance at living a great life after his prison sentence. He'll serve five years, be out in his mid-sixties, and he can go off and do whatever he wants in his retirement."

"I'll take it to him again, but he won't accept it." Hennessy leaned forward, resting his elbows on the table. "The missing witnesses hurt your case."

"Maybe." Garrett nodded and looked at the wall. "But they've made statements we can use in court."

"You must know that I'll dispute the use of those statements."

"Of course." Garrett nodded and let the silence hang between them for a while. When the moment dragged on for too long, Garrett felt the need to fill the gap in the conversation. "I'm sure you've figured out who Witness Two and Three are by now."

"John Tilly and Debra Fisher."

Garrett nodded. "Both parties have disappeared

off the face of the planet, and nobody knows where they are. They were both reported missing by their respective spouses, and I must say that both parties' disappearances were similar—their cell phones were left at home, they disappeared on the same day, and none of the children are talking. Their vehicles are still in the driveway, most of their clothes are still in the bedrooms, and their valuables have been left behind."

"Did they withdraw any cash?"

Garrett didn't answer, pressing his lips together and looking away.

"How much did they take out?"

"I'm not at liberty to say."

"I'm going to receive the missing persons file as part of discovery for this case this week. I'll get the information one way or another."

Garrett looked away and then sighed. "Tens of thousands each."

"Enough to start a new life."

"Maybe."

"This better not be a cheap tactic by your team, Aaron. If they reappear in two weeks, I will dispute their appearance at the trial."

"Is that what you think this is? No way. That would be a very underhanded move. I can assure you that we have no idea where they are. It's been five weeks, and no one has found them." Garrett scoffed and shook his head. "And we know what you're going to do. You're going to target them as part of your third-party culpability defense, suggesting that they were hiding the cash before their getaway. You're going to blame them for the despicable actions of Bernard Palin."

"Two members of an accounting firm are having an affair, they quit the same day, and then disappear without a trace before a criminal trial. That sounds like more than a coincidence."

"Come on, Joe. This case isn't about catching a couple having an affair—this is about catching a career-long criminal who has gotten away with so much that he couldn't remember what innocence is. This is about justice. This is about all the people he's ripped off and betrayed. This is about the struggling children he stole money from."

"Palin is claiming he's innocent."

"You and I both know that man is far from innocent. He's spent a lifetime ripping people off and using his connections to wield power over vulnerable people. There are so many witnesses who will testify that Palin has ripped them off in the past. That's not a good look, and the jury will take one look at him and understand the type of man he is."

"Your duty is to the courts and the justice system. Your duty is not to convict someone because you think they're guilty. If you put people away because you 'think' they're guilty, you're going down a slippery slope to tyranny."

"There's no tyranny here. We all know the truth. Palin was embezzling money from a children's charity foundation to set up his retirement in Costa Rica. There's no moral good in that." Garrett held his stare for a few moments before looking away. "And no matter how you play this with Fisher and Tilly, there's still a long witness list willing to testify against Palin. He's guilty, no doubt about it."

"You're not the jury. You don't get to decide who's guilty or innocent."

"But I'm the prosecutor. I get to decide who is charged or not, and let me remind you, I have a ninety-five percent win rate. I don't take cases to court unless I'm sure I can win it. I'm almost certain of the outcome if I end up in court. And in this case, well, it's about as solid as they come. I don't even know why he's trying to weasel out of it. He's going to prison, and there's nothing you can do to stop that."

"He deserves a fair trial."

"Fair?" Garrett scoffed. "That's a matter of opinion. He certainly wasn't thinking about fairness when he stole all that money. Do you think it's fair to the children?"

Hennessy didn't answer.

"I can see we're getting nowhere today," Garrett said. He reached down and picked up his briefcase, opening it on his lap. He removed a file and placed it on the edge of Hennessy's desk before he closed his briefcase and stood. He tapped his finger on the file. "Here's the redacted witness list, which is accompanied by several pieces of evidence. We'll email you a copy as well, but I thought I'd personally drop this one off. I'm sure it'll make for good reading."

"What's the new evidence?"

"A bank statement from the account in question. Palin gave one witness a copy of the bank statement to prove he had the money. We couldn't release this evidence before now because it would've identified the witness. It's an important piece of the puzzle, so I'm sure if you apply for a continuance, Judge Clayton will allow you extra time to review it. We won't object to that."

Garrett nodded to Hennessy, and then left without another word. Once he had gone, Jacinta walked back into the office.

Hennessy looked at the folder, contemplating what was inside. When Jacinta sat down, Hennessy reached forward and opened the file.

His mouth dropped open as he read the first page.

"Who is it? Do we know any of the other witnesses?" Jacinta asked.

Hennessy stared at the first page of the file, examining the details. The first page listed the five witness names, followed by their aliases.

And it was Witness One that had caught his attention.

He'd been played. He'd been set up from the start.

"Who is it, Joe? Who is Witness One?"

He turned the file around and pushed the page before his assistant.

"Oh," Jacinta whispered. "Really?"

"Our mystery witness, Witness One, who made the tip-off and started all of this, is Clarence Berkley."

CHAPTER 21

"He played you?"

Barry Lockett sat at the head of the boardroom table, staring at the whiteboard. The name 'Clarence Berkley' had been circled and underlined in red.

Hennessy stood, pacing the room as he rubbed his brow. "Berkley played us all, but most of all, he played Palin. Berkley set this whole thing up."

The boardroom table was covered in documents, the whiteboard was covered in scribbles, and boxes of files were pushed into the corner of the room. Evidence was piling up, and a week out from the trial, they had been thrown a curveball.

"Berkley was the man who provided the tip-off and instigated all this," Jacinta said. "He set up Palin from the start. He's the one that called the police and he's the one that supplied all the information. It wasn't another staff member of Palin Accounting that provided the tip-off—it was Berkley."

"What's the motivation to do that?"

"Because Berkley had had enough of Palin. Palin had been blackmailing Berkley for years and pushed him too far. Berkley hated Palin." Hennessy grunted. "Palin kept harassing Berkley for help, and Berkley had enough of him. He wanted Palin out of the picture and saw this as the perfect opportunity to do so. We've been given the full witness statement, and in the previously redacted section, Berkley states Palin went to him for help to transfer the embezzled money to Costa Rica. Berkley stepped him through it, and then called the police."

"And Palin had no idea it was Berkley that set him up?"

"None. He was sure that Berkley was on his side. He even told me I should go to Berkley for help."

"And the new bank statement?"

"Palin gave Berkley a copy of the bank statement of the account to show that he had more than a million dollars in there. He tried convincing Berkley to help him and showed him the statement to prove he could pay Berkley and set up a property in Costa Rica. It's a piece of evidence that shows Palin was aware of the money and the account and was planning to withdraw it. Palin left the bank statement at Berkley's house to convince him, but Berkley took it to the police."

"Will you apply to the court for a continuance?"

"No," Hennessy shook his head. "That's what the prosecution wants. They want us to push the trial date back so they have more time to find Tilly and Fisher. But our case looks stronger without them testifying. We need to push ahead with the current trial date."

The pause sat over the room for a while. "What about the other redacted witnesses?"

"Witnesses Two and Three were who we thought they were—John Tilly and Debra Fisher," Jacinta confirmed. "They hadn't been sighted since they were reported missing weeks ago."

"Any indication it was foul play?"

"Not yet, but the police haven't ruled it out," Hennessy said. "The Rebel Sons need to protect Palin, and if they can prevent the people talking about their connection with Stanwell Construction, they'll do what it takes."

"Is the PD taking the missing person's report seriously?"

"They're attempting to contact them, but there

doesn't appear to be any urgency to it." Jacinta flicked a page in her notepad. "It's a missing person's report and nothing more. Any luck on your end?"

"One police contact said that Tilly accessed his bank account in Alabama," Lockett responded. "That information will be added to the missing persons report next week when the officers in that section get around to it. You'll have that information before the trial starts."

"Are they following up the lead?"

"No," Lockett shook his head. "My contact said that the missing persons officers would review the footage from the ATM but wouldn't make any great effort to find them. They're both consenting adults who chose to leave the state, and there's no evidence of foul play or witness tampering. They need to have a reason before they put hours into the case."

"They've been subpoenaed to testify."

"And they haven't missed that date yet," Lockett shrugged. "And until they do, the police won't do anything."

"Are we still going to use them as the third-party culpability targets?" Jacinta questioned. "We still have Maxine and Melissa?"

"Who are both squeaky clean." Hennessy tapped his hand on the whiteboard. "Tilly and Fisher need to remain our targets. Tilly had access to the bank account, they both had access to the accounting reports and most importantly, they had the motive. Whether or not they testify, our case against them is strong. It's enough to raise a reasonable doubt about Palin's guilt if we play our cards right."

"I'll keep an ear out and let you know if there's any more leads." Lockett nodded. "And the other witnesses?"

"Witness Four was a business owner Palin ripped off, and Witness Five is another former employee," Hennessy noted. "Berkley is our main problem. His testimony just about convicts Palin. And considering he's a former judge, the jury will think he's a trustworthy authority figure, no matter how untrue that is."

"Palin won't have liked that," Barry said, then tilted his head to look at Hennessy. "How did Palin react when you told him?"

Hennessy didn't respond, keeping his eyes on the whiteboard.

"You haven't told Palin that Berkley is Witness

One?" Lockett pressed.

"We only received this information this morning," Hennessy said. He exhaled loudly and picked up his cell phone. He turned on the speakerphone and placed it on the table.

After the fifth ring, Palin answered. "Tell me this is all sorted, and the charges have been dropped."

"No such luck," Hennessy responded. "There's been a development."

"What is it?"

"Witness One, the person who made the tip-off, was Clarence Berkley."

The other end of the line was silent.

"Are you still there?"

"I am," Palin stated. "Are you sure it was Berkley?"

"I'm looking at the witness statements provided by the prosecution, and it has his name on top of it. The first two pages of the witness statement were redacted; however, it's now been released. That section states you went to talk to Berkley about your plans to move the money to Costa Rica to fund your retirement. The section even mentions that you've put an offer down to buy a waterfront home in Costa

Rica."

"Have you talked to him since you found out?"

"I tried to call him this morning. The nurse for his wife answered and said that he'd left town for a week and was uncontactable."

Hennessy heard the phone being placed down, and then Palin let out a few swear words, yelling into nothing. When he had finished yelling, he picked the phone back up.

"And you're sure it was Berkley?"

"We are. He's named in all the unredacted statements."

"Then I need to talk with him."

"He's a witness, which means he's protected, Palin."

"Nobody is that protected." Palin's anger seeped through the phone. "I'll find that lying scumbag."

Palin ended the call without another word.

Hennessy looked at his colleagues. They were all thinking the same thing—Berkley might not make it to the stand to testify.

CHAPTER 22

Garrett stood firm on his deal—five years in exchange for an early guilty plea.

He said it was as low as he could go. There was too much media coverage to go lower, he explained. There was an election coming up, and they couldn't let someone who stole from sick children to walk away. Garrett saw the case as an easy win for the prosecutor's office, and a chance to get their faces on the front page of the papers.

Palin rejected the deal. He said there was no way he was going to prison. Hennessy was sure if the State hadn't frozen Palin's accounts, he would've been on the next plane out of the country. And he was sure as soon as the accounts were unfrozen, Palin would withdraw every cent and make a run for the airport. If they won, Hennessy would need to ensure he was paid straight away.

Hennessy approached the courthouse for another

pretrial hearing and paused outside, letting the early morning sun soak into his face. It had been years since he first walked these steps, a wide-eyed twenty-five-year-old fresh out of law school and hungry to make his mark. Back then, he'd been full of determination, buzzing with idealism and the belief that justice was absolute and that the law could fix anything. A lot had changed since then.

Ten years with the Circuit Solicitor's Office had hardened him, each case leaving a mark. But it was the murder of his son that finally broke him. Charleston became unbearable after that—a city filled with ghosts and unanswered questions. He'd left, vowing never to look back. Yet here he was, on the other side of the fight, defending the people he used to prosecute.

Hennessy walked through security and stepped into the cool hallway. He stopped at its end, letting the familiar scent of varnished wood and old paper wash over him. He closed his eyes, inhaled deeply, and slowed his breathing. A few seconds later, he gave himself a small nod. He was ready.

The courtroom was quiet when he entered, the kind of quiet that always felt heavy with judgment. He moved to the defense table, setting down his laptop, files, and pens. He adjusted his legal pad so its edges aligned perfectly with the table. The black pen went beside the red, a small ritual that brought him calm before the storm. Another nod. Another breath. He was ready.

Five minutes after Hennessy arrived, Garrett arrived with one of his assistants. Garrett was well-dressed in a fitted suit, and an air of woody cologne followed him. When both lawyers were seated, the bailiff called the court to order. Hennessy stood and watched as Judge Clayton strode to the bench with purpose.

Judge Clayton sat down, opened his laptop, adjusted his files, and nodded to the bailiff. He confirmed the lawyer's names and opened the floor for pretrial motions.

"Mr. Garrett, let's begin with your pretrial motions." Judge Clayton moved a file in front of him. "I see you've submitted a motion to add fifteen names to the witness list. This seems late to be introducing new witnesses, Mr. Garrett."

"Yes, we understand this is late, Your Honor. However, there are no surprises on the updated witness list." Garrett stood behind his desk. "We have added experts in white-collar crime and further specialists in forensic accounting. We've also added a former employee of the defendant and another law enforcement officer."

"Any objections from the defense?"

"None, Your Honor," Hennessy responded.

"The motion to amend the witness list is granted," Judge Clayton stated. He typed several lines into his laptop and then looked at Garrett with raised eyebrows. "Next, there is a motion in Limine to exclude information from the trial that Mr. Tilly and Mrs. Fisher have been reported as missing persons. Mr. Garrett, I'll need a good argument for this one."

"Your Honor, it's prejudicial to include information that these two witnesses have been reported as missing persons. We don't know why Mr. Tilly or Mrs. Fisher have gone missing. We don't know whether they've chosen to or whether they've been the subject of foul play."

"Your Honor," Hennessy interrupted. He stood to emphasize his point. "That's an inflammatory statement. There's no evidence that foul play was involved, and in fact, the two missing witnesses were having an affair for years before they went missing. It's very likely that they've chosen to leave together and leave their spouses behind."

"And this is the sort of language we wish to exclude from the trial." Garrett spread his arms wide for the argument. "The defense is trying to concoct a make-believe tale that these witnesses have had something to do with the charges, and they're leveraging their disappearance to confuse the story."

"We're not leveraging anything, Your Honor. We're merely telling the truth. Two former employees of the defendant were having an affair, and those two former employees had similar access to the bank accounts and computer systems as the defendant. Those employees have gone missing only days before the criminal trial when their information would be scrutinized in public. That's the truth, and that's what the jury should be presented with."

"I agree, Mr. Hennessy," Judge Clayton stated. "This information is relevant, and excluding this information would impact the defendant's right to a fair trial. I find the information that these two former employees of the defendant are recorded as missing persons is admissible to the court. The jury is entitled to hear all the facts pertinent to this case. The motion is denied." Judge Clayton typed several lines into his laptop. "And next, we have a motion for continuance. Please explain, Mr. Garrett."

"Your Honor, given that the information about Mr. Tilly's and Mrs. Fisher's disappearance will be presented to the court, we wish to exhaust every avenue to find them. We're aware that we're close to the trial date; however, we have received information that may help us find them. We believe their testimonies are important to uncovering the truth, and we believe we will locate them given a little extra time. This information only came to us this morning, and we request extra time to explore this lead." Garrett passed a file to the bailiff, who passed the file to the judge. Garrett handed Hennessy a copy. "The Charleston Police Department received this information and are following this line of investigation."

"Your Honor, this information is dated several weeks ago," Hennessy argued as he flicked through the two-page file. The file referenced the video footage from an ATM at a gas station in Alabama. "The police have had weeks to act on this information, and if there's no further development, I cannot see how any extra time will help them. In fact, I would argue further time would make it less likely to find the witnesses. It's already been several weeks since this information was made available to the police. If there's no further development, in the interest of fairness, we should continue the trial."

"Mr. Garrett, is there any further development from the Charleston Police Department other than these photos dated weeks ago?"

"Not at the moment, Your Honor, but we're getting closer."

"The defense objects to the motion, Your Honor," Hennessy responded. "The prosecution's intent is obvious—they want this case to play out in the media and drag it out to win political points. However, I must state that this trial should progress in the interests of fairness and justice. In earlier pretrial hearings, the prosecution made it clear that the trial date was important, and this shouldn't be changed. There's no evidence of any foul play, and based on the witness's statements, it's the defense's belief that the witnesses left because they wanted nothing further to do with this case. There's no indication that extra time will assist the prosecution in finding these witnesses."

"I agree, Mr. Hennessy. Given that weeks have passed since this sighting, and there have been no further developments, I don't find any sufficient evidence that extra time would lead to finding these witnesses. Motion for a continuance is denied," Judge Clayton stated. "Any further motions from the State?"

"No, Your Honor."

Judge Clayton looked over his notes. "And the defense motion, Mr. Hennessy?"

"Your Honor, the defense has lodged a motion in Limine regarding the written statements of the witnesses of Mr. John Tilly and Mrs. Debra Fisher. These witness names were redacted for the defense until a few days ago. Under your ruling, we were not given information about the witnesses until a week before trial, however before that time, the witnesses have gone missing, and we have not been able to question them about their statements. There is vital information missing from their statements that is relevant to the trial."

"The defense had the opportunity to question the

witnesses via email, yes?"

"We did, however, once the names were confirmed, we found information that Mr. Tilly and Mrs. Fisher were in an extra-marital relationship. That is not mentioned anywhere in their witness statements. We have not been able to question them about that relationship and how their affair affected the evidence that they gave. Allowing these written statements to be presented without cross-examination would be a clear breach of the Confrontation Clause of the Sixth Amendment. The defendant has a constitutional right to confront his accusers, and these statements are not complete. We have not had the chance to confront them about it."

Judge Clayton nodded. "Mr. Garrett, can you please confirm that neither of those witnesses mentions this relationship in their statements?"

"That's correct, Your Honor, however, the witnesses were not questioned about their relationship either."

"It's clear that important information has been left out of the written statements." Judge Clayton stated. "Mr. Garrett, were you aware that Mr. Tilly and Mrs. Fisher were in an extra-marital relationship?"

"We're aware of it now, however we were not aware of their relationship when we originally questioned them. And we maintain that their relationship had nothing to do with this case. Their personal relationship had nothing to do with Mr. Palin's criminal actions."

"Important information was left out of the witness statements, and the defense has had no chance to question that information. Considering that, I have no choice in this matter," Judge Clayton groaned. "After considering the arguments presented, the Court finds that the written statements of the missing witnesses are missing important details, and therefore denies the defendant their constitutional right to confront their accuser. The motion to exclude the written statements is granted. However, if Mr. Tilly or Mrs. Fisher were found before the trial date, I will allow them to testify in person. Any objection to that, Mr. Hennessy?"

"No, Your Honor."

When Judge Clayton confirmed there were no further motions, he tapped his gavel and exited the room without fuss. It was a good morning for the defense. Hennessy looked at Garrett. Garrett's jaw was tight, and his hands were clenched into tight fists.

"This isn't over, Joe," Garrett growled through gritted teeth. "Not by a long shot."

CHAPTER 23

Hennessy stepped out of the courthouse and into the midday heat, the kind that clung to his skin and made the pavement shimmer like a mirage.

He crossed the street without looking, his mind miles away, and wandered into Washington Square Garden. The park was quiet this time of day, the hum of distant traffic muted by the thick canopy of ancient oak trees. He stopped beneath one of the larger oaks, its branches sprawling like arms, offering shade from the unforgiving sun. Tilting his head back, he stared up at the endless blue sky, his eyes unfocused, lost in thought.

With a sigh, Hennessy loosened his tie and rolled up his sleeves, the fabric clinging to his damp skin. He sank onto a wooden bench, its surface warm from the sun. For a while, he just sat there, letting the stillness settle over him. No arguments, no files, no ticking clock. Just the shade, the heat, and the distant chirping of birds.

After a few minutes, he stood, the moment of peace fading as the weight of the day returned. He walked the fifteen minutes back to his office, the sun beating down on his shoulders with every step. Outside the building, he paused to wipe the sweat from his brow, already feeling the cool promise of air conditioning through the glass doors. Inside, the chilled air hit him like a blessing. He let out a long breath, grateful for the reprieve.

"Good afternoon," Jacinta said as she sipped her coffee. "Why are you smiling so much?"

"The air-conditioning," Hennessy pointed to the vents above their heads. "I'm so happy it was invented. I'd hate to think about what life was like before air-conditioning."

"Well, it's not all positive." Jacinta placed her mug down and sat behind her desk. "My Grandma says air-conditioners put an end to evening socializing in the Southern states. She remembers when people had to leave their houses in the evenings and sit on the porch to enjoy the cooler weather. People would be inclined to wander over to the neighbors' porch or visit friends down the street just to get out of the house and enjoy the cooler air. She says that once people started putting AC in their homes, nobody went outside in the evenings anymore. She says that comfort put an end to the sense of community."

"The side effect of progress," Hennessy said as he sat down. "How are we going with our expert witnesses?"

"Good. They've all provided their statements and their availability. They're clear about the case they're testifying in and have all the details about the potential dates and times. The IT specialist took some time to respond, but he's confirmed his availability now." Jacinta tilted her head slightly. "But something's wrong. What is it?"

"How could you tell something was wrong?"

"Are you kidding me?" Jacinta laughed. "You can't hide your emotions. You might be tough, and you might be stoic, but every one of those emotions is written on your face. You can't hide from me."

Hennessy smiled. He loved his team. Working with Jacinta had been an absolute pleasure. She was hard-working, smart, and kind. Her presence lit up the room, and he was happy to have found her. When she first started working for the law firm, she requested flexible working hours to help with her family, going to school and volunteering, coaching, or being present as a mother. Having not been in the law for twenty years, Hennessy initially found the request jarring, but once she started, he realized it mattered little. Her work ethic was unmatched.

He sat on the chair beside her desk, huffed, and shook his head. "Garrett requested to add fifteen names to the witness list. Fourteen were nothing witnesses, experts and specialists, and people who will make little difference to our trial tactics, but there was one name that we haven't seen before. Richard Dunstall. He's listed as an eyewitness, and his witness statement makes for interesting reading. And with his name in the middle of the list, it appears like Garrett was trying to bury his presence."

"And the fourteen new witnesses aren't important?"

"They're not inconsequential, but they'll add nothing we haven't already prepared for. They're all experts. Some are forensic accountants, some are white-collar crime specialists, and others are expert financial witnesses. I don't expect Garrett will use all of them, but he's showing us that he has a lot of firepower when it comes to analyzing the money trail."

"And the unexpected witness?"

"Richard Dunstall has provided a witness statement that makes for interesting reading. His statement says he used to work for Palin and quit two years ago when he saw Palin embezzling money from several companies, not just the Foundation. The statement also says that he saw the discrepancy in the Foundation's accounts and approached Palin about it. Palin brushed him off."

"Interesting," Jacinta said. "But why has he come forward now?"

"Because Garrett has lost Tilly and Fisher. They were his big witnesses, the employees who would point the finger at their boss. I imagine Garrett knew about Richard Dunstall this whole time but didn't use him because he had Tilly and Fisher. Without the affair couple testifying, Garrett needs someone to fill their place."

"Who are the new companies that Dunstall claims Palin stole money from?"

"His written statement doesn't mention the company names." Hennessy looked at his watch, huffed again, and then stood. "And that's what I need to find out."

CHAPTER 24

Hennessy spent the afternoon researching Richard Dunstall. He found out everything he could from the publicly available information. Dunstall had a wife and two kids. Coached his son's basketball team with passion, according to his social media profile. Volunteered for the fire department. He was a member of his local church. According to his work profile, Dunstall worked for Palin Accounting for five months before he quit. He had held every other job for over ten years.

Hennessy drove to an office block in North Charleston to find Dunstall's current employment with a large trucking company. Dunstall was the bookkeeper in the company, which seemed to have a sign on every second truck that drove through Charleston.

Richard Dunstall was waiting for Hennessy in the parking lot, smoking a cigarette, leaning against the front of his twenty-year-old sedan. Dunstall was average height, average build, and had average looking facial features. His blue shirt was creased and a size too big, his black slacks slightly too long, and his brown hair was cut short. He looked at the prime age for a mid-life crisis.

Hennessy parked next to Dunstall's car and exited his pickup truck. Dunstall offered him a slight nod. As Hennessy approached, he could only smell the strong odor of cheap cigarettes.

"Mr. Dunstall, thank you for agreeing to meet," Hennessy said as he approached. "I understand this will be a stressful time for you."

"You didn't give me much choice." Dunstall shook Hennessy's hand. "It was either here or we did a deposition. My employer doesn't like me taking time off and is already angry that I need to take a day off to go to court."

"Then why come forward at all?"

Dunstall put one hand in his pocket, as the other held his cigarette. He avoided Hennessy's question and nodded to his pickup. "Not the sort of truck I'd expect a lawyer to be driving. Most of them around here drive brand new city sedans."

"I own a vineyard Upstate. A city car wouldn't last a week out there." Hennessy placed his hand on his truck. "But this old girl has been my best friend for almost two decades."

The answer seemed to ease the reluctance out of Dunstall. "That's the dream, isn't it? Retire to make wine, or fish, or hunt all day. That's my dream, anyway. Wish it could pay the bills, though."

"That's why I'm a defense lawyer in Charleston."

"Ha!" Dunstall liked the answer. "You're close to living the dream, then."

With a rapport built between them, Hennessy pressed. "So, why come forward for Palin's case now?"

"Conscience got the better of me."

"I don't believe that."

"That's fair enough because it's a lie." He rubbed the back of his neck and looked away. "The prosecution had something on me."

"What is it?"

"Just some stuff."

"We can talk about it here, or I'll find out through them. But if I find out through them, that information will be exposed in court and will be on

189

the public record."

"Ah," he groaned and rubbed the back of his neck again. "And if I tell you now, will you keep it out of court?"

"I can't promise that, but if it doesn't affect your credibility or testimony, then I won't use it."

"It has nothing to do with the case."

Hennessy shrugged. "It's your choice."

Dunstall looked at Joe's pickup, sucked back on his cigarette, and looked out into the distance. "Twenty years ago, I might've had a criminal record in another state. Drugs. Not dealing, just taking them. A small amount, but I was chased by an overzealous cop and a prosecutor who was determined to win everything. The judge sealed that record in the case after I completed a five-week drug treatment program. The drug treatment program was the hardest thing I ever did, but I haven't touched the stuff since. After the program, the judge said she was proud of me and sealed the record. But still, it's not a good look for my current employer. They're a trucking company with a strict drug policy. Zero tolerance. And in the interview for this job, I said I'd never been arrested. If they found out about my record, I wouldn't have a job."

"And that's what the prosecution threatened you with?"

He nodded. "Aaron Garrett came to me after Palin was arrested, but I told him I wanted nothing to do with the case. He left me alone, and I thought that was the end of it. But when Tilly and Fisher went missing, Garrett came to my house. He came prepared. I said I wanted nothing to do with the case, but he threatened me with my old record. I told him it was twenty years ago, and it'd been sealed, but he knew the trucking company has a zero tolerance for drug offenses. He told me the files would find their way into the hands of my manager, and I'd be without a job the next day. I had no choice."

"Are you telling the truth about what you saw Palin do?"

"Yeah. I approached him about the discrepancy in the accounts, and he said it was nothing." He glanced at Hennessy and then looked back at the end of his almost fully smoked cigarette. "But I'm not telling you everything."

"What else do you know?"

He looked around the half-empty parking lot and

then back at Hennessy. "I didn't come forward earlier because there are people around Palin who are dangerous. They're the type of people you never want to cross."

"The Rebel Sons."

"And Stanwell Construction." He nodded. "They don't care about Palin, but they do care about their business."

"You think they'll come after you?"

"That's what I'm afraid of, but I don't have a choice. I either lose this job, or I take a risk with them. Garrett said he'll protect my family if there are any threats." He looked at the end of his diminishing cigarette for a while and then took a long final drag. "I gave these up years ago," he explained. "But this whole court case forced me back to them. My wife wouldn't like me puffing again."

Hennessy nodded. "Your written deposition also says that you witnessed Palin embezzle money from various companies around Charleston."

"That's what I said."

"You said that you saw him embezzle tens of thousands of dollars through false invoices. Among those were a mechanic, a building supplier, and a concreting firm. That's small-time stuff and nothing to do with Stanwell Construction."

"That's right." Dunstall eyed him for a few moments, considering the next options. "I'm telling you what I'm allowed to tell you. And that's all I'll testify about. I'm not saying a word more. I'll talk about those small companies, and that's it."

"But there's more to your story."

"Maybe there is, maybe there isn't," Dunstall looked away and flicked the cigarette to the ground. He trod on it with his foot and walked toward his car door. "But I'm not talking about everything I know. It's too dangerous. You're going to have to figure the gaps out yourself."

CHAPTER 25

Hennessy spent the evening back in the office.

It was clear that Dunstall wasn't telling the whole truth. He was skirting around the issue and not telling Hennessy what he knew. Hennessy was sure that Dunstall hadn't told Garrett the whole truth either. Dunstall wanted nothing to do with the lawyers, nothing to do with Palin, and nothing to do with justice. He wasn't interested in the truth; he was only interested in keeping his job.

Hennessy didn't even know where to look for Dunstall's hidden evidence. Palin had over two hundred and fifty companies on his books. Hennessy would have to spend months looking for it. Still, he called several companies and tried to gather as much information as possible. They had all heard of the charges against Palin, and none of them had anything nice to say about him.

He reviewed all the mechanics on Palin

Accounting's books, the building suppliers, and all the concreting firms. None had discrepancies. The only anomaly was a company called 'JR Concreting Supplies.' Hennessy couldn't find a number to contact them, and their website had been shut down years earlier. Hennessy left a note for Jacinta to continue digging into information about 'JR Concreting Supplies.'

As the time ticked past 10:55 p.m., Hennessy turned off his computer, packed up his desk, and finished for the night. He stepped out of the office, locked the door behind him, and sucked in a lungful of thick evening air. Even at night, the humidity was still lingering over Charleston.

He heard the motorbikes before he saw them. Five Harley-Davidson cruisers turned the corner of the street, rumbling toward him. Hennessy looked around. A man was sitting in the front seat of a white pickup on the other side of the road, under the direct shine of the streetlight. The man was a spotter, waiting for Hennessy to leave the office.

Hennessy groaned. The loud rumble of the motorbike parade was all for show. An attempt at intimidation. He stepped toward the edge of the sidewalk and waited for the inevitable.

The bikes rumbled up the street and stopped in front of him. Hennessy watched as the loud beasts circled around him.

Behind the bikes, a black SUV rolled forward. When the car was near Hennessy, the dark-tinted back window rolled down.

Tony Stanwell sat in the rear seat. He didn't look in Hennessy's direction.

Intimidation was important for Stanwell's business. It was how he ruled the streets. In the highly competitive city of Charleston, the pressure to win jobs was intense. Not many companies bid when Stanwell Construction put their name forward. In turn, Stanwell Construction left the smaller jobs for everyone else to fight over. And if the unions came knocking, they got knocked out.

The bikers stepped off their bikes. One of the bikers, the largest, stepped toward the SUV and opened the back door.

Hennessy eyed the biker, unmoved by the suggestion.

The biker smiled slightly, impressed by Hennessy's stoic determination. He gave Hennessy a nod of respect.

The biker leaned down to the SUV's back seat and talked to the person inside. A moment later, Tony Stanwell climbed out of the SUV.

He stepped toward Hennessy.

"Quite the show." Hennessy quipped as the bikers returned to their bikes. They leaned against the cruisers, and one pulled out a cigarette packet, sharing it with the others. "You should put this in the theater."

"This isn't acting, Hennessy," Stanwell responded and looked at the bikers. When one nodded back, Stanwell continued. "I've heard there are new witnesses, and you've been digging deep into Palin's past. I received two phone calls this evening that said you've been calling a lot of his former clients."

Hennessy nodded.

"And why did you go digging into his business interests?"

"Because Palin's trial starts next week, and I need to know what'll be said in court. A new witness will give information about some of Palin's older clients. The man is a former employee of Palin Accounting, and he presents a problem for us. I need to be prepared for whatever happens in court."

Stanwell scoffed. "Richard Dunstall will tell you what we've allowed him to tell you. What will be uncovered is what we allow to be uncovered. It's all in his statement. He can talk about what he saw Palin do with the Foundation, but that's it."

"How did you know his name?"

"I have connections."

"And will Dunstall tell the truth?"

Stanwell laughed. "What even is the truth? Your memory? My memory? Because the facts of the world differ depending on who you talk to. If I talk to someone and you talk to someone, then the situation might be different. Our memories might differ depending on what we can or can't recall. The truth is but a memory."

"That's very insightful for a man with a tendency for violence."

"Prison gives you a lot of time for philosophy," he quipped, lowering his tone. "And it gives you a lot of time to plan bloodshed."

"What do you want?" Hennessy stepped closer. "What's this whole show for?"

"It's to remind you that there are areas of Palin's

business that need to be kept out of the trial. Chase the truth, investigate the accounting, but don't spread your net too far. Everything that's outside the net has been handled. You don't need to do anything else. The only thing you need to do is back off and focus on Palin's case."

"I'll do what I need to do for my client."

"Your client? We say what the rules are. We dictate what happens in this world."

"I don't play by your rules. I go by the law."

"The law!" Stanwell laughed again and walked back to the open door of the SUV. "If that's all you care about, then there's trouble coming your way."

CHAPTER 26

Hennessy sat on his balcony, laptop on the small table next to him, staring at Jacinta's email about the media coverage.

The media had run with the story, and true crime podcasters were already sniffing about. They had been contacted by every major news channel in the state, radio stations, and even national news broadcasters. It was an outrageous Southern scandal—an accountant embezzling money from a charity foundation for his own personal gain. The hatred for Palin spewed into every comment section of the news stories, onto social media, and into the streets. At dinner two nights earlier, Hennessy heard a group of rowdy men loudly discussing what they wanted to do to Palin. It wasn't nice.

"It's getting a lot of attention," Wendy said, leaning over his shoulder. "It seems the entire nation wants to read about the latest southern fraud scandal."

"We go to court in two days, and it seems the public has already decided on his fate."

"All that hate is not good, Joe. People hate him for stealing from sick kids. They want to hang him for his crimes. And then they see your face standing next to him and wonder how you could defend him. Someone even asked me in church how you could do it."

"Who?"

"Mrs. Hoover."

Hennessy nodded with a grin on his face.

"Don't say it," Wendy laughed. "We all know her husband likes to spend time with other men, and you don't need to make any jokes about her. She might be mean to everyone around her, but that doesn't mean we should stoop to her level."

"Hey, I didn't say a word," Joe smiled and closed his laptop. He tucked it under his arm and walked inside. "I've done enough for today. Let's cook."

Joe wanted to forget about work for a while. He wanted to forget about Palin and his repulsive demeanor. He wanted to forget about Garrett and his desire to win the case. And he wanted to forget about the law, how the pressure of the court case was giving him headaches, causing him sleepless nights, and sending him to the edge of exhaustion.

Joe went to the fridge and took out two beers. He held them up, and Wendy shook her head. "I was thinking about cooking some oven-fried chicken with roasted vegetables. I think a nice white would be great, perhaps a Riesling."

"I have just the thing," Joe said, returning to the fridge. He took out the bottle, uncorked it, and poured two glasses of the sweet white wine.

"Thank you," Wendy said and reached up to kiss him on the cheek. "Now, get the vegetables and start chopping."

"Yes, ma'am," Joe smiled, walked to the other side of the kitchen bench, pulled out the chopping board, and started cutting up the vegetables.

"No," Wendy complained when she saw him cutting. "Smaller pieces, please. Like this." She pulled the knife from his hand and showed him how to cut smaller pieces of vegetables. "See?"

"Yes, ma'am." Joe smiled again and started cutting again.

"Thinner," Wendy moaned and took the knife

again. She cut up the potato how she wanted. "You know, we put a man on the moon years ago."

"Ok?" Joe responded, confused.

"Well, why did we stop?" Wendy smiled. "I mean, we should've had all the men up there by now."

"Ouch," Joe laughed. He leaned back and teased her. "You know, I hate it when guys say that women belong in the kitchen. I mean, how are women going to clean the rest of the house from there?"

"Oh," Wendy laughed and tossed a piece of potato at him. "You know what the difference between certificates of deposit and men is? CDs eventually mature."

Joe laughed as he poured another glass of wine. Together, they finished cooking, served up the delicious meal, and ate sitting around the kitchen bench. Joe praised Wendy's cooking, and Wendy praised Joe's ability to stay out of her way.

As they ate, they talked and laughed, discussing news, rumors, and the happenings around town. It was one of Joe's best meals in weeks.

After they finished their meal, they retired to the front porch to catch the evening breeze. They sipped their wine in the moonlight, listening to the cacophony of bugs fill the Southern night air.

The conversation remained light on the porch for the first part of the evening, but it soon became apparent that something was weighing Joe down.

"Are you sure you're ok?" Wendy asked.

Joe looked out to the street, catching a glimpse of the moon hanging over a nearby house.

"I'm done with this, Wendy. I'm done with all this. I'm done dealing with people like Bernard Palin. I'm done dealing with criminals, felons, and corrupt people who take advantage of others. It makes me angry that these people still exist in the world."

"That's what capitalism does," Wendy said. "It makes people greedy. That's the whole idea of capitalism. It's not about helping each other or looking after the planet. The idea of capitalism is to win. It's not to look after your community, help your fellow person, or care for nature. It's about winning, and to win, you need to be greedy."

"Are you turning into a communist?" Joe smiled. "I think you're too late. The Cold War's over, remember?"

"I've been talking to Casey about her studies. She's taken a political science class in her first year, and she's been talking about communism, socialism, and capitalism. She's being taught that we're at late-stage capitalism, and something will change soon because it needs to. People are getting sick of inequality and how wealthy the top are getting."

"Is there another option?"

"I don't know," Wendy said. "But it worries me that our grandchildren will grow up in a world where such inequality exists."

"Is Casey pregnant?" Joe laughed.

"Thankfully, there aren't any grandchildren yet." Wendy slapped his arm lightly and then snuggled into it. "It'd be good to have you back at the vineyard full-time. I miss nights like this. We don't do it enough."

"Agreed," Joe said. "I need to be home at the vineyard."

"Well, Joseph Hennessy," Wendy's tone was soft. "You better win this case, then."

CHAPTER 27

INDICTMENT

STATE OF SOUTH CAROLINA

COUNTY OF CHARLESTON

IN THE COURT OF GENERAL SESSIONS

NINTH JUDICIAL CIRCUIT

INDICTMENT NO.: 25-CR-6575

STATE OF SOUTH CAROLINA, V.

BERNARD KENNETH PALIN, DEFENDANT

At a Court of General Sessions, the Grand Jurors of Charleston County present upon their oath: Breach of Trust, Fraud, and Forgery.

COUNT ONE

BREACH OF TRUST

That BERNARD KENNETH PALIN, in the County of Charleston, State of South Carolina, entrusted with the transfer of funds from the

WOLFGANG BERGER FOUNDATION, of a value exceeding one million dollars, did unlawfully and fraudulently breach that trust, with intent to permanently deprive the WOLFGANG BERGER FOUNDATION of said funds, in violation of Section 16-13-230 of the South Carolina Code of Laws, 1976, as amended.

COUNT TWO

FRAUD

That BERNARD KENNETH PALIN, in the County of Charleston, State of South Carolina, did unlawfully and willfully devise a scheme to defraud the WOLFGANG BERGER FOUNDATION by means of false pretenses or representations, with the intent to obtain money, property, or other benefit, to which the Defendant was not entitled, contrary to the statutes in such case made and provided, in violation of Section 16-13-240 of the South Carolina Code of Laws, 1976, as amended.

COUNT THREE

FORGERY

That BERNARD KENNETH PALIN, in the

County of Charleston, State of South Carolina, did knowingly and unlawfully forge or counterfeit a document, instrument, or signature, with the intent to defraud the WOLFGANG BERGER FOUNDATION, and did attempt to use or utter said forged document as true and genuine, in violation of Section 16-13-10 of the South Carolina Code of Laws, 1976, as amended.

Each of the acts described in Counts 1, 2, and 3 constitutes a separate and distinct violation of the laws of the State of South Carolina.

FINDINGS

WHEREFORE, the Grand Jurors say that the Defendant be made to answer to this indictment in a court of law, and that such proceedings be had as are in accordance with the laws of the State of South Carolina.

This indictment is true and correct to the best of the knowledge and belief of the undersigned.

*****

The Charleston Judicial Center Courthouse was in the beating heart of downtown Charleston. Tourists strolled by, admiring the city's history. Lawyers hustled between cafes and the courthouse. Office workers hurried through the nearby city and county administration buildings.

After months of posturing and months of turmoil, Bernard Palin had his day in the criminal court.

Dressed respectfully in a fitted black suit with a white shirt and a red tie, Palin met Hennessy in the courthouse foyer. They greeted each other with a handshake and spoke about the humidity for a few moments before they turned their attention to the court case. Palin couldn't stand still, moving from one foot to the other, trying to disperse his growing nerves. The significance of his life choices had become clear—his life of crime and corruption was calling for its fee to be paid.

He followed Hennessy through the courthouse and into the courtroom, settling at the defense table. While Hennessy set up his desk, Palin's eyes remained locked on the empty jury box. Those seats would soon be filled by people holding his fate in their hands.

After twenty-five minutes, the prosecution team walked into the courtroom. Garrett and his two assistants greeted Hennessy and sat at the prosecution table. They spoke loudly, confidently, and joked with each other. They felt this win was already in the bag.

The bailiff announced Judge Clayton's arrival. The judge walked into the courtroom, greeted everyone present, and called for any final pretrial motions. When none were presented, he called for voir dire, the jury selection process, to begin.

In some criminal cases, jury selection was a routine exercise, wrapped up within a single session. But the more intricate the case, the more grueling the process became. A fraud and forgery trial demanded precision. The lawyers had to probe every potential juror's biases, tease out hidden prejudices, and expose every preference. It wasn't just about finding twelve impartial people—it was about uncovering who could be swayed, who could be trusted, and who might see the world through a lens that worked against their client. Every question mattered. Every answer could tip the scales.

The lawyers probed the potential jurors' opinions on law enforcement, and dug into their religious views, searching for beliefs that might color their judgment. They asked about their attitudes toward law and justice, pressing to see if they leaned too far toward punishment or forgiveness.

No detail was too small. They inquired about professions, the jobs that shaped their days, and the families that filled their nights. Education mattered, too—what they'd studied, where, and how far they'd gone. Then, they turned to the heart of the case: fraud. Did they understand it? Could they grasp the intricacies of deception in the banking system? How did they feel about office work—the endless spreadsheets, the dull hum of fluorescent lights?

They asked if the jurors had ever donated to a charity, and if so, why. Did they lend a hand to others? How did they celebrate the holidays? These weren't idle questions; they painted a picture of values and priorities.

Numbers became the next battleground. Accounting, bookkeeping, tax law—did these terms mean anything to them? Did they always pay their taxes on time, or had they ever been tempted to bend the rules? And, perhaps most revealing of all: what did they think of the IRS?

Every hesitation, every inflection, gave the lawyers another piece of the puzzle, another hint at who might decide the fate of their case.

After a day of jury selection, progressing through group after group of potential candidates, the lawyers had their final twelve.

There was a business consultant, a teacher, and a wedding photographer. A retired administration worker, a bus driver, and a nurse. Two construction workers, a gardener, and a hotel manager. The final two selected were retail sales staff, although not known to each other. Two alternatives were also selected—people who would hear the case but take no part in deliberations unless one of the other jurors was excused.

Judge Clayton called an end to the day at five minutes past 5 p.m. Palin didn't talk much as he exited the court. His nerves were too much.

They returned to the courtroom the following morning for opening statements. The gallery filled behind them. Row after row, people walked into the courtroom, interested in the fraud case that irked the public. Garrett had held to his threat to make it a trial through public opinion. The prosecution released a media statement after jury selection, and every news website ran Palin's case as their headline story. Hennessy briefly looked at the early comments that morning. They weren't nice.

"All rise," the bailiff called out. "The court is now in session, the Honorable Judge Clayton presiding."

Judge Clayton walked into the courtroom, sat in his chair, and looked over the crowd.

He expressed his surprise at the full gallery before he greeted the lawyers and confirmed Palin's name. Once the formalities were completed, he called for the jury members to enter. The sound of the door opening and the shuffle of footsteps filled the room as the jurors entered and took their seats. Clayton waited for the rustling to subside before leaning forward slightly, his voice steady and deliberate as he addressed them. He provided them with preliminary instructions on the case, explaining the relevant legal definitions, the charges, and the responsibilities of the people in the courtroom. Satisfied they understood, he spoke to them about their role and how they were required to leave any biases at the door.

When everything was settled, Judge Clayton invited Assistant Circuit Solicitor Aaron Garrett to begin his opening statement.

*****

"Your Honor, ladies and gentlemen of the jury. My name is Aaron Garrett, and these are my colleagues, Michelle Saltmarsh and Maxwell Smith. Together, we will present the State of South Carolina's case against the defendant, Mr. Bernard Palin. As prosecutors, we represent the commitment of the Ninth Circuit Solicitor's Office to combat the devastating effects of fraud in our community.

Mr. Palin is charged with three felonies: Breach of Trust with Fraudulent Intent, Forgery, and Financial Identity Fraud. Mr. Palin is accused of transferring funds from the Wolfgang Berger Foundation. The foundation trusted Mr. Palin to manage their accounting, and instead of transferring the money to help sick and disadvantaged children, Mr. Palin transferred the money into his own account. Over the course of five years, Mr. Palin transferred more than one million into his business bank account. That's one million dollars that was taken away from sick and disadvantaged children.

That's right—Mr. Palin stole from sick and disadvantaged children.

Don't fool yourself and think that because there was no violence, this wasn't a serious crime—it was. This is one of the worst crimes I have seen. This man, Mr. Palin, put his own personal needs above the needs of sick and disadvantaged children. We cannot let this crime go unpunished. This crime must have real consequences.

The impact of his actions is far-reaching. The stolen money was supposed to go to the children's hospital to assist in purchasing new equipment. This stolen money was supposed to help families. This stolen money was supposed to help treatments.

Here, in this trial, we have the opportunity to show our great community that these actions are unacceptable.

The Charleston Police Department, led by Sergeant Danielle Young of the White Collar Crime Unit, investigated a tip-off that Mr. Palin was preparing to withdraw the stolen funds and move to Costa Rica to begin a very comfortable retirement.

The first charge, Breach of Trust with Fraudulent Intent, is South Carolina's version of embezzlement laws. This felony offense occurs when a person who is trusted to manage another person's property steals money for personal use.

The second charge against Mr. Palin, Fraud, is straightforward. The South Carolina Code of Laws makes it a crime to falsely counterfeit a recording instrument. It also makes it illegal to publish any such false documents. Mr. Palin did both those things.

The third charge is Financial Identity Fraud. This section of the law makes it unlawful for people to use information with the intent to defraud. The creation and use of false information for financial gain are clear elements of Financial Identity Fraud.

Over the coming days, we will present witnesses to you, and they will provide the evidence in this case. Nothing you hear from me now can be considered evidence. This opening statement is given to you to provide a roadmap of what will be shown during this trial.

During this case, you will hear from Sergeant

Young, and she will detail the investigation into the crimes, and why they arrested Mr. Palin before he could withdraw the money and flee the country.

You will hear from Mr. Palin's friend, respected and now retired Judge Clarence Berkley, about why he provided the tip-off. He will testify that Mr. Palin provided him with a copy of the bank statement, which indicates that Mr. Palin was aware of the funds. Judge Berkley will testify that Mr. Palin came to him to help purchase a property in Costa Rica. Mr. Palin was going to use the funds in that account for his own benefit.

You will hear from several of Mr. Palin's former employees about how they were threatened not to disclose his fraudulent behavior. You will hear from the CEO of the Wolfgang Berger Foundation, who will describe the shock and betrayal she felt when she was told that Mr. Palin was stealing from them. You will hear from forensic accountants describing how Mr. Palin made forged documentation that showed the money was being transferred. You will hear from accounting experts who will detail how Mr. Palin got away with this crime for five years.

Mr. Palin had the intent and motivation to

defraud, steal, and trick the Wolfgang Berger Foundation into transferring money into his business bank account.

Mr. Palin does not have the right to defraud charities. He does not have the right to steal from sick and disadvantage children. He does not have the right to destroy our communities.

This was an inexcusable crime, a horrible and tasteless act, and it deserves to be severely punished.

At the end of this case, I will address you again and ask you to consider all the evidence we have presented and to conclude beyond a reasonable doubt that Mr. Bernard Palin is guilty of all three charges.

Thank you for your time."

*****

During the opening statement, most jurors studied Palin, judging his demeanor to check if he looked capable of performing such a despicable crime. Most of them had already appeared to mark him as guilty, shaking their heads any time his name was mentioned.

During voir dire, Garrett had argued for polite and honest jury members, the type of people who had never stepped a foot wrong in their lives. He needed people who believed everything that was told to them. The type of people who would never question authority. He had five people on the jury that fit that mold. It wasn't enough, but it was a start.

Hennessy needed the opposite. He needed people who could question the information presented to them, people who could look at the big picture and see the missing elements, people who questioned the government, people who questioned authority, and people who were strong enough to stand up for what they believed in. Hennessy had five of those people on the jury.

The remaining two jurors seemed to be somewhere in between, people who could be easily swayed by the group's decision.

There were two leaders in the jury box, likely to be on opposite sides, and both seemed ready to fight for what they believed in. The leaders would be Hennessy's target throughout the case. They would be the people he talked to, made eye contact with, and watched for their reactions.

A leader in the jury room was an invaluable asset.

Jurors were susceptible to herd mentality, as were most normal people. A strong voice in the deliberation room could sway the timid, the uncertain, even the stubborn. One dominant personality, one persuasive argument, and suddenly twelve individual minds became one collective force.

As soon as Garrett finished his opening statement, Hennessy stood, folder in one hand, ready to begin. Garrett sat down, and when Judge Clayton invited him, Hennessy moved to the lectern, opened his folder, and looked at the jury.

With a loud and projecting voice, Hennessy began his statement.

*****

"Ladies and gentlemen of the jury, Your Honor, my name is Joe Hennessy. I'm a criminal defense attorney, and I'm here to represent the defendant, Mr. Bernard Palin.

There's a saying in aviation that if there's any

reasonable doubt, then there's no doubt. If there's any reasonable doubt about safety, whether it's due to the weather conditions, the mechanics, the navigation, then there's no doubt. The pilot will not take off.

This trial is the same. If there's any reasonable doubt at the end of this trial, then there's no doubt.

If you have any reasonable doubt, you must find the defendant not guilty.

And you will have reasonable doubt because there's not enough evidence against the defendant.

The legal system in our great country is called an adversarial system. This means that two parties, the prosecution and the defense, present opposing evidence and challenge the validity of the other parties' claims. Because we're in an adversarial system, you will hear the defense challenge the prosecution's evidence. This isn't a personal attack or an attack on anybody's reputation. We challenge the evidence because we're working toward a truthful, reasonable, and fair result in this case. We challenge the evidence because you need the truth to make a decision. And we challenge the evidence because there's reasonable doubt about what it shows.

There's no doubt that money was transferred into

a bank account other than the intended recipient. That's not in doubt. That's a fact. The money was transferred from the Wolfgang Berger Foundation into a bank account managed by the firm, Palin Accounting.

What the prosecution did not tell you in their roadmap is that another person had access to that bank account. Another person was a signatory on that bank account. Another person had the opportunity, and motive, to forge the invoices to the Wolfgang Berger Foundation.

This other person was an employee of Palin Accounting.

They also did not tell you that another person employed by Palin Accounting had the access to change the financial reports. They had the access to change the documentation presented to the Wolfgang Berger Foundation. They had the access to change the financial files.

These two employees were Mr. John Tilly and Mrs. Debra Fisher, and they were having an extramarital affair for five years.

Why is the timeframe of their affair important?

Because that's also the timeframe for the fraudulent transfers.

When Mr. Palin was arrested, Mr. Tilly and Mrs. Fisher left their respective partners and drove to another state to begin new lives. We don't know where they drove to because their partners reported them as missing persons. Mr. Tilly and Mrs. Fisher intended to use the money they transferred from the Wolfgang Berger Foundation to begin a new life together.

In addition, in the State of South Carolina, Breach of Trust with Fraudulent Intent is only a crime if the intent is clear. There will be no evidence presented to you to show intent by Mr. Palin. None. That's because Mr. Palin did not commit this crime.

There are other people who had the means, the motive, and the ability to commit this crime. That will be clear to you at the end of this trial.

And when it comes to the end of this court case, in your role as a juror, you'll be asked to make a decision based on the evidence, or lack thereof. In making your determination at the end of this case, the only evidence that can be considered is the evidence that has been presented during the trial.

And in making your decision, you must be unbiased. You must be impartial. And above all else, you must be fair.

When this case draws to a close, I will stand before you again and point out how the prosecution has failed to present enough evidence to convince you beyond a reasonable doubt. At that point, you will use your common sense to make a decision. You are the pilots in this trial, and you must remember that if there's any reasonable doubt, then there's no doubt.

Your decision must be not guilty.

Thank you for your service to our great justice system."

CHAPTER 28

Charleston Police Department Sergeant Danielle Young was called to the stand as the prosecution's first witness.

She presented herself as a strong and intelligent woman. She wore a brown jacket, white shirt, and brown skirt. Her black heels were minimally high, and her brunette hair was tied back. Over the course of her career, she had built a reputation as a no-nonsense investigator, someone who took their job seriously and had no time to play office politics. Her commitment was to the city and to the community, and nobody could convince her otherwise.

Flanked by two junior lawyers, Garrett typed into his laptop, read over the lines and lines of notes, and then greeted his first witness.

"Sergeant Young, thank you for taking the time from your busy schedule." Garrett began. He stood at the lectern at the side of the room, one hand resting on the file while the other moved with purpose, punctuating his words and giving his speech an air of conviction. "Can you please tell the court your profession and connection to this case?"

"My name is Sergeant Danielle Young, and I've been proudly employed by the Charleston Police Department for over ten years. In my current role, I lead the White Collar Crime Unit in the Central Investigative Division, and I've served in this role for more than ten years. I believe it's a great honor to serve your community, and I'm proud to expose people who fraudulently use the system for personal gain." Young rested her hands on her thighs. "And I was the lead detective in the investigation into Mr. Palin's activities with the Wolfgang Berger Foundation."

"Thank you, Sergeant Young. Have you previously led investigations into fraudulent activity?"

"I've led many investigations into fraud and its associated activities. In fact, I've been involved in hundreds of investigations into fraudulent behavior, although I must say I've never been involved in a case where someone has taken money from a charitable foundation."

"Is it rare to find someone stealing money from a charitable foundation?"

"Extremely. I've never seen it, and I can't recall a case within our county that has involved a charity foundation, especially not a children's charity foundation. As a society, we respect charities and what they provide to vulnerable people."

"Can you explain why the Charleston Police Department's White Collar Crime Unit opened an investigation into Palin Accounting?"

"We received information from a former client of Palin Accounting. This tip-off came from retired Judge Clarence Berkley. Judge Berkley stated there was evidence that Palin Accounting was embezzling money from the Wolfgang Berger Foundation and transferring it into a personal bank account. Judge Berkley informed us that Mr. Palin had approached him and asked for legal advice about his financial situation. Mr. Palin explained to Judge Berkley that he was about to withdraw the money from the account and fly to Costa Rica to retire."

"And how was this tip-off delivered?"

"In person. Judge Berkley arrived at our office and asked to speak with me on the condition of anonymity."

"And were you able to provide anonymity to Judge Berkley?"

"I explained that if we found evidence that what he claimed was true, we could apply to the courts to have the witness names redacted, however, if it made it to trial, then legally, the accused has the right to confront the accuser. I explained that Judge Berkley would need to be prepared to testify if the case came to trial. He stated that, as a former judge, he understood this and thanked us for keeping him safe until he could testify."

"And what made you think this tip-off was legitimate?"

"We trusted the tip-off because it came from a source close to Mr. Palin. Judge Berkley had explained that Mr. Palin had left a copy of a bank statement at Judge Berkley's home, and he bought this to us as the piece of evidence."

"Is this a copy of that statement?" Garrett introduced the bank statement as evidence to the court.

"It is," Young confirmed. "Palin had shown the bank statement to Judge Berkley to confirm he had the funds. Mr. Palin wanted to show the judge he had the money, and the bank account statement was to convince him the money was available."

Garrett studied the paper in front of him before he asked the next question. "Sergeant Young, do you have a transcript of this tip-off?"

"Not a transcript, but we have a report that was filed."

"And is this the report here?" Garrett handed a piece of paper to the bailiff, who then handed it to the witness.

"It is," Young confirmed.

"And did Judge Berkley explain why Mr. Palin came to him?"

"Judge Berkley explained that Mr. Palin came to him for legal advice and assistance in purchasing a property in Costa Rica. Judge Berkley had contacts in Costa Rica and traveled there often. Mr. Palin wished to leverage those contacts."

"Interesting," Garrett noted. "Can you please describe the investigation process that occurred after the tip-off?"

"After confirming the information was legitimate, we issued warrants to the five banks used by Palin

Accounting, requesting financial documents for all his accounts. We also requested the financial documents kept by the Wolfgang Berger Foundation. We warned the members of the Foundation not to request the documents from Palin Accounting because we didn't want to alert Mr. Palin of the investigation. Once we received the documents from both sources, we studied the incomings and outgoings from the bank accounts and compared that against the information from the Foundation. We confirmed that Mr. Palin was transferring money from the Foundation into a different account than intended. The documentation from the Foundation showed two annual payments of $200,000 each to the MUSC Shawn Jenkins Children's Hospital, a practice in place since the hospital opened five years earlier. However, the hospital received only one of these annual $200,000 payments because the second $200,000 payment was transferred to an account with Palin Accounting. In our initial investigation, we tracked five different payments made over the past five years, and they were all transferred into an account that belonged to Palin Accounting."

"What happened next?"

"We approached a judge, and they issued an order to the financial institutions to freeze all his assets. The judge issued a broad asset freeze to prevent Mr. Palin from fleeing the country. At the same time his assets were being frozen, we went to his home and arrested Mr. Palin."

"And during your investigation, did you understand how Mr. Palin could make those payments undetected?"

"The Wolfgang Berger Foundation made two annual donations of $200,000 each to the MUSC Shawn Jenkins Children's Hospital. The first was to support education for sick children within the hospital, and the second was to support the purchase of new equipment for the hospital. Mr. Palin transferred one of the payments to the hospital; however, he doctored the invoice for the second payment. The second payment was transferred into an account that was opened by Palin Accounting. Because there were still payments being received by the hospital, nobody within the Foundation suspected anything was wrong."

"Did Mr. Palin doctor the financial records of the Wolfgang Berger Foundation to show the payments were being transferred to the hospital?"

"That's correct, yes. Although the Foundation's records show both amounts of money going to the hospital, the second amount was never received."

"When did you make the arrest?"

"Although the money hadn't yet been withdrawn, we believed Mr. Palin was preparing to access the funds and flee the country. Numerous crimes had been committed, and we were concerned that Mr. Palin was winding down his business activities and considering moving to Costa Rica to retire. We couldn't wait for Mr. Palin to withdraw the money, so we requested a judge to issue a freeze order to his bank accounts and made the arrest while the order was being applied to his financial institutions."

"And where did you arrest Mr. Palin?"

"At his home in the neighborhood of South of Broad."

"What was the state of his home when you arrived?"

"Everything was packed up inside. All his belongings were in boxes, all his clothes were packed, and there was minimal food in his cupboards. We believed he was going to leave within the following week."

"His house appeared like he was leaving?"

"Objection," Hennessy called out. "Leading the witness, and the question is based on speculation."

"Sustained," Judge Clayton responded.

The objection didn't faze Garrett. He rephrased the question and received the answer he needed.

For the next five hours, Sergeant Young painfully walked the court through step after step of the case—how they investigated it, how they monitored the accounts, and how they ensured they had the right person. Hennessy lost focus at times, as he was sure the jury would, and when Judge Clayton called out to him to begin cross-examination, he wasn't sure what the last question from the prosecutor was.

"Mr. Hennessy?" Judge Clayton asked. "Would you like to question the witness?"

"Certainly, Your Honor." Hennessy stood to begin questioning. "Sergeant Young, would you say the tip-off was essential to this case?"

"It was the starting point for our investigation, yes."

"And did Judge Berkley tell you how he was involved with Mr. Palin?"

"As I explained earlier, Mr. Palin approached Judge Berkley to provide legal advice about his illegal activities. Mr. Palin also requested Judge Berkley's help purchasing a property in Costa Rica, but in both cases, Judge Berkley declined to assist him."

"Why would Judge Berkley be approached to be involved?"

"They were friends and Mr. Palin thought Judge Berkley could help. As Judge Berkley explained, he had many connections to help transfer the funds to Costa Rica, and Mr. Palin wanted to do that without raising any alarms."

Hennessy nodded, leaving a long pause between questions. He knew the power of a well-timed pause, how it forced people to lean in, to fill the void with their own thoughts. He watched the jurors, waiting for the exact moment when their gaze locked with his. When he was sure he had the jury's full attention, he continued. "During your investigation, did you find out who else had access to the bank account where the money was transferred?"

"We did. The accounts were registered by Palin Accounting."

"That's not what I asked. I asked who else had

access to those accounts?"

"Nobody else had withdrawn money from that account."

Hennessy paused and looked at Judge Clayton. "Your Honor, can you please instruct the witness to answer the question? The witness is deliberately not answering the question."

Judge Clayton leaned closer to the witness. "Sergeant Young, please answer the question put to you. I know this isn't your first time in court, and I would hate to hold you in contempt."

Young grunted. "What was the question again?"

"How many people had access to the bank account to which the money was transferred?"

"Two."

"And the names of those two people?"

"Mr. Palin." She paused for a long moment, clenched her jaw, and continued. "And Mr. John Tilly."

"Did you investigate Mr. Tilly as a suspect?"

"We talked to him, yes. We had extensive interviews with him. In fact, we spent over two hours interviewing Mr. Tilly."

"Was he considered a suspect at any point?"

"No."

"Are you aware that Mr. Tilly and fellow senior employee Mrs. Fisher were having an extra-marital affair?"

Again, another long pause. "Yes."

"Were you aware that Mrs. Fisher had access to the reports that were changed?"

"Yes."

"And were you aware they had been in that extra-marital relationship for five years?"

"Yes."

"Did you interview Mrs. Fisher?"

"Yes. We interviewed her for more than two and a half hours."

"Did you question either Mr. Tilly or Mrs. Fisher about that relationship?"

"No."

"Why not?"

"Because at the time we were questioning them, we were not aware that they were having an affair."

"During your extensive police interviews, over many hours, neither Mr. Tilly nor Mrs. Fisher told you they had been in an extra-marital affair together over the past five years?"

"They did not, but an affair is not something that people talk freely about. As far as I'm aware, not many people knew they were having an affair at the time."

"How about later? Did you question them about the affair once you found out about it?"

"No."

"Can you please tell the court why you didn't question them?"

She looked at Judge Clayton. The judge nodded, indicating she should continue. "Because their respective spouses reported them as missing persons."

"When were they reported as missing?"

"Several weeks ago."

"Interesting. When was the account in question opened?"

"Just over five years ago."

"And when did the funds start to be transferred into the account in question?"

"As I've said earlier, it was five years ago."

"And how long had Mr. Tilly and Mrs. Fisher been having an extra-marital affair?"

Young's jaw clenched again. "As far as we know,

they've been in a relationship for five years."

A ripple of unease passed through the jury box. One juror leaned forward, furrowing their brow, while another shifted uncomfortably in their seat. Hennessy's line of questioning was striking a nerve.

"Sergeant Young, are you telling the court that two people—who were having an affair, worked for Palin Accounting, had access to the account in question, and disappeared just before this trial—were never considered suspects?"

"That's correct."

"And even though they didn't tell you the truth during the police interviews, you still didn't consider them as suspects?"

"We didn't because the tip-off was regarding Mr. Palin. The tip-off came from a retired judge, and we believed the information he provided to us. And it must be said the information he provided was correct. Without his tip-off, nobody would've noticed the money was missing."

Hennessy exaggerated his surprised expression for the benefit of the jury. One nodded in return. "No further questions."

CHAPTER 29

Garrett called Ms. Melissa Stevenson next.

As she swore her oath, her face looked etched out of stone. Her eyebrows didn't move as she talked, most likely the result of too much Botox. Her jaw was clenched as she looked at the jury. She wore a black and white dress, covered with a black jacket. She glared at Garrett, her impatience evident as she exhaled loudly when he took more than fifteen seconds to ask his first question.

"Thank you for coming to court to testify today," Garrett began sitting behind his desk. "Can you please tell the court your name and occupation?"

"My name is Ms. Melissa Stevenson, and I'm the CEO of the Wolfgang Berger Foundation and have been for the past five years."

"And what is your role, exactly?"

"I'm the Chief Executive Officer of the Foundation. I was granted that position by the board and have held the position since the inception of the Foundation. My father's estate provides most of the funds for the Foundation to disperse."

"Why did your father leave money in his will to the Foundation?"

"My father grew up very poor after World War Two in Germany, and those experiences shaped him. His younger brother was always sick when they lived in Germany, and his brother died when my father was young. That stuck with him throughout his life. After I was born, he moved us to South Carolina, hoping for a better life. He was a hard worker who built his wealth by selling cars. First, he did it privately while working as a janitor, but the car business grew, and he was able to open a used car lot. He then expanded and bought another used car lot and several new car dealerships. Eventually, after more than fifty years of hard work, he owned twenty-five dealerships and used car lots."

"And can you please tell the court how the Foundation can give away more than a million dollars a year in donations?"

"When my father died, his estate was worth over thirty million dollars. His will instructed the executor, or personal representative, to sell all his assets, including the businesses he had built from the ground up, and put all the money into a high-interest account. The interest from the account was to be used as donations to help disadvantaged children, which was to be distributed through the Foundation. We have some expenses, including my wage as CEO and the wage of the Foundation's assistant, but the remainder is distributed to various charities throughout the state. We donate more than a million dollars per year. We have a board of five people, and together, we choose who receives the funds. We chose the MUSC Shawn Jenkins Children's Hospital as the place where the majority of our donations go, but we also make donations to other places as well. We liked that the new hospital opened around the same time we started to make donations."

"And as CEO of the Wolfgang Berger Foundation, how do you know Mr. Palin?"

"He took on the accounting for the Foundation five years ago when we first started as a charity foundation. He offered to do the first year of accounting for a reduced rate if we signed on for another two years. We took the contract, and he's been doing the accounting ever since."

"And did you have personal interactions with Mr. Palin?"

"Many. My role is to ensure all the organization's moving parts work well. We would talk monthly on the phone, and he would attend two or three board meetings a year. He would provide comprehensive reports about our financial situation and discuss where all the donations were going. He talked to us about the interest on the accounts and calculated how much we had to donate each year."

"And how were your interactions with Mr. Palin?"

"Fine. There was never any cause for concern."

"And did you notice any discrepancies in the accounting?"

"No. Never. I trusted Mr. Palin, and he instructed us on where to send the payments. Nothing ever looked illegitimate, and we never had a reason not to trust him. The other board members and I attended functions set up by the MUSC Shawn Jenkins Children's Hospital, and they often thanked us for the donations. We never had any reason to question whether the money was being received or not. Since this instance of stealing, we've set up safeguards to prevent it from ever happening again, but at the time, we were trusting of Mr. Palin."

"And Mr. Palin had the power to transfer the payments to these organizations?"

"He transferred all the payments from the accounts. The board met monthly, and part of the meeting was to review the donations, but we never thought the donations were going anywhere else. Every year, the hospital, along with all the other recipients, thanked us for the donations."

"How did you feel when you discovered this was not correct?"

"It wasn't my father's intention for the money to be transferred to an accountant. His goal was to transfer the money to sick children."

"Did it make you angry?"

"Objection. Leading the witness."

"Withdrawn," Garrett was quick to respond. "How did it make you feel, Ms. Stevenson?"

"Angry."

"Thank you, Ms. Stevenson. No further questions."

Garrett closed the file, nodded to the jury, and sat down. If Stevenson had shown more emotion,

Garrett might have prolonged her testimony to sway the jury's sympathy. But her detached demeanor wasn't working in his favor. She hardly even seemed upset that the money was missing.

When invited by Judge Clayton, Hennessy stood to begin his questioning.

"Ms. Stevenson, did you ever check the location of the payments made by the Wolfgang Berger Foundation?"

"No. I received the reports from Palin Accounting and trusted that the information was correct. I never double-checked the bank account numbers to ensure the correct payments were being made."

"And what was your relationship with Mr. Palin like?"

"Very good. We chatted monthly, and he helped me with several questions about taxes."

"Did you ever ask him to open an account for you?"

"I don't recall."

"In May, two years ago, you emailed Mr. Palin requesting that he open a new bank account in the Foundation's name, asking him to put fifteen thousand dollars aside every year. Is that correct?"

"I don't recall that."

"In another email, you asked Mr. Palin to write off the money from that account as work-related expenses. When Mr. Palin asked about the nature of those expenses, you wrote back and said that five thousand dollars had been spent on dinner dresses. Is that correct?"

"I don't recall."

"I have the email here." Hennessy handed a piece of paper to Garrett and two to the bailiff, who handed one paper to the judge and another to the witness. "You told Mr. Palin that you had spent five thousand dollars on dinner dresses and asked him to assign that as a business expense. Is that correct?"

"It's important for me to attend events to fundraise for the Foundation. The dresses were used to attend the functions. It's an important part of my role as CEO of the Foundation."

"Is it?" Hennessy expressed his surprise to the jury. "And in the five years you've run the Foundation, how many extra funds have you brought in?"

"I wouldn't know."

"Zero is a hard number to forget."

"I…" She bit back on her words. "I haven't had much luck with fundraising, but I must remind you it's my family's estate that funds this foundation. We've donated over five million dollars to the sick and disadvantaged children of South Carolina."

"And that's wonderful. The money from your foundation has changed lives," Hennessy said. "But I put it to you that you have no intention of fundraising at any point. When you attend events, you're merely socializing and enjoying the elite company the Foundation affords you. Is that correct?"

"Objection," Garrett stood. "Relevance."

"Your Honor, we're trying to establish the procedures and intention of the Foundation."

"Overruled for now," Judge Clayton stated. "You may answer the question, Ms. Stevenson."

She took a moment to settle herself. "I enjoy socializing, yes."

"Your father's estate was worth more than thirty million dollars. Can you please tell the court how much money your father left you personally in his will?"

She stared at Hennessy for a long moment before responding. "My father was… very charitable to other people, but he also believed in the value of hard work. He believed I should work for the money."

"You didn't answer my question, Ms. Stevenson. How much money did he leave to you in his will?"

"None."

"Not a cent?"

"That's correct."

"Your father was a man worth tens of millions of dollars, and spent his entire life being frugal but left no money to his only child. Is that correct?"

"That's right."

"How did that make you feel?"

"Objection. Relevance. We're straying into family issues here."

"We're getting to the point, Your Honor," Hennessy said. "Just a few more questions."

"The objection is overruled, but get to the point, Mr. Hennessy." Judge Clayton was quick to respond. "You may answer the question, Ms. Stevenson."

She took a moment to adjust her jacket before she answered. "I was angry at my father after the will was read out. I had expected he would leave some money in the will, but we had a… strained relationship for most of my life."

"Did you dispute the will?"

"Legally, yes."

"What were you wishing to receive when you disputed the will in court?"

"Some inheritance, which I believe I was entitled to after putting up with my father for all those years."

"The will said that you had to be employed as head of the Foundation, is that correct?"

"Yes. The will states that I need to be employed as CEO or the thirty million dollars will be donated in full to different charities."

"And how much do you earn as CEO of the Foundation?"

"Around $150,000 per year."

"And how many hours do you do each week?"

"It's hard to quantify. Like I said, I attend a lot of functions on behalf of the Foundation."

"But you don't work full-time?"

"Not every week, no."

"That's a very good wage for your role," Hennessy said. "Ms. Stevenson, if you could pay yourself more from the Foundation, would you?"

"Yes. I would. I believe that my family estate can afford to pay me more."

Hennessy paused and looked to the jury. Two jury members were squinting in confusion, and another was busy writing notes.

"No further questions," Hennessy said. "However, we reserve the right to recall Ms. Stevenson as a defense witness."

CHAPTER 30

"The State calls Mr. John Lockhart."

Forensic Accountant John Lockhart walked to the stand with an effortless grace. He wore broad-rimmed black glasses and a nice suit. His hair was trimmed, but his shoes were scuffed. He held himself well, and on looks alone, he looked like an expert in something.

Garrett walked to the lectern in front of the jury, placed a folder down, opened it, and read over several lines before he turned his attention to the witness. "Mr. Lockhart, can you please describe your professional expertise?"

"Certainly. I've been employed as a consultant with the Charleston Police Department for the past ten years. I've been certified as a fraud investigator, and I'm also certified in financial forensics. The Association of Certified Fraud Examiners and the American Institute of Certified Public Accountants issued those certificates. Before this employment, I was a corporate accountant for fifteen years."

"And what was your role in this investigation?"

"My role was to review all the records associated with Palin Accounting, including IRS statements, bank accounts, and financial reports. Along with my team, I searched through the last five years of the bank accounts managed by Palin Accounting and reviewed all the accounting linked to the Wolfgang Berger Foundation. Due to the complex nature of the payments, I ensured I followed each lead and each avenue for the potentially fraudulent activity. It was a painstaking process, but I thought it was important to leave no stone unturned during this investigation."

"Did you find any irregularities in the files connected to the Wolfgang Berger Foundation?"

"Yes. In the files associated with the Foundation, I found ten donations registered to the MUSC Shawn Jenkins Children's Hospital. These were legitimate donations, approved by the board. There was documentation about the donations and records about the board's decisions to make the donations. But when I searched where the money was transferred to, I could see that five payments didn't match any account numbers that belonged to the

MUSC Shawn Jenkins Children's Hospital. However, once I looked through Palin Accounting's bank accounts, I could match payments made by the Foundation. It should be noted that Palin Accounting had twenty-five bank accounts with five different financial institutions, and it took some time to find all these links."

"Interesting," Garrett stated. "Is it normal for an accounting firm to have this many bank accounts?"

"No. It's unusual. Most firms around this size would have between five and ten bank accounts, most likely with one or two banks. Having twenty-five bank accounts across five different banks sets off alarm bells."

"Did you investigate all the deposits into those bank accounts?"

"Yes. After I looked at the five deposits from the Foundation, I began to look at other transactions going into the Palin Accounting bank accounts."

"And what did you find?"

"A lot were legitimate deposits from customer invoices. However, some deposits had a very long paper trail where money was transferred into one account, then another, then another, being split up more and more each time. All these transferred amounts were under the regulatory threshold of $10,000. This is typical behavior for places trying to avoid detection for money laundering. There were fifteen unusual transactions that I focused on. When I traced the money back to the original source, I found that most of the funds had come from cash deposits into ATMs. However, I could not prove this was associated with money laundering."

"How were the funds recorded?"

"As payments from clients for billable hours, but there was no way the firm could've billed for as many hours as it did. For instance, in documentation from Palin Accounting, I found that they were overcharging most of their clients. While they had ten employees, including two support staff who couldn't perform billable hours, they should've only been charging 15,000 billable hours per year. Still, some years, they were charging as much as 45,000 billable hours, which would've been physically impossible for the staff to work. When I investigated the billing, it became clear that they were overcharging most of their clients."

"Would you say there was an established pattern

of fraudulent behavior in Palin Accounting?"

"It appeared that way."

"I'd like to ask you some specific questions about the money being transferred from the Foundation. How much money was transferred from the Foundation to the bank account owned by Palin Accounting?"

"Over five years, just over a million dollars was transferred, or two hundred thousand a year. Two annual payments were made to the children's hospital. The hospital received one payment and never received the second."

"Did the MUSC Shawn Jenkins Children's Hospital ever receive the money transferred into the Palin Accounting bank account?"

"No."

"And in your professional opinion, was this behavior intentional?"

"Absolutely. There was no doubt that this was intentional. Even if it happened in only one year, it would be hard to understand how a mistake like this might happen. However, every year, the documentation was deliberately doctored. That shows a concerted effort, year in, year out, over five years."

Garrett shook his head several times, making a 'tsk' sound when he did. For the next fifty-five minutes, Garrett led Lockhart through the details of the fraud case. They reviewed the reports, the bank deposits, and the timing of the funds. When it was clearly established that the money had been transferred directly to Palin Accounting instead of the hospital, Garrett finished questioning.

Judge Clayton invited Hennessy to begin his cross-examination after a short recess. Hennessy stood and walked to the lectern, resting one hand on it. He then stood close to the jury members.

"Mr. Lockhart, can you please describe the limitations in your investigation?"

"I only had limited access to the accounts and didn't have access to the documentation outside of the accounts registered by Palin Accounting."

"Have you testified in cases of fraud that later turned out to be mismanagement of funds and unintentional errors?"

"Yes."

"Did you consider whether there were other alternative explanations for transferring funds?"

"Yes, but this was too deliberate for that to occur.

The reports were changed yearly, and Mr. Palin presented those to the Foundation's board."

"Was the money ever withdrawn from the bank account?"

"No, but only days before the arrest, the bank records show that Mr. Palin requested an online statement to verify the funds."

Hennessy paused and went for the big questions.

"How many people had access to the account where the money was transferred?"

"Two."

"And their names?"

"Mr. Bernard Palin, and Mr. John Tilly."

"Mr. John Tilly," Hennessy repeated. "Thank you, Mr. Lockhart. We have no further questions."

CHAPTER 31

Redacted Witness Five, former Palin Accounting employee Jane Smith, was called to the stand next.

Smith was in her mid-fifties and had a quiet demeanor. She was well-dressed, had short-cropped gray hair, and a healthy figure. She contemplated each question and took her time to respond. While it was a good look in a courtroom, Hennessy would've hated to have a drink with her. Any conversation would've been infuriatingly slow.

"Can you please describe your role in Palin Accounting?"

A long pause. "I was employed as a taxation consultant for Palin Accounting for five years before I resigned. My role included assisting businesses, organizations, and foundations in navigating the complexities of federal, state, and local tax laws. I provided advice on tax planning strategies to minimize liabilities while ensuring compliance with all relevant laws. My specialty was in payroll tax, but I also advised on corporate tax, income tax, property tax, and sales tax. I also represented clients during audits. Currently, I work for a large accounting firm in Savannah."

"On the day you resigned, were you the only person to resign?"

"No. The entire office quit on that day. There were ten employees of Palin Accounting, and we all quit on the same day. We walked in on Monday morning, left a letter of resignation each on our desks, and walked back out."

"Was it a coincidence that all ten staff members of Palin Accounting quit on the same day?"

"No. Mr. Palin was terrible to work for, but over the last year, he got even worse. He would often come into work drunk, smoked in his office, and he was always yelling at us. He slapped me on the behind one time, and I saw him try to grope another two of the female staff members. One day, I found one junior staff member in the restroom crying. When I asked her what was wrong, she said that Mr. Palin had groped her breasts and said they weren't big enough. She quit that afternoon. I offered to take her to the police to file a report, but she declined. And then one Saturday, after one of the junior staff members had her bottom groped by Mr. Palin, two senior staff members called for a meeting. We met at a café and planned a mass walkout two weeks later."

Garrett let that statement linger in the courtroom for a while. He was trying to establish that Palin was immoral, corrupt, and abusive. It was working. One of the female jury members scrunched her face up whenever she looked at Palin.

"Mrs. Smith, during your time with Palin Accounting, did you notice any unusual transactions?"

Another long pause. "Yes. I noticed a lot of transactions that could be deemed unusual. There were unusual transactions happening with most of the clients, and before I resigned, I noticed there was unusual transactions with the Wolfgang Berger Foundation account. There was money being transferred to pay for invoices for work that hadn't been conducted, such as consulting services that were never provided."

"Can you please explain the process of approval for transfers of this nature?"

"There were no processes of approval for

transactions like that. Mr. Palin had the final say on everything."

"How do you know those services weren't provided?"

"Because the invoices had my name on them. The invoices stated I provided the services to the Wolfgang Berger Foundation, even though I never talked to them. One invoice was worth $15,000 dollars. I never did that work, and I never advised them on their tax practices. I was angry that he was using my name to defraud other companies and foundations."

"So, you never performed the work?"

"No, I didn't do any work for the Foundation."

"If you were so angry, what did you do about it?"

"I raised the invoice with Mr. Palin, but he told me to stay quiet and forget about it. He told me it was an error and he'd fix it. He never talked to me about it again."

"And who had final approval of those invoices?"

"Mr. Palin signed off on those invoices."

"Did Mr. Palin ever instruct you to act in a way that would be considered unethical?"

"He made me charge more money than I did

hours. In some instances, he suggested I charge double the billable hours, but I was uncomfortable with this. He said he would sack me if I didn't, and threatened to tell any future employer that I was a terrible employee."

"At any point, did Mr. Palin try to keep information private and away from you?"

"Yes. He tried to keep lots of invoices private from me, even though they were attributed to my earnings within the firm."

Garrett asked Jane Smith several more questions, but the damage was done early. It was becoming clear that Palin conducted his business fraudulently and had no moral compass. The weight of evidence was building, and it was starting to convince the jury of Palin's guilt.

When invited by the judge, Hennessy stood and walked to the lectern.

"Mrs. Smith, was Mr. Palin the only person who had the authorization to transfer money from the Wolfgang Berger Foundation?"

"No. The most senior accountant in the office, Mr. John Tilly, also had access to the accounts."

"And did multiple staff members have access to

the system used to create the reports presented to the Foundation?"

"Yes."

"Was Mrs. Fisher one of those staff members who had access?"

"Yes."

"Can you please tell the court about the relationship between Mr. Tilly and Mrs. Fisher?"

"They were having an affair. It was rumored for a long time, and they confirmed it after we quit. The entire time I was working there, they were having an affair."

"And who were the two senior staff members who organized the mass walkout?"

"Mr. Tilly and Mrs. Fisher organized it after Mr. Palin groped one of the junior staff members."

Hennessy nodded. "Did Mr. Tilly or Mrs. Fisher talk to you about what they were going to do after the mass walkout?"

"They chatted informally about retiring to a ranch in Texas. They both loved Texas, and it seemed to be a common goal of theirs."

"Are you aware of where they are now?"

"I don't know."

"Why not?"

"Because they've been reported as missing persons."

Hennessy nodded. The case against Tilly and Fisher was building. "No further questions."

CHAPTER 32

To open the next day of the trial, Garrett called Richard Dunstall.

Dunstall walked to the stand with his head down. He avoided eye contact with the jury and avoided looking in Palin's direction. He kept his eyes down while swearing his oath and then raised his eyes to look at the prosecution table and only the prosecution table. He wore a blue shirt, one size too big, and faded black slacks. His blue shirt had an orange stain near the pocket; although faded, it was eye-catching.

"Can you please tell the court your name, your profession, and how you are associated with Palin Accounting?"

"My name is Richard Dunstall, and I'm a bookkeeper. I've received my certificates from the National Association of Certified Bookkeepers. Two years ago, I was employed by Palin Accounting for a period of five months, however, I quit after five months and am now employed as a bookkeeper in a transport company."

"And how does your role as a bookkeeper differ from that of an accountant?"

"As a bookkeeper, my primary tasks are to record transactions, process payroll, and create documents for accountants to review. We mostly look at ledges and financial records. An accountant analyses and interprets financial data, prepares financial statements, and advises on tax planning, budgeting, and financial management. Accountants can also transfer money for business and ensure that invoices are paid on time."

"Why did you leave after only five months at Palin Accounting?"

"I resigned from the role at Palin Accounting because I noticed some transactions I wasn't comfortable with. I approached Mr. Palin about it, and he said they were legitimate transactions, but I wasn't convinced."

"What transactions were they?"

"When I was reviewing the reports for the Wolfgang Berger Foundation, I found that one payment was being transferred to an account number that I recognized. I am good with numbers, and once I see an account number, it tends to stay stuck in my head. I checked the business account records and found the bank account that belonged to Palin Accounting."

"Did this raise alarm bells for you?"

"It did."

"And what did you do next?"

"I asked Mr. Palin about the reports. He explained the payments were being transferred into the firm's bank account first and then to the hospital. He said it was a process decision and nothing more. Then he reminded me I had signed a non-disclosure agreement about my employment with Palin Accounting, and also reminded me he had connections to dangerous people."

"Did you feel comfortable with this?"

"No."

"What did you do?"

"I quit. It was clear to me this was illegal, however, I wasn't going to risk my life for it."

"Were you sure that the payments weren't going to be transferred to the hospital at a later time?"

"They could've been, but the money wasn't

transferred to the hospital while I worked there."

"Are you sure of that?"

"Yes."

"And when you talked to Mr. Palin, was he aware that the funds were being transferred directly from the Wolfgang Berger Foundation into a bank account in Palin Accounting?"

"Yes. When I presented the report to him, he said he knew that the money was going to that account, and he had the approval of the board to do that."

"When I questioned if the board was expecting the funds to be transferred at a later time, he became angry and started calling me names."

"Did you press the topic or leave it at that?"

"I wanted to keep my job, so I didn't ask any more questions."

Garrett tapped his hand on the side of the file before him, buying time to allow the jury to absorb the testimony. When he was sure they had thought enough about Palin's guilt, he continued. "Mr. Dunstall, did you notice anything else unusual in your time with Palin Accounting?"

"In my first week there, I realized Mr. Palin instructed his staff to overcharge for every transaction. He was creating billable hours from nothing, and changing the reports to show more work was performed than necessary."

"Any other unusual transactions or reports?"

"I was reviewing one set of reports, and there were cash deposits into some bank accounts that had no link to reports or invoices. When I enquired about the transactions, Mr. Palin informed me I should list the payments under whichever business I liked. He told me as long as the reports lined up, he didn't mind which business I assigned the money to. And there were several accounts that raised alarm bells. There was money being assigned to payments from a concreting account, a building supplier, and a consulting firm."

"That seems very unusual. Have you ever encountered that before in your time as a bookkeeper?"

"No. And it's unusual because it's illegal."

"Thank you, Mr. Dunstall. No further questions."

When asked by Judge Clayton, Hennessy went to begin questioning, but Palin grabbed his wrist.

"Don't ask him too many questions," Palin whispered. "He knows too much."

Hennessy glared at Palin for a few moments and then stood, walking to the lectern to create distance between himself and his client.

"Mr. Dunstall, thank you for talking with us today. What first alerted you that there was a problem in those accounts?"

"The payments appeared to match exactly to payments from the Wolfgang Berger Foundation. The dates lined up with the amounts being deposited into the business bank account."

"Are you aware which staff members had access to that account?"

"No."

"Two staff members were signatories on that bank account—Mr. Palin, and Mr. Tilly. Did you approach Mr. Tilly, the senior accountant, about the information you found?"

"No. I was working directly with Mr. Palin, and I thought it was best to go straight to him with my concerns."

"And after Mr. Palin threatened your job, did you talk to the staff manager, Mrs. Fisher?"

"No. I didn't talk to Mrs. Fisher. Mr. Palin made it very clear to everyone that he was in charge of the firm, and whatever he said was final."

Hennessy turned and looked at Palin, who glared at the witness with squinted eyes. Hennessy drew a breath and continued. "Mr. Dunstall, were there any other transactions that you thought were unusual?"

"I don't recall." Dunstall's body language changed. He folded his arms, tucked his shoulders forward, and brought his chin toward his chest. "It was two years ago, and I didn't work at the firm for long."

"In your testimony, you mentioned there were several accounts that raised alarm bells. What were the other accounts? Were they managed by Mr. Tilly or Mrs. Fisher?"

He sat back. "I don't recall."

"But you recall more than one account raising alarm bells?"

He looked out at the crowd, his eyes scanning over the audience. "Maybe. I can't be certain."

"What other companies raised alarm bells?"

"I don't recall."

"You mentioned a concreting supply company. Was that one of the accounts that raised alarm bells for you?"

Dunstall froze. When he didn't respond, Hennessy

squinted and tilted his head.

Palin coughed loudly behind Hennessy. Hennessy turned and looked at his client. Palin shook his head slightly. Hennessy turned back to the witness. He had to move on quickly.

"In your time with Palin Accounting, were you aware that Mr. Tilly and Mrs. Fisher were having an affair?"

"No, I was not."

"Did you see any unusual behavior from them?"

"Not that I can recall."

"Were you aware that they were preparing for retirement?"

"I don't recall having a conversation with them about retirement. Everyone in the office kept to themselves. It wasn't a good working environment, and the turnover of staff was high."

Hennessy nodded. "No further questions, Your Honor."

When Garrett declined to redirect, Hennessy breathed a sigh of relief.

They had dodged a bullet.

CHAPTER 33

"You embezzled money from Stanwell Construction?!" Hennessy slapped a file on the table in front of Palin. "Why didn't you tell me there was evidence you did this?"

The meeting room in the courthouse was small. A table took up much of the space, with five office chairs squeezed around the outside. A potted plant was in the corner, and a small hand-drawn, framed picture of Charleston was hanging on the wall.

"I don't know what you're talking about."

"JR Concreting Supplies." Hennessy glared at Palin. "It's an anomaly through your accounts. Richard Dunstall talked about an anomaly with the records for a concreting company. JR Concreting Supplies is not a registered business, but Stanwell Construction made several payments four years ago, totaling more than $50,000."

Palin sat back, taking his time to think over his

following answer. He shook his head and then groaned. "I told you not to ask Dunstall too many questions."

"This is what you've really been scared of, isn't it? You didn't care about the Foundation or the children or your reputation. This is what you've been scared of. You made fake invoices for Stanwell Construction and stole their money."

"I didn't steal their money." Palin paused for a moment, and a look of defeat spread across his face. "Maybe I sent them fake invoices from a fake company, but that was before they started providing muscle for the Rebel Sons. They weren't winning many contracts then, and they were small-scale. At that time, Tony was nasty but wasn't a threat. And when I first came on, their books were a mess. They had no idea how to run a business, and they had no idea how to balance their books. A few dollars here and there didn't hurt anyone."

"$50,000 is more than a few dollars. Do you have a death wish?"

"I have a life wish. That's why I created the fake invoices. I wanted to live a little. I had a great vacation in the Bahamas. And I stopped when they started working with the Rebel Sons. Tony knew someone who knew someone, and then they started working together to launder money through the construction business. I didn't touch his records after that."

"That's a dangerous game to play."

"It's four years ago, and Tony wouldn't even know where to look. That man struggles to work out a calendar, let alone complex accounting systems. The only records the company has from those days are with me. If I don't show him, then he never knows." Palin stood, the stress becoming too much. He leaned against the back of the chair. "We're lucky Dunstall didn't say anything on the stand."

"How did he even know?"

"He was like a savant. Numbers were his thing. He had no personal skills and zero common sense, but he could read records so fast, and the numbers just stuck in his brain. He came to me with questions about records that were seven years old, and I told him to forget it. I told him to put the physical records through the shredder and delete them from the computer. He refused, saying it wasn't best practice, and then I took the paper records and put them through the shredder while he was sitting in my office. He quit a week later."

Palin sat down, and Hennessy leaned his tall frame against the far wall. He looked at the ceiling for inspiration.

"We're lucky Dunstall didn't say anything," Hennessy said. "But the longer this case goes on, the worse it looks for you. There are so many people willing to testify that you ripped them off, and it's convincing the jury that this pattern of behavior extended to the Foundation."

"I know I'm not squeaky clean, but it had to be Tilly and Fisher. Everything is pointing to them. They were planning their retirement and saw these funds as an easy way out. They were ready to take the money before I was arrested."

"That doesn't explain why you gave Berkley a copy of the account statement. That is the piece of evidence that's going to stump the jury. Even if they think it's Tilly and Fisher, they'll be stuck on the bank statement Berkley gave the police."

"It's a set up. Berkley wanted me out of his life and saw this as an easy way to set me up. The jury will see that when he testifies. Tilly probably gave him the bank statement to set me up."

"Berkley will be the key. You're done if he comes to the stand confidently and presents a trustworthy image. But if we can link Tilly and Berkley, we might have a chance of raising suspicion about where the bank statement came from."

"I'll see what I can do about Berkley."

"Don't touch him. This is a court of law, not a schoolyard."

"You've got your rules, and I've got mine." Palin shrugged. "If the prosecution wants to pin me for everything else I've done, they should go ahead and try. I always covered my tracks well. They won't find a thing. And just because I've done questionable things in the past, doesn't mean that I should pay for this crime when I'm innocent."

Hennessy hated, deeply hated, that Palin was right.

CHAPTER 34

The following days of the trial moved past in a blur of activity.

Garrett called several more witnesses who were involved in Palin Accounting. One former employee testified Palin used to grope her bottom on regular occasions. Another said he would often make sexual comments and talk about how much he'd love to see photos of her naked. A third employee said Palin tried to kiss her at work one evening. She quit the next day.

None of it proved his guilt about embezzling money from the Foundation, but it added to the character assassination the prosecution was pushing. Not that it was hard. After one woman testified, Palin turned his head to watch her leave the room. When he turned back around, he licked his lips. It was a horrible look, and the disgust on the female juror's faces was clear.

At the start of the second week of the trial, once

Palin's character was clear to the jurors, Garrett began calling in the experts. He called accounting specialists, who all testified that the transfer to the account could not have happened in error. He called ethics experts, and they detailed how bad stealing from a charity foundation was. And he called fraud experts, who testified about the changes in records.

Garrett called a document examiner, a compliance expert, and a computer technician. He called forensic specialists, criminal investigative accountants, and fraud investigators. As the expert witnesses testified, Hennessy objected at every opportunity. With each witness, Hennessy crossed examined, but it was of little use. Their testimonies were factual, focused, and involved little emotion.

They all said the same thing—this could not have been an error.

By the second Friday of the trial, the case was firmly in the prosecution's favor.

Law enforcement made no indication that they had found Witnesses Two and Three, and Garrett was doing their best to prevent Hennessy from referring to them.

Berkley was their star witness to bring everything

together, and Hennessy expected him to hit the stands after the weekend.

Hennessy had done everything he could to prepare for his testimony. He read the witness statement so many times that he knew it word for word and knew everything about Berkley's previous indiscretions. To discredit Berkley on the stand, Hennessy would have to place his questions well. Berkley was a former judge, intelligent, and he appeared trustworthy. Hennessy couldn't accuse Berkley of fraudulent behavior but instead had to allow the jury members to come to that conclusion themselves.

The closer the trial came to exposing the truth, the more Hennessy could feel the threats. There were people who needed to protect Palin. There were people who needed to ensure their names weren't mentioned in court. And there were people who had no care for the rule of law.

Publicly, Garrett was going hard after Palin. He repeated the term 'stealing from children' over and over and over again. He knew what he was doing. He thought the case was an easy win, and he was painting Palin as the worst sort of criminal. The public was outraged, angry that someone could stoop so low. It all looked good for Garrett and his boss's re-election chances.

Hennessy dug deep into Stanwell Construction and their activities. He found Palin had been embezzling money from the construction company under invoices paid to the fake firm 'JR Concreting Supplies,' which matched Palin's bank account.

Tony Stanwell didn't know it, nor did the Rebel Sons.

And Hennessy hoped they never found out.

The nerves were beginning to show for Palin. There were bags under his eyes, and he was slouching at the defense table.

Before Hennessy returned to his apartment after another long Friday night in the office, he entered The Blind Tiger, a legendary bar in downtown Charleston. The bar was a captivating alehouse that opened in 1803 and was almost always full. It featured a brick-walled courtyard at the rear and dark décor inside.

Hennessy greeted Lockett with a handshake and a pat on the shoulder. He then went to the bar, ordered two locally brewed Pale Ales, and returned a moment later.

"I have a lead on Tilly and Fisher," Lockett explained. "John Tilly's brother owned three cars. When I checked, there were only two in his driveway. I've put out feelers on his brother's car, got a hit in Texas. Someone has put the car up online for sale in Austin. If it's Tilly, he must be trying to ditch it and buy another one. I can contact them, arrange to meet up, and bring them back here if you need it."

"They're two consenting adults who have fled town, and I don't blame them. With everything that Palin is connected to, I'm surprised the prosecution hasn't charged them with being accomplices."

"Don't need me to drag them back?"

"Leave them there," Hennessy said. "Right now, the jury believes they've run away scared. Let's not break that myth."

Lockett nodded. "Think you can win it?"

"It's in the prosecution's favor. Right now, Palin looks guilty," Hennessy said. "But Clarence Berkley is about to testify. He's the key to the prosecution's attack and if we can break him, we might have a chance."

CHAPTER 35

Hennessy's stress remained throughout the second weekend of the trial.

He spent most of it in his office, focusing on the upcoming witnesses, their statements, and their backgrounds. He reviewed every line of every statement, studied every piece of evidence several times, and spent hours examining the witness profiles.

When his focus waned, Hennessy questioned his choice to defend Palin. Were his morals for sale? No, he concluded. The justice system was based on the idea that everyone, regardless of actions, wealth, or skin color, received a fair, non-biased, and impartial judgment from the jury. Hennessy knew the reality of the courtroom was far from that. There was an unconscious bias in the courtroom, as there was to human behavior. It was his job to ensure that unconscious bias didn't affect the outcome of Palin's trial. Yes, Palin was dirty. Yes, Palin was a sleaze. Yes,

Palin was corrupt. But none of that proved he was guilty of this crime.

Hennessy was certain Garrett would open the week by calling Judge Berkley to the stand. Garrett used primacy and recency effects well and knew that the first witness on a Monday morning had more impact on the jury than a witness on a Wednesday afternoon after lunch.

By the time Hennessy walked into the courtroom to start the week, he felt like half his blood was coffee. He wiped his eyes and focused on the case. Palin arrived twenty minutes later, followed in by Garrett and the prosecution team. When the gallery doors opened, they filled steadily with members of the public until most of the seats were full.

Hennessy turned and looked to the crowd. The usuals were there—the reporters, the casual onlookers, the future law students—but one person caught his eye. Dressed in a black shirt and black jeans, the man was heavily tattooed and scarred. Hennessy turned back to Palin. "What's he doing here?"

"Who?"

"The biker."

Palin turned around and looked at the crowd. "No idea," he replied but his voice was unconvincing. "It's nothing to do with me."

Hennessy glared at Palin as the bailiff called the court to order. Judge Clayton walked to his bench, unaware of the threat in the room. He welcomed everyone back after the weekend, confirmed there were no further motions, and then asked the bailiff to bring the jury in.

When invited by Judge Clayton, Garrett stood and confirmed Hennessy's suspicions. "The State calls Judge Clarence Berkley."

Berkley entered through the rear doors of the courtroom. Dressed in a black suit, complete with a black tie and polished shoes, his movements were slow but elegant.

As he reached the front of the courtroom, the tattooed man stood.

In one swift movement, he leaped toward Berkley, throwing a heavy left hook that connected with Berkley's face.

Berkley crumbled. Other members of the gallery yelled in fear.

The bailiffs were quick, tackling the tattooed man

within seconds. They flung him to the floor, diving on top of him, and using their body weight to subdue the attacker.

The gallery was quiet as they pinned him down.

"Don't move!" They yelled as they held the man to the floor, pushing his head down, and holding his arms behind his back. "Don't move! Stop resisting!"

Members of the public went to the assistance of Berkley, who was dazed and bloodied, sitting on the ground. He looked barely lucid.

The bailiffs called for backup on their radios, and soon, the courtroom was filled with officers who had no sympathy for the tattooed man. They pulled him to his feet and stormed him out of the courtroom. Hennessy looked at Garrett. His mouth was hanging open in shock.

Courthouse staff assisted Berkley, and Judge Clayton asked the remaining bailiff to lead the jury out and then clear the gallery.

Once the bailiff cleared the gallery, EMTs arrived to check on Berkley. Judge Clayton left the room in a huff, clearly angry that his courtroom had been the subject of such violence.

When the commotion started to subdue, Hennessy

turned to Palin. "Did you do this?"

"No idea." Palin smiled. "Whatever happened to Berkley was out of my control."

CHAPTER 36

"A motion for a mistrial," Judge Clayton groaned as he leaned back in his leather chair. "It's understandable, given the circumstances that occurred."

Law books lined the walls of Judge Clayton's chambers. It was a dark and narrow room, with the curtains drawn. A black leather couch sat near the door, next to a table with five different whiskey bottles. A thick Persian rug led to the judge's large mahogany desk. Two armchairs sat on one side of the desk, and the judge sat on the other. The smells of wood, leather, and whiskey filled the air.

In the twenty-four hours since the assault on Clarence Berkley, Hennessy had drafted the motion.

"You need to declare a mistrial," Hennessy stated. "The jury saw what happened, and there's no way they can remain impartial after that event. This is a fundamental issue that will prevent fairness or impartiality. The jurors' opinions on this case will be biased by the actions of someone not involved in the trial. The integrity of this court is paramount, and we must acknowledge that the jurors' opinions will be tainted by this."

Judge Clayton stared at the piece of paper in front of him for a long moment before he shook his head several times. "I understand why you've lodged this, but this courtroom will not be manipulated by the defendant or the people he's associated with. Mr. Garrett, what do you have to say about this motion?"

"We're against it, Your Honor. We believe the case can continue with the right instructions to the jury members. Mr. Palin did not attack the witness, and he did not appear to be involved at any point. From the juror's point of view, there's no indication that he had anything to do with the assault. We believe we can continue the trial."

"Did Mr. Palin know anything about the assault?"

"Not that I'm aware of," Hennessy responded. "But this is about what the jury will think."

"Your Honor, this case needs to continue," Garrett argued. "We cannot allow this to become a precedent in South Carolina. If a criminal thinks he's going down, he can set this up every time. We must not allow our courts to be dictated by thugs. This fight cannot change the course of this trial."

"Wasn't much of a fight," Judge Clayton quipped. "How's the witness?

"He's shaken but is ok. He has bruising on the side of his face, and given his age, it will take some time before that bruising reduces," Garrett explained. "But he's still willing to testify. Given his injuries, he would be able to take the stand later this week. We've talked to him, and he said he won't be scared off by these thugs. He wants to come to court and tell the truth."

"Any testimony he makes will be tainted," Hennessy said. "The attack happened in full view of the jury. We cannot pretend that the attack will not bias their opinions. This case needs to be declared a mistrial. If it's not, it's a reversible error."

Judge Clayton ignored Hennessy and looked at Garrett. "And what do we know about the man who assaulted Judge Berkley?"

"Jimmy White. Forty-five years old and has spent most of his adult life in and out of prison. Currently wanted on various warrants, including assault charges, weapon charges, and probation issues. He was already looking at another stretch in prison, and this will only add to his time back there."

"We'll throw the book at him. We can't allow this behavior to go unpunished. We need to send a message to say this behavior is not acceptable in the court." Judge Clayton leaned forward and picked up the motion. He glanced over it again before he huffed and looked back to Garrett. "Why did Mr. White attack the witness in my courtroom?"

"The police have questioned him, and he claims he had a personal issue with Judge Berkley," Garrett explained. "He says that he attacked Judge Berkley in the courtroom because Berkley had gone missing in the weeks before. He couldn't find him, but he knew Berkley would arrive for this testimony. And he said he has no connection to Mr. Palin or his associates."

"But why in the courtroom? Why not in the hallway outside?"

"I have no idea what he was thinking. That's a question you'll have to ask of Mr. White, Your Honor."

Judge Clayton looked at Hennessy. "Any ideas?"

"I was unaware of Mr. White or his intentions."

"And your client?"

"He has told me he was unaware of the attack as well."

"We've had threats against witnesses, we still have two missing witnesses, and another witness was physically assaulted in my courtroom." Judge Clayton threw his hands up in the air. He took a moment to think before he continued. "People who think they're above the law will not intimidate this courtroom. I will explain to the jurors that this incident had nothing to do with Mr. Palin and that this was a personal matter for Judge Berkley."

"Your Honor—" Hennessy tried to argue.

"My decision is made. The motion for a mistrial is denied, and the trial shall continue on Thursday morning." Judge Clayton indicated to the door. "Now get out of my chambers."

CHAPTER 37

Joe Hennessy sat in the booth, staring at his whiskey instead of drinking it.

Barry Lockett nursed a pint of pale ale in his large hands on the other side of the booth, and Jacinta Templeton sipped a glass of chardonnay next to Lockett.

Big John's Tavern was a legendary bar in Downtown Charleston. Refurbished after a fire ten years ago, the rustic tavern was one of Charleston's favorites. First opened in 1955 by a former New York Giants player, the bar now had different owners but held onto the dive bar feel, if only a more upmarket version. The lighting was dim, the décor was dark, and the smells of aged bourbon wafted from every corner of the building.

"No mistrial?" Lockett asked.

"Judge Clayton doesn't want to give into thuggery in the courtroom, and it's understandable," Hennessy said. "It gives us grounds for appeal, but it doesn't help us now. The jury is almost convinced of Palin's guilt, and Berkley is going to be the one to slam it home."

"Well, the timing is good," Lockett said. "I found something for you this afternoon. If Berkley had testified on Monday, then we wouldn't have been able to use this information."

"What is it?"

Lockett took out his cell phone, opened the screen, and passed it across to Hennessy. Jacinta leaned over his shoulder to look at the picture.

"John Tilly and Clarence Berkley together?" Jacinta questioned as she looked at the picture. The picture showed Berkley standing next to Tilly at a golf game, both men dressed in white polo shirts, one arm around the other.

"It's from two years ago," Lockett explained. "They were at a charity golf game together in Florida. I ran their faces through our facial recognition program, which took days to process. The program picked up this hit from a photo on Facebook promoting the golf day. It's not much, but it might help the case."

"This is good," Hennessy agreed. "Berkley will retake the stand on Thursday, and now we've got new ammunition to attack him with. If we can suggest to the jury that Tilly gave Berkley the bank statement, we might be able to create enough reasonable doubt about Palin's guilt in this one instance."

"Yeah. This 'one' instance," Jacinta said. "He still looks like he's guilty of so much more."

Hennessy and Lockett nodded their agreeance.

"Are you all set for the defense case?" Lockett asked.

"Almost," Hennessy responded. "All our expert witnesses have agreed to testify, and their statements look good. We've got financial investigators, fraud experts, and IT specialists all lined up to support our claim that there's doubt about who did the transfers. In our defense case, we're not going to dispute it happened, but we will claim there's reasonable doubt that Palin did it. Jacinta, can you please call Harrison Reid and Jeremy Flynn tomorrow and confirm they're ready to testify? They'll open our defense case, and I need them to be ready."

"I'll do it first thing," Jacinta said. "Do you think we've got a chance to win?"

"John Tilly wasn't investigated as a suspect, and that failure by the investigators has left a reasonable amount of doubt. The question is whether the jury sees it the same way. We won't know their thoughts until they deliver the verdict."

"Think they'll be more trouble before then?"

"I don't know," Hennessy responded. "But the closer we get to a decision; the more things escalate. Palin doesn't want to go to prison, and I'd hate to think what he'll do if it looks like we're going to lose."

"You could request to leave the case," Jacinta said as she sipped her drink. "Forget about the money and walk away. You don't owe Bernard Palin anything."

"I can't do that," Hennessy shook his head. "I'm in too deep. Ethically, I can't walk away from the case now."

"How many more chances will you give him?" Jacinta asked. "He's going to keep pushing the boundaries. How many more witnesses will be beaten up or go missing because of this case? And what if his anger turns to you?"

"He wouldn't be that stupid," Hennessy replied. "But that's not my biggest worry. My biggest worry is that if we win, he'll be on the first plane out of here, and it'll be a long time before I get paid."

"Didn't he put his house up as collateral?"

"He did, but that's a long legal process to claim. It could take years for that to happen. I'd have to go through so many hearings and court appearances. It's an option, but it's the last option."

Two gray-haired men at the bar started arguing loudly, catching everyone's attention.

Words were thrown around about the Clemson Tigers, and Hennessy started to move to defend his team. Jacinta held out her hand and then shook her head at Hennessy. Hennessy conceded and made no further moves. Still, the older men in their late seventies continued to argue until one stood up and pushed the other. They scuffled in slow motion, not having the strength to nudge each other off their feet. As they became physical, the bartender raced to break them up, pulling them apart. He pushed both back onto their barstools and cautioned them like they were children. The two men didn't argue any further, and after the bartender instructed them to shake hands, they did so. Once the hands were shaken, the bar went back to its normal business.

"If this is all about money," Jacinta turned back to

Hennessy. "Then you need to make sure you get paid. Otherwise, we've just defended a despicable human for nothing."

It wasn't a statement Hennessy wanted to think about. He'd become tangled in a web of corruption, lies, and violence, and the thought of not getting paid for it was too much.

"I need to defend him," Hennessy said. "If he didn't do this, then I need to convince the jury of the truth. That's my job. That's my part in the justice system. Dirtbag or not, I need to defend his right to a fair trial."

CHAPTER 38

Every prosecution case has a big star, the witness who can tie all the evidence together and place the final piece in the puzzle. Clarence Berkley was that witness. He was the man to complete the picture, tying everything into a neat bundle and confirming all the information laid out previously. He appeared respectable, trustworthy, and intelligent. None of it was true, but appearances matter. The jury members would believe every word that rolled off his tongue. He was almost the perfect witness. Almost.

On Thursday morning, the courtroom felt empty and soulless.

Judge Clayton had ordered that Berkley testify behind closed doors, away from further threats. Judge Clayton began the day by taking twenty-five minutes to explain to the jury that the attack on Berkley had nothing to do with the case. It was a personal vendetta and had nothing to do with Palin. The assailant had been arrested and charged, and he would look at a long stretch in prison, Judge Clayton said. He asked the jury several questions about their understanding, and when he was satisfied, he called for the case to continue.

Garrett called Berkley to the stand. Sitting in the front row of the empty gallery, Berkley stood.

The bruising was evident on the side of his face. His cheek was purple, his eye was red and slightly swollen, and he limped as he walked to the stand. He swore his oath and sat in the witness box with his bruising clear for the jury to see.

"Please state your name and occupation for the court." Garrett began.

"My name is Judge Clarence Berkley. I've spent most of my career as a judge in Charleston County; however, I retired several years ago. I served this county, and this court, with respect. I'm very proud of my career and to have been of such service to the people of Charleston County."

"And how do you know the defendant?"

"Mr. Palin used to be my accountant for many years. He stopped being my accountant several years ago; however, since that time, we've remained associates."

"And are you still employed now?"

"No. My wife was diagnosed with dementia, and I've been her caregiver for several years. We have nurses who help during the day, but much of that responsibility falls to me."

"And how are you involved in this case?"

"I provided the first tip-off to the police."

"And did you have anything to gain by providing that tip-off to the police?"

"No."

"How did you come across the information?"

"Mr. Palin approached me with several legal inquiries. He wanted advice from me, because of my many years in the justice system. We met in a bar off King Street, however, Mr. Palin requested we use a private booth to discuss the matters. When he did that, I knew it would be a serious chat."

"And what did he ask you?"

"He asked me the best way to take embezzled money from a business account to a private one. He explained he would transfer the money to himself and retire to Costa Rica. He said it was enough money to retire with."

"His intention was to retire, and—"

"Objection," Hennessy called out. "Hearsay."

"Sustained," Judge Clayton stated. "Please move on, Mr. Garrett."

Garrett nodded his response and then continued. "Did he send you any emails about moving to Costa Rica?"

"Objection. Leading the witness."

"Sustained."

Garrett took a moment to consider his statement. "How did Mr. Garrett tell you he was moving to Costa Rica?"

"Via email," Berkley stated firmly.

"And are these the emails here?" Garrett handed two sheets of paper to the bailiff, who passed it to the witness and another copy to the judge.

"That's correct."

"In these emails, Mr. Palin talks about retiring to a Costa Rica waterfront property and asks you to assist him in buying it. Did you help him?"

"No. I told him that the people I know usually deal with cash only, and I said I didn't think he had the cash. When we met for drinks, he showed me his bank statement to show he had the money in cash."

"And is this the bank statement he showed you?" Garrett introduced the bank statement as evidence.

"It is. It shows that he had more than a million dollars in that account."

"And can you please read the account number on the bank statement?"

Berkley read out the account number, and when Garrett stated it was the same account number where the funds were being transferred from the Wolfgang Berger Foundation, one jury member gasped. The connection between the bank accounts wasn't a surprise. Either the woman hadn't been paying attention to the entire case or she was easily shocked. Looking at her, Hennessy wasn't sure which it was.

"Were you aware that Mr. Palin was transferring money from the Wolfgang Berger Foundation—"

"Objection," Hennessy stated. "The question assumes facts not in evidence. There's no evidence that Mr. Palin made the transfer into that account."

"Sustained," Judge Clayton stated.

"Let me rephrase," Garrett tapped his hand on the file before him. "Were you aware that the money transferred into that bank account came from the Wolfgang Berger Foundation?"

"Yes, that's what Mr. Palin told me."

"And were you aware that someone within Palin Accounting made that transfer?"

"Yes. Again, that's what Mr. Palin told me."

"And were you aware that the million dollars in that account was fraudulently gained?"

"Yes. Mr. Palin informed me that the money had come from a charity foundation. When I told him that was terrible behavior, he informed me that he'd been doing it for years, and nobody in the Foundation said anything. They weren't missing the money."

"What did you say to that?"

"I told him it was terrible behavior."

"How did he respond to that?"

"He didn't like it. He said he never withdrew the money from the account so if he was caught, he could claim it was an accounting mistake. He also said that after nobody discovered the transfer in the first year, he kept doing it. Now he was ready to move away and take the money out. I made it clear it was illegal."

"What did you do after that?"

"I told Mr. Palin I wanted nothing more to do with him and took the bank statement. I sat with the information for another day before I decided to talk with law enforcement. I couldn't live with myself if I allowed him to steal all that money from those children."

"Thank you, Judge Berkley. No further questions."

Hennessy stood to begin his cross-examination. It was his turn to tear Berkley apart.

CHAPTER 39

"Thank you for taking the time to discuss the case, Judge Berkley." Hennessy moved to the lectern with a folder in front of him. He stared at Berkley for a long moment and then began his questions. "Would you call yourself friends with Mr. Palin?"

"Mr. Palin and I have been friends in the past, yes. He did my accounting for years, although he no longer does it. Since he began doing my accounting, we've been friends and associates."

"You mentioned you were friends in the past. How is your relationship currently?"

"We have a strained relationship."

"Why is that?"

"I never trusted Mr. Palin. And it's hard to be friends with someone you don't trust. I think he's devious, deceitful, and dishonest. He told me about some of his actions, which I find despicable."

Hennessy opened the file and read over the first

line. "Did Mr. Palin know any secrets about you?"

Berkley drew a breath and glared at Garrett. Garrett stood. "Objection. Relevance. The witness is not on trial here."

"We're questioning the credibility of the witness, Your Honor. He's called the defendant devious, deceitful, and dishonest. We wish to establish how Judge Berkley came to that conclusion."

"The objection is overruled. You may continue establishing the credibility of the witness, Mr. Hennessy."

"Judge Berkley," Hennessy pressed. "Did Mr. Palin know any secrets about you?"

"I'm not sure what you're referring to." Berkley was evasive. "I'm not friends with Mr. Palin anymore if that's what you're asking."

"No, that's not what I asked. I asked if Mr. Palin knew any secrets about your behavior?"

"Not that I'm aware of."

"Interesting," Hennessy said and picked up a folder. "Judge Berkley, was Mr. Palin aware that you paid several 'female companions' to travel with you on work trips? These female companions were not known to you before the trip, is that correct?"

Berkley's mouth hung open and then he looked back to the prosecution. When Garrett saw Berkley's shock, he stood. "Objection. Relevance."

"The question establishes his credibility, Your Honor."

"Again, the objection is overruled. You may answer the question, Judge Berkley."

"Mr. Palin was my accountant, so naturally, he had information on where I spent my money. I had work expenses and items that needed to be claimed."

"Did you ask him to hide the money you spent on female companions titled under work expenses?"

"My memory is not what it used to be, so I don't recall. I can't recall what my IRS statements claimed all those years ago."

"Judge Berkley, are you aware that claiming work expenses under taxpayer dollars is fraudulent?"

"I'm aware of that."

"And are you aware that in the ten years before your retirement, you spent more than fifty thousand dollars on 'female companionship,' as you've called it in one of your emails?"

He sat back. "I don't recall."

"Do you recall spending any money on 'female

companionship?'"

He shook his head. "I don't recall doing that."

"This should refresh your memory." Hennessy handed one sheet of paper to the prosecutor and the other to the bailiff. The bailiff handed the piece of paper to Berkley. "These are the transactions where you transferred money to the bank accounts of female companions, averaging five thousand dollars per year, and the corresponding emails where you ask Mr. Palin to list these transactions as work expenses. In one email, Mr. Palin asks what expense the money was for, and you respond by saying, 'a great night with a twenty-five-year-old girl.' Is that correct?"

"I don't recall."

"It's on the paper in front of you, Judge Berkley."

"I can see that, but I don't recall what the statement refers to." Berkley looked over the sheets of paper. "None of these transactions were listed in my IRS statements as work expenses."

"Then why bother listing them as work expenses on your accounting statements?"

"I don't recall why that happened."

"Do you recall sleeping with prostitutes?"

"Objection! This is a personal attack on the

witness and has nothing to do with credibility. When done within the law, the personal actions of the witness are not relevant to this case, nor their credibility."

"Sustained," Judge Clayton agreed. "You've overstepped the line there, Mr. Hennessy. Judge Berkley's lawful actions aren't on trial, and unless you have evidence of unlawful actions, we will move on."

Hennessy nodded to Judge Clayton. "Judge Berkley, you mentioned you were married. How long have you been married to your wife?"

"Fifty-two years."

"And in that time, how many female companions did you have sex with?"

"Objection! Relevance!"

"Sustained. It's time to move on, Mr. Hennessy."

"Judge Berkley," Hennessy continued. "Were you forced to retire from being a judge?"

"No. I did it of my own accord."

"Were there allegations of sexual assault against you by staff members when you retired?"

"Objection!" Garrett stood again. "There's no relevance to this case. Judge Berkley is not on trial and shouldn't be subjected to such a personal attack."

"Judge Berkley is the person who presented the tip-off to the police, Your Honor," Hennessy argued. "We have the right to establish his credibility and we believe this information establishes his motive to provide that tip-off."

"Overruled," Judge Clayton agreed. "You may answer the question about your employment."

Garrett sat down, disappointed.

"Nothing was ever proven against me," Berkley said. "And like I said, I retired of my own choice. My wife has dementia, and I spend most of my days looking after her."

"But when you retired, there were allegations of sexual assault?"

"There were no charges."

Hennessy raised his eyebrows and looked at the jury. One nodded in return. "Judge Berkley, do you know Mr. John Tilly?"

His mouth hung open for a long moment.

"Judge Berkley?"

"Yes. I know John Tilly."

"And how do you know Mr. Tilly?"

"He worked for Palin Accounting, and they handled my accounts. I've interacted with all their staff over the years. And Charleston is a small city. Everyone has links to everyone here."

"You've played golf with Mr. Tilly, is that correct?"

"Not just the two of us playing together. We've interacted at tournaments. We didn't plan to go on golf trips together."

"But you have played golf together?"

"Yes."

"Were you aware that he was having an affair and had planned to elope with Mrs. Fisher?"

"Objection!" Garrett raised to his feet again, but the damage was done. The jurors were already making the links in their heads. "This question assumes facts not established. There's no evidence that Mr. Tilly was planning to elope."

"I'll withdraw the question," Hennessy said. "Judge Berkley, did you and Mr. Tilly arrange the bank account statement so that you could set Mr. Palin up for this crime?"

"Objection!" Garrett shouted. "Your Honor, this is an outrageous accusation."

"Withdrawn." Hennessy looked to the jury and saw several sitting with their mouths open, staring at the witness, stunned by all the coincidences. "No further questions."

Hennessy returned to his seat at the defense table, knowing his cross-examination had gone well, but there was still a long way to go.

CHAPTER 40

After Berkley's testimony filled most of the morning, Judge Clayton called for a recess for lunch. Garrett was evasive and avoided eye contact with Hennessy. That worried Hennessy. He was sure Garrett still had something up his sleeve.

When the lawyers returned to the courtroom after lunch, the gallery filled behind them, eager to see if the prosecution had changed tactics after the morning testimony. But it was Garrett's first witness after lunch who would have the most significant impact on the trial.

"The State calls Mr. John Tilly."

"Objection!" Hennessy leaped to his feet as the courtroom doors opened. John Tilly stood at the rear of the gallery, unsure whether or not to continue toward the stand. "Your Honor, this witness has been listed as a missing person, and we were not made aware that he'd been located, and we were not made aware that he was going to testify."

"He's on the witness list, Your Honor," Garrett stated. "We received information at lunchtime that Mr. Tilly had arrived back in Charleston, and he's an important witness to this case. The defense has been positioning the witness as someone with knowledge and access to the accounts, and we would like to give the witness a chance to clear his name."

"Your Honor, the prosecution claims that they located the missing witness on the last day of their case when it looked like they were losing. That's more than a coincidence."

"I agree it's an unusual coincidence, Mr. Hennessy," Judge Clayton glared at Garrett. "But Mr. Hennessy, you have positioned this witness as someone who's very important to this case."

"The defense has not had the chance to depose the witness after the truth was revealed about his false and misleading witness statements. There's information that wasn't revealed to the defense until after he was reported as a missing person."

"Understood, Mr. Hennessy," Judge Clayton sighed. "Mr. Tilly is listed as a witness in the discovery information, however, I agree with Mr. Hennessy that

314

his return to Charleston is new information and outside the scope of reasonable notice. I will grant a recess for an hour to allow the defense to either depose Mr. Tilly in person or make other arrangements as necessary. This witness is important to the case, but this court must also maintain due fairness. We will reconvene in an hour and assess the situation then. After the hour, if the defense wishes to have more time, I will consider the proposal."

"Thank you, Your Honor."

Judge Clayton cleared the courtroom, and fifteen minutes later, Hennessy was sitting inside a conference room questioning Tilly. He didn't need to depose Tilly, but the tactic bought him time to prepare for the upcoming testimony. Garrett knew it, and his frustration during the deposition was apparent.

Hennessy spent five minutes in the deposition before he went to a separate conference room to focus on his legal tactics. He wondered why Tilly returned but reasoned that Garrett had found him and threatened him with legal consequences if Palin got off. Someone had to be convicted for the crime, and if it wasn't Palin, they would go after Tilly and

Fisher. Tilly had returned to save his own skin, Hennessy concluded.

When he returned to the court an hour later, he was ready. Judge Clayton confirmed Hennessy had no further objections and then invited Garrett to recall the witness.

"The State calls John Tilly," Garrett began.

As he had done an hour earlier, John Tilly stepped through the courtroom doors. This time, he wasn't interrupted. He walked through the courtroom, swore his oath, nodded to the jury members, and sat in the witness box.

Dressed in a light brown suit and striped shirt without a tie, Tilly looked presentable. But his twitchy movements, avoidance of eye contact, and a thin layer of sweat on his brow showed his nerves.

"Thank you for testifying today," Garrett stood behind his desk. "Can you please tell the court your name, profession, and how you are associated with Palin Accounting?"

"My name is John Tilly, and I've been an accountant for over thirty years. I worked for Palin Accounting as the senior accountant for five years, before I resigned earlier this year."

"And while you worked for Palin Accounting, did you notice any unusual, fraudulent, or immoral behavior?"

"Absolutely. Mr. Palin was a terrible boss. I witnessed him groping some of the younger women. He physically pushed me on several occasions, and he would yell and swear and throw things around the office. It was a horrible working environment."

"If it was so bad, why did you stay? A man with your experience could get another job."

"Because Mr. Palin would threaten us. He said if we ever left the firm, we would never get another job in the State. And it happened. Several experienced accountants quit when I started, and Mr. Palin spread rumors about their poor behavior and terrible working habits. Those accountants had to go to another state just to find work. So, if I wanted to stay in South Carolina around my children, I had to stay at Palin Accounting."

"Did you witness any fraudulent behavior while working there?"

"I witnessed many occasions of unlawful and fraudulent behavior by Mr. Palin. He was the owner of the firm and had the final say on all the processes.

As the senior accountant, I had access to the same reports and bank accounts as Mr. Palin, and I witnessed many instances of fraud. One of the most common ways Mr. Palin was fraudulent was to overcharge clients. I believe he overcharged more than ninety percent of our clients."

"Is that the only instance of fraud that you witnessed?"

"No. Mr. Palin also created fake invoices for work that was never performed. He would create invoices for business consulting services and would send these invoices to the companies to pay. As a firm, we rarely delivered business consulting services, and when we did, it was only minor work. Some years, Mr. Palin would charge tens of thousands of dollars to particular companies for consulting services that were never delivered."

"If the fraud was so prevalent, why would any clients stay with Palin Accounting?"

"Because Mr. Palin would dig and dig and dig until he found something on the clients. No business is squeaky clean, and Mr. Palin would leverage that information. He would tell the companies if they didn't pay, he could expose them to the IRS or law enforcement. He also ensured every client and employee signed a non-disclosure agreement, and he was diligent in monitoring those agreements."

Garrett nodded and looked at a note from one of his associates. It was a pre-planned routine. They didn't need the note but were buying time, allowing the jurors space to think about the terrible working conditions within Palin Accounting. Once enough time had passed, Garrett continued. "During your time with Palin Accounting, what was the worst instance of fraud you witnessed?"

"I witnessed a fraud involving the Wolfgang Berger Foundation."

"And can you please explain what you witnessed?"

"When I first started in the job, Mr. Palin forced me to become a signatory on several new bank accounts. I was told I would be fired from my position if I didn't sign. I didn't think much of it then, but I later found that money was being transferred into one of those accounts directly from the Wolfgang Berger Foundation."

"When did you discover that?"

"Around one year ago."

"And what did you do?"

"I called a friend who worked in law enforcement and discussed my position. My friend advised me that because my name was on the bank account and the transfers came from a computer within Palin Accounting, then I could be charged as an accomplice to the crime. That made me realize why Mr. Palin made me sign on as a signatory to the bank accounts. If he was ever charged, he could blame me for it."

"What else did your law enforcement friend advise you to do?"

"They told me to gather as much information about the fraudulent behavior as possible. Once I had all the evidence, I could take it to the police, and Mr. Palin would be charged."

"Did you take it to the police?"

"No. When Mr. Palin was arrested, I was still gathering evidence."

"But by this point, you had finished work with Palin Accounting?"

"That's correct. I had resigned, but I was still a signatory on some of the accounts. Mr. Palin hadn't removed me from them yet."

"And were you able to present this evidence to the police when Mr. Palin was arrested?"

"I did."

"Did you directly see Mr. Palin transfer money from the Foundation into the Palin Accounting bank account?"

"I saw the reports, which made it clear that Mr. Palin had transferred one payment of two hundred thousand to the MUSC Shawn Jenkins Children's Hospital and an equal payment to his bank account. He made that transfer every year. The hospital would receive half, and he would receive the other half. It made me feel sick that he would steal from vulnerable children."

"If it made you feel so sick, why didn't you go straight to the police when you first discovered the fraud?"

"Because I was scared of what Mr. Palin and his contacts could do. He threatened us numerous times, and we signed several non-disclosure agreements. Mr. Palin physically threatened me on more than one occasion, and once, he told me he would hurt my family if I ever double-crossed him."

"And you're not scared of him now?"

"My children have left the state and attend college in New York and Chicago. I don't believe Mr. Palin will chase them there."

"And your wife?"

"Ah," Tilly shrugged. "We're in the process of separating, and she owns several firearms. I don't believe she's in any danger."

Garrett continued the same line of questioning for the next hour, and several times, Tilly repeated that he was scared of Palin. It was a convincing testimony.

When Garrett finished his questioning, Judge Clayton turned to Hennessy and signaled for the cross-examination to begin. Hennessy rose to his feet. It was time to dismantle Tilly piece by piece.

CHAPTER 41

"Mr. Tilly, thank you for coming to court to testify." Hennessy stood behind the lectern. His voice was firm, and his stare was intense. "Are you having an intimate relationship with anyone who was previously employed by Palin Accounting?"

"Objection. Relevance." Garrett stood. "Mr. Tilly's personal relationships are not a matter for this court. The defense is trying to humiliate the witness publicly, and we believe the questions are outside the scope of this trial."

"The question goes to the witness's credibility, Your Honor. Considering Mr. Tilly's statements in this courtroom about his employment, we believe it's important to establish all the details of his time in Palin Accounting."

"Agreed. Overruled," Judge Clayton stated. "You may answer the question, Mr. Tilly."

"What was the question again?" Tilly squinted and

leaned forward.

"Are you having, or have you ever had, an intimate relationship with anyone that Palin Accounting previously employed?"

"Yes."

"Who?"

Tilly drew a long breath. "I'm currently divorcing my wife, and we're separated. We are going through that process amicably, and yes, I have started a relationship with Debra Fisher, who also worked for Palin Accounting. We met at work and were a great match for each other."

"So, this was an extra-marital affair?"

"Yes, but as I said earlier, my wife and I are in the process of separating."

"And how long has this affair been happening?"

"Five years."

"Five years?" Hennessy expressed surprise. "That's a long time to lie to your wife, Mr. Tilly. Do you lie often?"

"Listen, I regret that it was an affair, but my marriage was failing, and Debra is amazing. She's my soulmate."

"If she's your soulmate, why didn't you leave your

marriage five years ago?"

"Because my children were still at home. I didn't want them growing up in two houses. I wanted them to have a stable home."

"So you've been preparing to leave your marriage for the last five years?"

"I was…" he paused and then exhaled loudly. "I was looking forward to my children finishing high school and going to college so that I could end the marriage."

Hennessy nodded and returned to the table. He picked up a folder and then walked back to the lectern. "Apart from Mr. Palin and yourself, who else were the signatories on the bank account where the money was transferred to?"

"Nobody."

Hennessy looked at the jury. Several heads were nodding. "Mr. Tilly, you mentioned you didn't report the crime you witnessed because you didn't want to hurt your family. Is that correct?"

"That's correct. I was fearful of what Mr. Palin, or his connections, would do to my family if I went to the police."

"But you were happy to hurt your family via the

affair?"

Tilly sat back. "Come on, man. That's different. Debra and I love each other, and we've planned a future together."

"Without consideration for your wife's emotions," Hennessy said. "Mr. Tilly, were you comfortable with the activities of Palin Accounting?"

"Of course not. That's why I helped organize a mass walkout of staff. I was never comfortable with all the fraud he committed."

"What did the mass walkout involve?"

"Convincing all the staff to quit on the same day. It didn't take much convincing. Mr. Palin groped one of the junior members, and that was the final straw for all of us. Nobody wanted to stay there."

"And how long before Mr. Palin's arrest did this happen?"

"We walked out a week before Mr. Palin was arrested."

"Did you go to the police in that week?"

"No."

"So, even though you quit and had a week, you still didn't take your so-called evidence to the police?"

"I wanted everyone to be safe first. I wanted to

ensure my family was safe and I wanted to ensure Debra was safe. I was preparing all the evidence, but before I had the chance to present the evidence, Mr. Palin was arrested anyway. They came and asked questions about his activities, and that's when I could present the evidence to the police."

"What a remarkable coincidence," Hennessy said. "Mr. Tilly, can you please tell the court if you were preparing for retirement when you quit?"

"I'm an accountant. Numbers and finances are what I do. I've been preparing for an early retirement for years. There's nothing wrong with that, and it's best to plan for retirement in advance."

"What did your planning involve?"

Tilly didn't respond for a few moments. It was clear he was considering whether he should tell the whole truth.

"Mr. Tilly?" Hennessy pressed.

"I opened a separate bank account and had some money in there. I decided to retire when that bank account reached a certain amount."

"Was your wife aware of this bank account?"

Tilly looked away. "No."

"How much money was in the bank account?"

"I'm not sure."

"An estimate, please."

Tilly drew a breath and then exhaled loudly. "Around two million."

One jury member gasped. One audience member muttered, 'Woah.' Even Hennessy expressed his surprise with raised eyebrows. "Two million dollars?"

"That's right."

"On a senior accountant's wage, while supporting a family, you put away two million dollars over the last five years?"

"Yes." Tilly's answers were deliberately short. The regret of coming to court was painted on his face.

"Was all that money legally acquired?"

"Yes," Tilly scoffed. "I got lucky and won two million on the lottery."

"Lucky indeed," Hennessy said. He hadn't seen that coming. "And how much money was in the account before the lottery win?"

"A hundred and fifty thousand."

"So, when you were planning for retirement, one million would've helped a lot in your retirement plans?"

"Two million."

"That's not the money I was referring to, Mr. Tilly." Hennessy paused, and when no objection came from the prosecution, he continued. "When did you win the money in the lottery?"

"Earlier this year."

"And did you plan the mass walkout before you won the lottery?"

He bit his lip. "No."

"You planned the mass walkout after winning the lottery, knowing you would never work again?"

"That's right."

"Mr. Tilly, I put it to you that you were diligently planning for your retirement, preparing to move away with your affair partner, and then you won the lottery. This was the catalyst that meant you could quit work and run away with Mrs. Fisher. Does that sound right?"

"That's about right."

"Is that why you left the million dollars behind? Because you didn't need it anymore?"

"Objection," Garrett rose to his feet but was slow to react. The question was already planted in the juror's minds. "That's an accusation."

"Withdrawn," Hennessy said. "Mr. Tilly, where

329

have you been for the past five weeks?"

"Texas."

"The Charleston Police Department has a missing persons file on you. You were reported as missing by your wife several weeks ago."

"I knew where I was."

"Were you with anyone in Texas?"

"Yes."

"Who?"

"Debra Fisher."

Hennessy shook his head while staring at the witness. Tilly looked away, uncomfortable under Hennessy's glare. "How long had you planned your trip to Texas?"

"I don't remember. Maybe a year."

Hennessy's voice rose. "Mr. Tilly, you had the opportunity. You had the access. You had the motive. I put it to you that you set up that account and you were gathering the funds to prepare for retirement next year. Did you transfer the money from the Wolfgang Berger Foundation into an account that you had access to?"

"That's ridiculous."

Hennessy shook his head. Several jurors did the

same. "No further questions."

"Redirect, Mr. Garrett?" Judge Clayton asked once Hennessy had sat down.

Garrett conferred with his associates for a few moments and then stood. "Just a few questions, Your Honor." He turned his attention to the witness. "Mr. Tilly, did you witness Mr. Palin set up those accounts?"

"Yes."

"Did you see Mr. Palin prepare those fraudulent reports to cover his fraudulent transfers?"

"Yes."

"Did you witness the amounts Mr. Palin transferred from the Wolfgang Berger Foundation?"

"Yes."

"Were you aware that Mr. Palin was doing this illegally?"

"Yes."

"Then we have no further questions."

When asked to call his next witness, Garrett looked at his notes and spoke briefly to his associates again. They nodded their response, and Garrett looked up at Judge Clayton.

"Your Honor, the State rests."

CHAPTER 42

Hennessy spent the weekend in the office, calling each defense witness on the phone to confirm their availability and discuss their testimony. There were no surprises. He was prepared, he was thorough, and he was determined to defend his client. The State had built an almost perfect case against Palin, but their star witnesses, Berkley and Tilly, had only thrown more doubt into the trial. When Hennessy entered court on the third Monday of the trial, he was lifted by the fact the case was winnable.

When asked by Judge Clayton, Hennessy stood and called his first witness. "The defense calls Mr. Harrison Reid."

A former accountant for thirty-five years, Harrison Reid was now a financial investigator, reveling in his second career. As he walked to the stand, he appeared solemn, focused, and trustworthy. Dressed in a blue suit, he wore a yellow bowtie, showing a little splash of color in his otherwise formal appearance.

"Mr. Reid, thank you for testifying today," Hennessy began. "Can you please tell the court your full name and occupation?"

"My name is Harrison David Reid, and I'm employed as a financial investigator with Marlin and Marlin Accounting in Columbia, South Carolina. I've been a financial investigator for the past year and have testified in many courtrooms, including civil trials, divorce cases, and criminal trials. I love looking at numbers and reports and following a trail of activity to uncover what happens behind those numbers."

"And what does your role involve?"

"My role as a financial investigator involves examining a business's accounting, reports, and bookkeeping to see if there's any fraudulent activity or suspect accounting. My primary goal is to search for the potential places where fraud can occur. Sometimes, I'm brought into a business to identify if there's potential for fraud and then advise the business on how to fix the holes in their process."

"And have you reviewed the accounting, reports, and bookkeeping at Palin Accounting?"

"I have."

"And what did you find?"

"I found there was the potential for fraud to occur as there weren't many checks or reassurances on transferring funds. There were no safeguards, and some of the bookkeeping was a mess. Some of it didn't make sense, some of it didn't add up, and numbers appeared to come out of nowhere. There were discrepancies that were approved by the senior staff in the firm."

"And during your investigation, did you discover the names of the particular staff members who approved the work?"

"There were two names that approved almost all the work. They were the owner and managing director, Bernard Palin, and the senior accountant at the firm, John Tilly."

"Did these two people have equal access to the accounting, reports, and bank accounts?"

"That's correct. Both people were approved to transfer money, approve reports, or change them however they saw fit. They had signatory access to all bank accounts associated with the firm, as well as access to all computers. The way the firm was set up was outdated, and only five logins were used for logging into the computers—senior accounting staff, management staff, accounting staff, junior staff, and administration staff. Mr. Palin and Mr. Tilly used the same login, so it was impossible to decipher who accessed which report or bank account."

"Did you review the files that were connected to the Wolfgang Berger Foundation?"

"I did, and it was clear that someone was changing the reports to present the information to the Foundation board and then transferring some of the donations into a bank account associated with Palin Accounting."

"Could you tell who was doing this?"

"Not exactly. According to the computer logins, I could tell it was a staff member in the senior staff band, but as they both had the same login, it was impossible to tell who did this."

"But both Mr. Palin and Mr. Tilly had the same access?"

"That's correct."

"Based on your review of the reports, could either party have conducted the transfer or changed the accounts?"

"That's correct."

"Do you see this sort of set up often?"

"We used to see it all the time when things were first becoming digitalized, but not anymore. Most workplaces have individual logins to identify the person performing the action."

"And in your professional opinion, could Mr. Tilly have changed the reports without Mr. Palin knowing?"

"Yes."

"And in your professional opinion, could Mr. Tilly have transferred the money from the Wolfgang Berger Foundation into a different bank account?"

"Yes."

"And in your professional opinion, is there any way to prove Mr. Palin made the transfer?"

"No."

"Thank you, Mr. Reid. No further questions."

Garrett stood before Hennessy had even sat down. "Mr. Reid, did Mr. Palin have the opportunity to transfer the money from the Wolfgang Berger Foundation into the bank account associated with Palin Accounting?"

"Yes, he had that opportunity. Along with—"

"And was the money transferred to the account?" Garrett interrupted.

"It was."

"And did Mr. Palin have the opportunity to change the reports that were presented to the Foundation's board?"

"That's correct. As well as—"

"And can you please tell the court who presented the reports to the Foundation's board?"

"Mr. Palin presented the reports to the board."

"I thought so." The smugness radiated off Garrett as he sat back down. "No further questions."

CHAPTER 43

Hennessy called Information Technology specialist Jeremy Flynn next.

Jeremy Flynn entered the courtroom looking like an IT expert. He wore a suit without a jacket, his shoes were clunky and looked one size too big, and his skin looked like it hadn't seen the sun in years. Hennessy almost suggested that he should wear a pair of thick glasses to complete the look, but Flynn's natural persona looked convincing enough.

"Thank you for testifying. Can you begin with your name and then tell the court about your field of expertise?"

"My name is Jeremy Flynn, and I'm an IT specialist specializing in digital forensics." His voice was soft and nervous. "IT stands for Information Technology. I have a master's degree in computer science from Duke University, and I've been working in the field for the past ten years. I've testified in several court cases and am always happy to review computer systems. My day-to-day work usually involves consulting with businesses and looking for holes in their security for potential fraudulent use."

"And did you review the systems associated with Palin Accounting?"

"That's correct."

"And based on your analysis of their accounting systems, were there any vulnerabilities in the system that could've allowed fraudulent transactions to occur?"

"Yes. There were so many issues with their processes. It's like they wrote their business workflows before computers were invented, and they haven't changed since. Every step of the business process was open to fraudulent activity. There were no checks, reviews, or instructions on the work performed. After reviewing the business processes, I couldn't believe that an accounting firm had operated like that for so long. I'm surprised there weren't more instances of fraud."

"Where were the holes in the process?"

"Mostly the lack of oversight. The senior staff had nobody checking their work. If a complaint wasn't raised, then it appeared like nobody looked twice. The senior staff could've transferred all the money into their personal accounts, and nobody would've known."

"Who were the senior staff in the office?"

"The owner, Mr. Bernard Palin, and the senior accountant, Mr. John Tilly. The business systems were so bad that those two senior staff members even had the same login. It's impossible to determine which staff member authorized which transaction."

"Impossible to determine?"

"That's right. With the same system login, and both being able to log on at the same time, the system can't tell who is who. Unless you were physically standing next to them, you wouldn't know who performed what action."

"Thank you, Mr. Flynn. No further questions."

Garrett stood and buttoned his jacket. He remained standing behind the prosecutor's table.

"Just a few quick questions, Mr. Flynn. Why would Mr. Palin set up work processes like that?"

"Most likely a lack of knowledge about business processes and fraud prevention."

"If a business owner was trying to cover up their

fraudulent transactions, would they use the same login as someone else?"

"That's possible."

"What I'm asking you is, could Mr. Palin have deliberately set up joint logins for senior staff so that if he was ever accused of fraud, there wouldn't be an information trail that pointed the finger at him?"

"I don't know the answer to that question. You'd have to ask Mr. Palin about that."

"I thought so," Garrett smiled. "As a specialist, can you please confirm that Mr. Palin had the access and opportunity to make the annual transfer from the Foundation to his business bank account?"

"Along with Mr. Tilly, yes."

"Thank you, Mr. Flynn. No further questions." Garrett sat down, and his smug smile grew even wider.

CHAPTER 44

Hennessy called auditing expert Joan Watson next.

Watson was in her fifties and was aging gracefully. She moved with effortless movements, had an inviting smile, and kind eyes. Dressed in a black skirt with a pink shirt, she presented an image of class, sophistication, and intelligence.

"Mrs. Watson, thank you for testifying today," Hennessy said as he stood behind his desk to ask his questions. "Can you please state your full name, qualifications, and experience in auditing and fraud detection?"

"Certainly. My name is Mrs. Joan Sarah Watson, and I have an MBA with a concentration in accounting that specialized in auditing, forensic accounting, and fraud detection. I received this MBA from the University of South Carolina and I'm also a Certified Public Accountant. I've lectured on the auditing process for the University of South Carolina and consulted on the auditing process for several businesses. I've testified in twenty-five civil and criminal cases where there have been questions about auditing, accounting, or reports."

"Have you reviewed the reports and financial practices of the Wolfgang Berger Foundation?"

"That's correct."

"And have you reviewed the reports and financial practices for Palin Accounting?"

"Yes, I have."

"As an expert in auditing, what are some common mistakes or discrepancies you typically see in accounting systems?"

"Typically, the most common errors are incorrect report details, incorrect filing of financial transactions, and incorrect money transfers. The possibility of these errors can be reduced by ensuring the businesses have stringent review policies and approval processes."

"Did the Foundation or the accounting firm use any review or approval processes?"

"No. No review process was implemented by any of the senior staff in either organization. Frankly, the accounting firm was one of the most careless businesses I have encountered."

Hennessy checked his notes, ran his finger over the next question, and continued. "In your auditing process, did you find that any other individuals besides the defendant had access to the Foundation's financial accounts or authorization to make a transfer?"

"Yes. The two most senior staff in Palin Accounting had equal access to all statements, reports, and bank accounts."

"And the names of the two most senior staff?"

"Mr. Bernard Palin and Mr. John Tilly."

"In your audit of the business, was it possible to see who performed each transaction?"

"No. The access given to Mr. Palin and Mr. Tilly was under one login. It was impossible to tell who made the transfer. The only thing that was clear was the transfer was made by a senior member of the staff at Palin Accounting."

Hennessy looked at Garrett and then back at the witness. "In your expert opinion, do you believe the evidence supports the prosecution's conclusions about the defendant's involvement in the alleged fraud?"

"There's no evidence in the auditing process that supports the assumption that Mr. Palin, and Mr. Palin alone, made those transfers. There's simply no way to distinguish between Mr. Palin and Mr. Tilly in the reports."

"And in your expert opinion, is there sufficient evidence to conclusively prove that the defendant acted with fraudulent intent?"

"No. There's nothing in the reports or transactions that support this conclusion."

"Thank you, Mrs. Watson. We have no further questions."

Hennessy sat down, and when invited by the judge, Garrett conferred with his assistants for a moment. He then began the cross-examination seated behind his desk. "Mrs. Watson, do you believe it's the responsibility of an accounting firm's owner and managing director to implement strong internal controls to prevent fraudulent activity?"

"Yes. I believe it's the responsibility of the managing director or owner to implement best practices."

"And as managing director and owner of the accounting firm, did Mr. Palin do this?"

"No, he did not."

"Would you agree it would be Mr. Palin's responsibility to have safeguards and processes that protect the funds entrusted to them?"

"I agree with that statement."

"And would you agree that the absence of these safeguards significantly increases the likelihood of fraud?"

"Yes. I would agree with that."

"In your professional opinion, if an accounting firm lacks these safeguards, does it make it easier for individuals to conceal fraudulent actions?"

"Yes."

"And do you believe that it's reasonable to assume Mr. Palin was responsible for ensuring these safeguards exist?"

"Yes."

"And is there any evidence to support the fact that it was someone other than a senior member of Palin Accounting who made those transfers?"

"No. The evidence clearly points to a senior member of Palin Accounting making those transfers."

"That's what I thought," Garrett noted. "No further questions."

CHAPTER 45

For three days, Hennessy brought in expert after expert, and it all amounted to one thing—there was reasonable doubt that Palin was involved.

He called data specialists, forensic accountants, financial consultants, and professional ethics experts. Their testimonies were dry, factual, and unemotional. Hennessy would've called character witnesses to testify on Palin's behalf, but nobody would stick their neck out for him.

Tilly had access to the accounts, he had access to the reports, and he had the motive to do it. Hennessy inferred Tilly was taking the money from the Foundation to put away for his retirement, but after his lottery win, he felt he didn't need to take the risk anymore.

There wasn't much left to do except continue to point the finger at Tilly and create doubt that Palin was guilty.

Palin suggested he could testify, but that idea was quickly shot down. It would expose him to questions about his past behavior, and even if he pleaded the fifth, his guilt would look almost certain.

After his surprise testimony, Tilly had gone back to Texas. Lockett called several contacts, and one of them tailed Tilly from the airport to a rental home in Austin. It looked comfortable. The tail also confirmed Debra Fisher was living there.

After Hennessy rested the defense case, Judge Clayton called for a twenty-five-minute recess before closing statements. Palin didn't leave his seat. His leg twitched under the table, and he continued to sweat. If he was found guilty, it was over. He couldn't do time in prison. He wasn't built for that sort of life. He was used to a life full of large meals, expensive drinks, and hired women. He wouldn't have any of that behind bars.

Garrett waited impatiently at the prosecution table, concerned but self-assured. When Judge Clayton returned, tension remained in the courtroom.

Before calling for closing statements, Judge Clayton addressed the jury about their civic duty and ensured they were clear about their responsibilities.

When called, Garrett walked to the lectern to begin his closing statement.

*****

"Ladies and gentlemen of the jury, thank you for serving this court and listening to this case. Being on a jury can be challenging, and this case has been long, and lots of information has been thrown at you. I'm going to walk you through what we've heard over the past two and a half weeks and give you a guideline for making your decision.

This is a simple case.

The facts are simple, the evidence is simple, and your decision will be simple. Don't let all the information that has been thrown at you confuse the facts. Don't let a good story distract you from the evidence.

The defense has stood up here and tried to convince us that the story is complex and that there are many factors at play. It's not true. This is not complex at all. Don't be fooled by the great tales of corruption and lies, misled by their impressive presentation, or deceived by the tricks.

The facts are simple.

Four hundred thousand dollars a year were due to go from the Wolfgang Berger Foundation to the MUSC Shawn Jenkins Children's Hospital. This amount was transferred in two separate payments.

However, only one payment was transferred to the hospital. The other payment was transferred to a bank account that belonged to Palin Accounting.

When presenting the financial reports to the board, Mr. Palin changed the bank account number on the file to make it appear like the money had gone to the hospital.

Two hundred thousand dollars per year was transferred from the Wolfgang Berger Foundation to Palin Accounting.

Those facts are indisputable.

And so is the conclusion—Mr. Bernard Palin was the only person who had control, motive, and opportunity to commit this despicable act.

Nobody else transferred the money, changed the financial reports, or printed out the bank statement to show Judge Berkley.

As jurors, you will be asked to decide on three separate charges. And while these charges are all connected to the defendant's pattern of fraudulent behavior, you must decide on each charge separately.

The Breach of Trust charges involve the defendant's abuse of the responsibility he was entrusted with. He used his position of trust for his own financial gain.

The Forgery charge is related to his actions of deliberately falsifying documentation for his own financial gain.

The Fraud charge is the culmination of his betrayal, as he intentionally manipulated the records for his own financial gain.

You've heard from many witnesses who have stated there was an established pattern of fraud occurring within Palin Accounting. You've heard from experts that there is no way this could've been an error. You've heard from experts that Palin Accounting overcharged most of their clients.

Judge Berkley testified that Mr. Palin came to him for legal advice and for his connections to Costa Rica. You've heard that Mr. Palin gave Judge Berkley a copy of the bank statement with over a million dollars in it. Mr. Palin did this to show Judge Berkley he had the funds available.

You've heard from the investigating officer that the evidence all links back to Mr. Palin.

You've heard from forensic experts that there is evidence of years of fraudulent behavior by Mr. Palin.

And you've heard from former employees who have testified that they witnessed the reports written by Mr. Palin to approve the transfer to the bank account.

This is not a coincidence. This is a despicable, disgraceful, and appalling crime.

You have the chance to show the people of South Carolina that we will not stand for white-collar crime, to show the public that we protect our most vulnerable people, not steal from them, and to punish a man who committed some disgraceful actions.

The only reasonable conclusion you can make after hearing all this evidence is guilty.

Justice demands that you find the defendant guilty on all counts.

Thank you for your time."

*****

Garrett walked back to his seat with a spring in his step. He looked at Hennessy and gave him a small wink. Hennessy ignored Garrett's swagger. He made several notes on his closing statement, then stood and walked behind the lectern.

Twelve regular people were about to make the decision on Bernard Palin's guilt or innocence, and Hennessy was determined to convince them there wasn't enough evidence to convict his client.

*****

"There's not enough evidence to convict Bernard Palin of this crime. That should be clear to you now. Really clear.

Our great legal system, the system that serves us all, is built around the principle that every person, regardless of their gender, their race, or their past, is presumed innocent until proven guilty beyond a reasonable doubt.

And that's the key—a reasonable doubt.

This is a doubt that is based on reason and common sense, and I can tell that you all feel it. I feel it. There's reasonable doubt that Mr. Palin committed this crime. The prosecution did not present enough evidence to prove Mr. Palin committed this act.

Every individual in this country deserves the right to be innocent until proven guilty beyond a reasonable doubt. That did not happen here in this courtroom.

In the jury deliberation, you will review the evidence and testimonies of what has been presented to you. While considering your decision, you must ask yourself if the prosecution proved their case. You need to consider the gaps in the evidence, the unanswered questions, and the inconsistencies that have left you uncertain.

Judge Berkley claims he received the bank statement from Mr. Palin, but did he? Someone else, Mr. John Tilly, had access to the bank statements and played golf with Judge Berkley. You've heard that Judge Berkley was cheating on his wife for over fifty years. It's up to you to decide whether this witness is reliable.

The prosecution claims that Mr. Palin was about to take the money and retire to Costa Rica, but was he the only person in the firm planning to retire? No, Mr. John Tilly was planning to retire before his lottery win.

The prosecution claims that Mr. Palin transferred the funds, but is there any evidence of that? No. It's just a theory. There was evidence that someone senior in Palin Accounting made the transfer, but who else had the computer login to make those transfers? Mr. John Tilly.

The prosecution claims that Mr. Palin was the only person with a motive to transfer the money, but was he? Mr. John Tilly was trying to elope with his mistress and run away from his family.

All these questions are more than a coincidence. It's an overwhelming pile of facts that you cannot ignore.

Witnesses have claimed that Palin Accounting had improper work practices, but is that what Mr. Palin is charged with? No. You're here to decide on the evidence about the funds transfer from the Wolfgang Berger Foundation. That's the only event you're deciding on.

You've heard from expert witnesses, technology specialists, and forensic accountants who agree on the facts. There's not enough evidence to say that Mr. Palin is guilty. There's not enough evidence to convict him beyond a reasonable doubt.

Finding Mr. Palin not guilty is not saying that you're sure he didn't do this. Finding Mr. Palin not guilty is saying to the prosecution that they didn't present enough evidence of this crime. That's it. Nothing more. Nothing less.

You should have reasonable doubt at the end of this trial.

Reasonable doubt is not certainty. It's not an absolute answer. It's not complete. If you hesitate, if your mind tells you something is not adding up, then that's reasonable doubt.

And that reasonable doubt means that you must find the defendant not guilty.

It's not a choice. It's not something that you get to select. This is your duty to your country, your state, and the legal system.

It's ok to want to punish someone for this crime. But you cannot, and must not, convict the wrong person. That's not justice. That's not what our great country is built upon.

Thank you for your time and thank you for your commitment to our great justice system."

CHAPTER 46

"Still no decision?" Barry Lockett looked at Hennessy. "Mate, this is the worst part of a trial. It's been two days and they still haven't decided on the verdict."

"I hate it too," Hennessy nodded as he rolled up his shirt sleeves to his elbows. "But it means there's conflict in that courtroom. At least one person doesn't agree with everyone else."

Lockett flipped the two large tenderloin steaks on the grill.

The yard at the rear of the Lockett household was large, a sea of lush green grass. A breeze blew off the nearby river, bringing with it the smell of magnolia blossoms and the salty tang of the pluff mud.

Lockett's grill under the back porch was an impressive set up. The grill had six burners and was next to a smoker and a pizza oven. He often said he loved to be outdoors and would take any opportunity to be outside, including cooking.

"This is the perfect Monday lunch," Hennessy said. He had spent the morning in the office drafting motions in his other cases when Lockett called and offered lunch. Hennessy couldn't say no.

Being Australian, Lockett was known for his straightforward approach to grilling, or barbequing as he called it. He often said that a great cut of meat needs nothing more than a sprinkling of salt and the quick burn of a hot flame. Don't overcomplicate perfection, he said.

"I've got a surprise for you," Lockett smiled as he wiped his hands on his black apron. He walked inside his house and returned with a small plate of brightly colored red meat. "I'm going to cook this for the family tonight, but I thought I'd give you a quick taste as an entrée for lunch."

"What is it?"

"Roo."

"As in... kangaroo?"

Lockett smiled. "That's right, mate."

"You eat your national emblem?"

Lockett laughed. "It's one of the lowest-fat meats in the world. When it's cooked right, it's a dream."

He took the steaks off the grill and rested them on a plate, covering them with aluminum foil and letting them simmer in their own juices for at least five minutes. He placed two thin strips of kangaroo meat on the grill, sizzled it for a moment, and then flipped it. He pressed it hard with his tongs, letting the juices sizzle onto the open flame. He removed the kangaroo and placed the two small pieces on a plate and handed it to Hennessy.

"Go on," Lockett smiled. "Taste a bit of Australia."

Hennessy shrugged and speared the thin strip of meat with his fork. He took a small bite, chewing before nodding in approval. "It's very gamey—almost like venison."

"Tasty," Lockett said as he picked up the second piece with his fingers and dropped it into his mouth. "Hmm. The taste of home. One of the best."

"I still can't believe you eat kangaroo." Hennessy shook his head. "They're such beautiful creatures."

"Did you know Ernest Hemmingway was part kangaroo?" Lockett smiled. "No joke. He had a car accident in the 1930s, and they repaired one of his tendons with a kangaroo tendon. That makes him part Australian. We welcome everyone in Australia, mate."

Lockett unwrapped the two steaks and served one to Joe. They sat at the outdoor table, and under the warm South Carolina sun, they ate in silence, enjoying the flavor of the tender steaks. They occasionally made sounds of approval and nodded to themselves.

"Life is good," Lockett said after he finished his steak. "How do you think they're leaning?"

"Hopefully not guilty," Hennessy confirmed as he wiped his mouth. "Juror five looks like he was convinced there wasn't enough evidence to convict Palin, but if you've got eleven people arguing against you, it'll wear you down."

"If it's a hung jury, think they'll retry it?"

"It's too high profile now. The prosecution wanted this trial to be a big news story, and they got their wish, but it might come back to bite them."

"And Tilly and Fisher? What happens to them?"

"If Palin is found guilty, we'll appeal based on Judge Clayton's decision to reject the motion for a mistrial. If a new judge grants us a new trial, Tilly and Fisher won't come back for it. It'll be too dangerous for them."

"And if Palin is found not guilty?"

"Then the prosecution is going to look like a group of fools. They'll want a conviction for at least something related to this crime, and I imagine they'll pressure Tilly and Fisher. If that's the case, they'll want to be as far away from Charleston as possible."

Hennessy's cell phone rang. He looked at the number. It was Jacinta. He answered the call, listened for a minute, and confirmed his understanding. After the call was finished, he placed his cell on the table and leaned back in his chair.

"They have a decision," Hennessy said. "It's time to find out whether or not that scumbag walks away."

CHAPTER 47

As Hennessy walked into the courthouse, Bernard Palin was waiting in the foyer.

He was leaning by a wall, arms folded, staring at Hennessy as he approached. He was dressed well in a black suit with a blue tie. His shoes were polished, and there was a sheen of sweat on his forehead.

"This is it, uh?" Palin asked. "After that whole trial, this is it?"

"This is it," Hennessy responded. "The jury has told the judge they've reached a unanimous decision."

"Any idea what it is?"

"No."

"But what do you think?"

"I think you're corrupt, crooked, and unlikable."

"Even after all the time we've spent together, we're still not friends. I'm heartbroken." Palin scoffed. "What happens if we lose?"

"If they find you guilty of any of the charges, we'll lodge the appeal today. It's already drafted and ready to go. We've drafted the appeal based on the rejection of the motion for a mistrial."

"But I would have to stay in prison until then?"

Hennessy nodded.

Palin looked at the ground, rocking side to side. "I can't do that. I'm not built for prison."

Hennessy ignored Palin's emotional moment and walked toward the courtroom. Palin followed a step behind.

They entered the courtroom and found Garrett already at his table with his assistants. They nodded their greeting but didn't talk to Hennessy or Palin. Once the bailiff allowed the crowd into the room, the seats filled quickly. Hennessy spotted Berkley in the crowd. He had a smirk on his face. That worried Hennessy.

The media had run headlines for the story, and everyone wanted to know if justice would be served. Once every seat was full, the door to Judge Clayton's chambers opened. Judge Clayton walked in without looking at the lawyers. Hennessy's breathing shortened.

When instructed, the bailiff went to the side of the room and bought in the jury. They looked anxious, avoiding eye contact with Palin as they entered. One juror bumped into a chair and almost fell over.

When instructed by Judge Clayton, Hennessy and Palin stood.

Judge Clayton turned to the jury. "Jury Foreman, have you reached a verdict in the case against Mr. Bernard Palin?"

"We have, Your Honor." The jury foreman stood tall and strong. "We've reached a unanimous verdict."

The jury foreman handed a piece of paper to the bailiff, who, in turn, handed it to Judge Clayton.

Judge Clayton took a few moments to read the verdict, nodded, and then placed the paper down.

Hennessy's heart was pounding.

"In the charges of Breach of Trust, how do you find the defendant, Mr. Bernard Palin?"

The moment they had been waiting for. The moment they had worked towards.

"We, the jury, in the charges of fraud, find the defendant not guilty."

"In the charges of fraud, how do you find the defendant, Mr. Bernard Palin?"

"Not guilty."

"And in the charges of forgery, how do you find the defendant, Mr. Bernard Palin?"

Hennessy closed his eyes. The moment lingered.

"Not guilty."

CHAPTER 48

After the verdict was delivered, Palin didn't wait around.

He raced out of the courtroom and back to his home. Hennessy was sure Palin would be blackout drunk within an hour. An hour after the verdict, Garrett talked to Hennessy in the courthouse's foyer. Garrett spoke through gritted teeth, talking about building a case of fraud against Palin for his overcharging and overbilling of other clients, but Hennessy doubted that would happen. There wasn't enough evidence to prove they weren't accounting errors.

They stepped out of the courthouse together, and Garrett faced the media.

"Today's verdict is not the outcome we predicted or expected, and we understand that the city of Charleston shares our disappointment," Garrett told them. "As Circuit Solicitors, our role is to present evidence and seek justice, and we have done this with the utmost integrity and commitment. However, the jury has made a decision, and we must respect the process. This verdict serves as a reminder that no case is guaranteed, no matter how terrible the crime or how strong the evidence is. We will review what transpired, and we will learn from this experience. We must move forward and continue to work to serve the State of South Carolina with diligence and fairness."

Hennessy was impressed with the delivery of the speech and told Garrett later via a text message. Garrett didn't respond. Hennessy understood why.

When he arrived back at his office, Jacinta and Lockett were waiting. Hennessy didn't want to celebrate. It was clear to him that Palin had spent most of his life as a corrupt individual, and that he had ripped off most of his clients. Hennessy felt no satisfaction that the man had walked away free from charges. The trio went for a meal to acknowledge the end of the case but avoided talking about Palin.

The stress wasn't over yet. Hennessy still needed to get paid before Palin fled the country.

The following morning, Hennessy parked his truck near the front of the Palin Accounting office, took a deep breath, and exited his vehicle. It was time to get paid. He needed to end his association with Palin, leave Charleston behind, and return to his vineyard.

Hennessy saw Palin's sedan parked near the entrance of the building, with two motorcycles on either side of it. That wasn't a good sign. The bikers stood near the entrance, puffing on cigarettes, and didn't acknowledge Hennessy's arrival.

Hennessy walked through the building and into Palin Accounting's office. He strode past the empty desks and stepped into the main office at the rear of the building.

Palin was seated behind his desk. He had sunglasses on, and he looked disheveled. His hangover was stinging hard.

"Ah, my favorite lawyer," he said without any enthusiasm. "Remind me to come to you if I ever get into trouble again. You're so good that you could convince a jury that the sun rises in the west."

Palin rubbed his brow, took a large swig of coffee, and groaned.

"What are the Rebel Sons doing outside?"

"Keeping an eye on me," Palin groaned. "I've told Stanwell Construction that I'm retiring, and they need a new accountant. They already found one during the trial, but the new guy wants me to send him all my documents. I'm too hungover to do this now, but he's demanding I do it today. I would go through the reports, but I can't be bothered. I'm just going to give him everything." Palin rubbed his eyes with the back of his hands. "But what do you want? Why are you here?"

"I've come to get paid."

"Ah," Palin whispered. "Here's the thing. The police won't unfreeze my bank accounts. They say it's clear the money was fraudulently acquired, even if I wasn't found guilty of it. My money is tied up in those accounts and I can't touch it. If you want the money, you're going to have to convince the courts to release it. But I'll warn you—that could take months or even years. I called Garrett this morning, and he told me that the freeze would remain on my accounts as they're investigating other claims of fraud. I told him where to go and that you'd deal with him for me again. I might've also put a few choice words in there as well."

"This isn't how it works. You signed a contract," Hennessy stated. "I got you off the charges, and now you need to pay up. It's time for you to get the money."

"Like I said, I don't have the cash until my accounts are unfrozen. I don't know what else to tell you." Palin leaned back in his chair and rubbed the back of his neck. "But there's another option."

Hennessy waited for Palin to continue.

"You see, Berkley has some of my money," Palin grimaced. "I gave him two-hundred-and-fifty thousand to put a down payment on an apartment in Costa Rica. I gave it to him in cash because he had the connections to get me a great price on a beautiful apartment, but it's clear to me now that he never did that. He still has my money."

Again, Hennessy didn't respond.

"He won't give me the money back," Palin continued. "I asked the Rebel Sons to convince him, but they said they don't feel comfortable beating up an old man. Considering our options, I think it would be easier if he just gave it to you."

"Berkley set you up from day one."

"And I didn't know it," Palin said. "I gave him a quarter-of-a-million dollars for a down payment. He was my intermediary and the one who would help me get away before the charges were laid. He even told me he had contacts in the justice system that said the charges would be laid in a month, but he was lying to me. And I had all this money from the Foundation, and I couldn't access it."

Hennessy squinted.

"Oh, come on, Joe. You didn't actually think I was innocent, did you?" Palin laughed. "I had planned it all from day one. Ensure Tilly had the same access and not withdraw the money until I needed it. If I did that, nobody could prove it was me or him. If it wasn't for Berkley, the plan was almost perfect."

The anger raged inside Hennessy. He stepped forward.

"The choice is yours, Joe. You can fight through the courts to get my accounts unfrozen, or you can go and talk to your old pal." Palin raised his hands in surrender. "I suggest you go and talk to Berkley. He always liked you. He has your money. You just need to convince him to give it to you."

CHAPTER 49

"He's not here," the nurse at the front door said. "I don't know where he is."

Hennessy stood at the entrance to Berkley's antebellum mansion on Murray Boulevard. The sun was shining brightly, and the area was bathed in warmth. Hennessy had been knocking on the door and ringing the doorbell for more than a few minutes before the nurse answered.

"I know he's here," Hennessy stated. He leaned forward and raised his voice. "And I know he's a coward."

The nurse didn't know how to respond. She hesitated and went to say something before someone else called out behind her.

"Alright. Fine." Clarence Berkley's tone was grumpy. "I'll deal with it. I'm coming."

Hennessy stood at the door, and the nurse stepped back. Berkley appeared behind her. He stepped around her and indicated that Hennessy should follow him. He led Hennessy down the mansion's steps and into the front yard.

"What do you want, Joe? To rub it in? To say that you're this great lawyer who has won again? You embarrassed me on the stand. That wasn't nice."

"You set him up."

"I didn't set him up. He stole that money. You know that, and I know that. Just because there wasn't enough evidence doesn't mean he didn't do it. The facts are the facts, and no matter how well you did in court, the fact is that he transferred the money from the Foundation into his own bank accounts. What type of man steals from a charity foundation?" Berkley shook his head. "After he was arrested, Palin asked me if I was involved. Of course, I denied everything, but I was the one who tipped off the police. He came to me, told me all about the money, and I told him I didn't believe him. When we met the next week, he bought the bank statement. Once I had that, I knew I had enough evidence to take it to the police and get him out of my life forever. Unfortunately, I didn't count on you spoiling the party."

"There wasn't enough evidence to convict him."

"There was," Berkley snapped back. "Any half-brained person could see Palin did it. He's been doing it for years for various companies. He was blackmailing everyone. And now, he's going to be on the next plane to Costa Rica, and he's never going to serve time for all his crimes." Berkley looked at Hennessy. "And you won't get your bonus."

"You have my money," Hennessy stated, not getting drawn into a further discussion about Palin. "Palin said he gave you two-hundred-and-fifty thousand in cash for a down payment on a property in Costa Rica that you never purchased."

Berkley scoffed. "He's skipping the country, Joe. I can guarantee that he'll be on a plane today or tomorrow. He won't wait for Garrett to smack him with further fraud charges. He'll go to Costa Rica, wait for the bank accounts to become unfrozen, and then live a very nice retirement."

"He doesn't have a passport. It was taken as part of the bail hearing, and it'll be another week before he gets it back."

"He doesn't need a passport," Berkley sneered. "He has connections with the Rebel Sons, and they'll smuggle him out of the country. He'll tell them he knows too much to be sent to prison, and they need to get him out of the country. They'll give him cash so he keeps quiet, and you'll never hear from him again."

"How do you know all this?"

"Because that big mouth Palin told me about his connections to Stanwell Construction and the Rebel Sons. I didn't bring it up in the trial because I don't need that sort of trouble in my life." Berkley wiped the sweat from his brow with the back of his hand. "He's got the money, Joe. He never gave it to me. He's got it in cash. He always bragged that he had two-hundred-and-fifty thousand in cash in a go-bag. I can almost guarantee that he's got that cash with him."

"How do I know you're telling the truth?"

"You don't, but I bet he sent you here as a distraction. My guess is that they're already on the road, driving south to somewhere in Florida where they smuggle drugs from. I don't have his money. Palin lied to you to distract you. My guess is that he's already on the road. You need to stop him if you want to get paid."

Hennessy thought about the bikes at Palin's office that morning and realized it was true.

He turned and walked away from Berkley without another word. The second he reached his truck, he took out his cell phone and called Roger East.

"Where's he going?" Hennessy snarled.

"Who?"

"Palin."

"How would I know?"

"Because he's running to Costa Rica through your connections. Where is he going?"

East was reluctant.

"East. I'm not going to ask again. Where is Palin going?"

"I've always liked you, Joe, and I've always hated Palin. That guy blackmailed me once, and I've never forgotten it." East paused for a long time before he clucked his tongue several times and then continued. "If he's running with the Rebel Sons, they're on their way to Jacksonville. The Rebel Sons have contacts at that airport. That means they can sneak money, drugs, or anything else in and out of the country. And if he makes it to the airport, you'll never see him again. But the Rebel Sons have a clubhouse on the way there, outside Midway, and they're obligated to stop if they're driving past. I'll text you the address."

Hennessy ended the call and raced to his truck.

It was time to get paid.

CHAPTER 50

"He's not here," Lockett said as Hennessy picked up the phone. "Berkley was right. Palin's gone already. The office is locked up."

Hennessy slammed his hand against the steering wheel of his truck as he drove. "And the Rebel Sons?"

"Gone as well."

"I'm five minutes away," Hennessy said as he raced through Charleston to Palin's office. "Wait for me there. I'll pick you up."

Hennessy roared his pickup truck around the streets, racing through intersections, speeding over humps, and ignoring traffic. Lockett was waiting for Hennessy as he pulled up to the front of the building that housed Palin Accounting.

Lockett jumped in, and Hennessy screeched the tires out of the parking spot and toward I-95.

"Where are we going?" Lockett asked as he

gripped the grab handle.

"South. We're headed to a stop outside Midway, Georgia." Hennessy paused as he weaved in and out of traffic. "It's a Rebel Sons roadhouse, and they need to stop there if they're driving past. They're escorting him to Jacksonville airport, where they have enough connections to get him out of the country. If Palin gets on that plane, we'll never see or hear from him again."

"And what are we going to do when we get there?"

"Berkley said that Palin often bragged about having a to-go bag with two-hundred-and-fifty-thousand cash in it. That's our money."

"And how are we going to convince him to give it to us?"

Hennessy hadn't thought that far ahead. He pointed to the glove compartment. Lockett opened it and saw Hennessy's Glock. "We're going to convince him to pay us before he leaves."

Racing through the traffic, they arrived at the roadhouse in under ninety-five minutes.

The bar was off the main road, with a dated and rundown hotel on one side and a gas station on the other. The red-brick building had seen better days, and judging by the almost empty parking lot, it didn't have many customers. That didn't matter, though. The bar was a front, a place where the Rebel Sons could relax and enjoy themselves without the pressures of the public.

"Two bikes and a black sedan," Lockett said as they rolled into the parking lot. There were two other sedans near the entrance, but the older cars looked like they had been parked there for days. "We won't be welcomed in there. They don't like strangers in a place like that."

Hennessy nodded but didn't respond. As they approached, his eyes were on Palin's sedan. The front seats were empty, and several suitcases were placed on the back seats.

As Hennessy parked, he noticed the pickup parked on the other side of the lot. It had a sticker on the door advertising Stanwell Construction.

Hennessy drew a breath and nodded to the glove compartment as he parked. Lockett opened it and took out the Glock. He handed it to Hennessy.

"Think we'll need it?"

Hennessy nodded as he checked the weapon.

Lockett took his handgun out of his belt and checked it.

"How do you want to approach this?" Lockett asked. "Wait until they come out?"

"There might be people around by then, and this might get messy," Hennessy responded. "We'll go in and ask Palin nicely for the money."

"Think that'll work?"

"I hope so." Hennessy looked at the weapon in his hand. "Because I don't like the outcome if it doesn't."

CHAPTER 51

With his weapon tucked into his belt, Hennessy pushed open the door to the roadhouse.

It took a few moments for his eyes to adjust. The lighting was dim and not even turned on in some parts, and the neon signs behind the bar did little to brighten the mood. The smell of beer and bourbon hung heavy in the air. Four people were seated around a table near the end of the room, and the bartender was wiping the bench top.

"We're closed," the older lady behind the bar called out. "We open for lunch after twelve, but I recommend going elsewhere. The chef is sick today, and you don't want me cooking your food."

"We're not here for food," Hennessy called back.

His voice caused everyone at the table to look up. The bartender saw the reaction and stepped back.

"Following me, uh?" Palin called out. "I don't know why you'd do that."

Hennessy walked toward the table. Palin was seated in the middle, and the two bikers were on either side of him. Beside them was Tony Stanwell.

"Joe Hennessy," Stanwell stood. "You're either very brave or very stupid. I haven't figured out which one you are yet."

"I'm here to get paid," Hennessy said. "I heard you were about to catch a flight from Jacksonville to Costa Rica."

Stanwell squinted. "Where did you hear that?"

"I have contacts." Hennessy turned his focus to Palin. "Berkley said you were going to run with my money. And looking at this situation, he was right."

"I can't believe you thought I would give my money to Berkley." Palin smiled. "I needed to get you out of the office, and you fell for it. I was quite happy with myself."

"Berkley said you had a to-go bag with two-hundred-and-fifty thousand in it. That's my payment."

"Really?" Palin scoffed and stood. "Berkley has betrayed me again. That stupid old man."

The two bikers stood and walked toward Hennessy and Lockett.

Lockett pulled back his black leather jacket to expose his handgun. Hennessy's hand went to his hip.

The first biker's hand went behind his back, reaching for something on his hip. He slowly moved his hand forward. The second biker did the same, and the two large men held their handguns in front of them.

Hennessy removed the Glock from his belt. Lockett followed and did the same thing. The four men held the handguns before them, pointing toward the ground.

The bikers' grips on their weapons were steady, their fingers hovering close to the triggers. The muted hum of the roadhouse grew quiet, the air thick with the weight of impending violence.

"Seems we're in a situation," Stanwell said. "Quite a predicament, isn't it?"

"It is." Hennessy kept his eyes on the bikers. He noticed Palin step into the shadows, but his focus was on the bikers.

"If you men don't want trouble, then you should back out now," Stanwell said. "I've come down to tie up loose ends before a friend of mine goes on a vacation. I didn't expect any trouble, so I'll let you boys leave here unharmed."

"And I came to get paid," Hennessy said. "Palin's got cash in his car to pay me."

Hennessy glanced at Palin, who had edged toward the side door.

The first biker stepped forward.

The side door to the bar swung open. Hennessy went to step toward it, but the biker held up his weapon. Hennessy stopped.

"We're helping him go on his vacation," Stanwell said. "And we can't let you stop him. He knows too much about us. He's going to help our new accountant understand the complexities of our business, and we need to protect him until then."

Hennessy stepped toward Stanwell. "Do you really think the Foundation is the only business he stole from?"

"When reviewing the files for this case, I found evidence that Palin embezzled money from Stanwell Constructions. It was before you got into bed with the Rebel Sons, and he thought he could rip you off. He said your books were a mess, and you'd never even notice."

"He wouldn't do that." Stanwell squinted at

Hennessy, his suspicion flickering into uncertainty. Stanwell glanced at the biker, who lowered his weapon. "If you're lying to me, I'll make sure you regret it."

"He stole your money. If you want proof, search for invoices to 'JR Concreting Supplies.'"

"And if we look at 'JR Concreting Supplies,' what will we find?"

"That the company never existed, and the money was going directly to Palin's bank accounts." Hennessy nodded. "I have no reason to lie to you. The payments went to the same bank account you used to pay his invoices. You'll find it all there."

Stanwell reached forward to the table. "Palin left his car keys behind. He won't get far if you need to talk to him." Stanwell dangled the keys in the air. "In the meantime, I need to make a phone call to my new accountant."

CHAPTER 52

Lockett pushed through the exit leading to the parking lot. Hennessy followed a step behind. It took a moment for their eyes to adjust to the midday sun blaring down on them.

The first gunshot echoed around the parking lot.

Hennessy and Lockett dove behind a sedan as a second shot rang out.

"Palin's going down fighting," Lockett said as he leaned against the truck's tire. "What do you want to do?"

"I want to get paid." Hennessy checked his Glock. "We've been shot at twice, and we have nowhere to retreat. Anything we do now is in self-defense."

Lockett leaned close to the ground and checked the surroundings. "I can see his feet. He's covering behind his car." Lockett explained. "I'll go right and hide behind the sedan over there. I'll draw his attention while you circle left and approach him from behind."

"No. This is my problem; I'll act as the diversion."

"You're too slow, Joe."

Hennessy nodded. It was no time for ego.

"Cover me," Lockett said. "In three... two... one."

Hennessy raised his Glock, fired two shots, and Lockett ran toward the older sedan. No shots were fired back.

Hennessy checked under the car and saw Palin's feet pointed in Lockett's direction. Lockett fired twice, and Palin went to his knees and sheltered behind his sedan.

Hennessy moved quietly to the right, toward a cluster of small trees near the edge of the lot. He caught sight of Palin, who began to rise to his feet again. Lockett fired again, and Palin went back to kneeling.

Hennessy moved toward Palin, careful not to make a sound. When another shot hadn't fired off, Palin peered over the sedan's hood.

Hennessy moved across the asphalt, crouched down with his weapon out.

Palin didn't see him coming.

"Don't move." Hennessy stood behind Palin. His Glock was focused on the back of the head of his former client. "And put the weapon down."

Palin froze for a long moment and then lowered his weapon to the ground. He raised both his arms out to his side. "Stanwell won't let you do this to me."

"He's busy on the phone." Hennessy kicked Palin's weapon away. "Now, where's my payment?"

Palin chuckled as Lockett came jogging around the back of the car. Lockett picked up Palin's handgun and put it into his belt while keeping his weapon trained on Palin. Hennessy nodded to Lockett and then put his Glock into his belt.

He grabbed Palin by the collar and turned him around to face him. Hennessy slammed Palin into his sedan, enough to wobble the car. "I'm not going to ask again. Where's my payment?"

Palin gripped Hennessy's wrist as he pushed it into Palin's throat, but Hennessy's strength was too much for him. When Palin stopped struggling, Hennessy eased off.

"It's in the car," Palin conceded. "It's in the black backpack on the passenger seat."

Lockett went to open the car door. It was locked.

Palin shrugged and smiled. "I guess you've got to go back in there and talk to Stanwell if you want the keys."

The car beeped.

Hennessy looked to his right.

Stanwell was approaching with the car keys in his hands. The two bikers flanked him on either side. Stanwell nodded toward the car. Lockett didn't hesitate. He opened the door and removed the backpack, unzipping it and looking inside. He showed Hennessy.

"That's a lot of cash," Lockett said. "All hundred-dollar bills."

"It's all yours," Stanwell said.

Palin's neck snapped to his left, staring at Stanwell. "But that's my money. That's how I get to Costa Rica and start again."

"You won't be going to Costa Rica today."

"What?" Palin's voice was exasperated. "Why?"

"I've just got off the phone with our new accountant. He checked the records that you sent him this morning and found there were invoices paid to 'JR Concreting Supplies.'"

"No," Palin whispered. "That's not right. That's a

mistake."

"JR Concreting Supplies never existed as a company. And when the new accountant checked the bank transfer, he confirmed the money went to your business."

"No, no, no." Tears welled in Palin's eyes. "It's a mistake."

Hennessy eased his grip off Palin's collar, and he looked at Stanwell.

Stanwell nodded. "I suggest you two get out of here before I change my mind about that money in the backpack."

Hennessy and Lockett nodded and backed away slightly.

"What will happen to Palin?" Hennessy asked.

"He ripped me off and now has a debt to pay. And I know the perfect way for him to pay me back."

"No, no, no," Palin whispered and fell to his knees. "Please, Tony, you need to understand. It was a mistake. An accounting error. That's all."

Hennessy didn't ask any further questions.

Lockett gripped the backpack tight, and the two men walked to Hennessy's truck.

They didn't look back.

CHAPTER 53

It took Hennessy five weeks to wind down his law firm operations.

He defended his clients, delegated long-term cases to other lawyers, and finalized his reports. He smiled most of the time he was in the office.

With the pressure off, he found he had a deep affinity and love for his home city. He often stopped and stared at the buildings he'd walked past so many times before, taking a moment to appreciate their beauty before he retired from the law.

The two-hundred-and-fifty-thousand-dollar payment had put the Hennessys in front of the bank loans, leaving them financially comfortable. His dream, his hope, and his fantasy had come true—he could retire to the vineyard.

Two weeks after the incident with Palin at the roadhouse, Hennessy received a call from Garrett. They were ready to press charges against Palin for further acts of fraud, but Hennessy explained he didn't represent Palin anymore. When Garrett asked if he knew Palin's whereabouts, he answered honestly— he had no idea. Garrett explained that Palin's accounts remained frozen pending the resolution of his next court case. Hennessy said he didn't think Palin would ever be found. He asked about Tilly and Fisher, and Garrett said they would testify against Palin in the new charges. They had started a new life in Texas and were both in the process of divorcing their previous spouses.

As Hennessy wound down the law firm, he used his contacts to get Jacinta another job. He gave Jacinta a glowing reference when asked, saying he had not worked with a more intelligent, fierce, and hard-working assistant. The larger firm offered her more pay, flexible working hours, and more responsibilities. Jacinta thanked Joe and told him she would miss working for him. Joe agreed and said he would miss her company.

Lockett picked up further work with another law firm. On his last day in the office, with a big smile on his face, he said Joe was the worst boss he'd ever had. They shook hands and then hugged for a moment, slapping each other on the back.

As he locked the office door for the final time, a wave of relief swept over him. The weight of endless motions, depositions, and trials was finally lifting. Yet, beneath the relief was a flicker of sadness. He was leaving behind not just a career but a part of himself—one that thrived in the pursuit of justice.

The team celebrated their last day with a long dinner at Poogan's Porch restaurant.

The restaurant was an institution in Charleston. Inside a charming Victorian townhouse, the iconic establishment had been serving Southern-style seafood for decades, pleasing locals and tourists alike with amazing dishes full of flavor and made with love.

Jacinta laughed most of the time as she ate her seafood, Barry told jokes and tales of Down Under, and Joe thanked everyone for their help and hard work.

Satisfaction was the strongest feeling for Joe— satisfaction that he was returning to the vineyard, satisfaction that Lockett and Jacinta had picked up better-paying jobs, and satisfaction that the house of justice, the house he had faith in, still stood strong.

The day after their last dinner, Hennessy received a call from Garrett. He was surprised at the news, and the next day, he drove south to Savannah, Georgia, and attended a packed court hearing.

Tension was in the air as Bernard Palin, dressed in an orange prison jumpsuit, was brought in via the side exit.

Palin looked skinnier. His head had been shaved, his face bruised, and he looked broken. His shoulders were slumped forward, and when the judge asked his name, he responded in a shaky voice.

When the charges of drug trafficking were read out, Palin began to cry. He was looking at fifteen years in prison. The prosecutor in the courtroom read out the charges and explained that Palin had been found driving a black sedan with five kilograms of heroin in the car. Palin claimed there was a chaperone with him, but the police didn't catch the other person. Palin told the court he had been forced to run drugs across the state borders by a drug smuggler. He told the judge that he hadn't been left alone in five weeks and always had someone by his side. He had been kidnapped, he explained. He had been beaten, battered, and abused by his kidnappers.

The prosecutor explained that when Palin was asked by law enforcement who the drug smugglers were, Palin kept quiet. And when asked to identify his kidnappers, Palin said nothing. Hennessy understood why. If he said a word, if he even mentioned the Rebel Sons, he wouldn't last a week in prison.

When the drug charges were officially read out, Palin's crying became louder.

His sobbing echoed through the gallery of the courtroom, and when asked to enter a plea, Palin wiped his eyes and said, "Guilty."

The prosecutor confirmed an early plea deal for ten years' prison time, and Palin was escorted out of the court, still sobbing as he went.

Hennessy smiled.

Justice had been served.

CHAPTER 54

On his first day back at the vineyard fulltime, Joe stood at the edge of the property, the late afternoon breeze brushing against his face, carrying with it the earthy scent of soil and grapes. He breathed in deeply, savoring the clean country air, and nodded.

He had done it.

After years of sweat and sacrifice, of wading through a world filled with crooks, criminals, and corruption, he had carved out his little piece of paradise. 'Luca's Vineyard' was his now, built on the back of hard work, sacrifice, and grit.

The land stretched out before him in an endless patchwork of rolling hills, farmlands, and untouched woodlands. Its vastness seemed infinite, stretching far beyond the reach of his gaze.

In the distance, storm clouds gathered over the mountains, heavy and dark, their edges silver-lined by the late sun. They loomed large, immovable, casting shadows over the valleys below, a reminder of nature's indomitable power.

Joe turned slightly, letting the evening sun warm his back. It burned low and strong, its golden light spilling over the fields and softening the cool bite of the breeze. This was his home. The place where he had raised his two daughters, loved his wife, and built a legacy in his son's memory. Charleston might hold his heart, but this land, these hills and fields, these vines and valleys, were part of his soul.

Above him, a bald eagle soared high, motionless in the sky, its wings spread wide as it floated effortlessly on the wind. It seemed timeless, like the land itself. Joe watched it for a long moment, admiring the way it moved without moving, gliding over the world as if it owned it.

As the sun kissed the horizon, the sky was painted in an array of colors—blue giving way to fiery orange, orange bleeding into crimson. The light bathed the land in a surreal glow, turning every blade of grass and every leaf into something almost otherworldly. The clouds shifted, casting long shadows and painting the landscape with shades of cosmic wonder. It was a scene too perfect, too profound, to feel accidental.

Joe stood there, watching the world change before his eyes, and felt the quiet pulse of something bigger, something eternal.

There was a rhythm here, a heartbeat, a pulse, a feeling of something bigger than one person, something profound, something spiritual.

As he looked at the lands before him, he felt at peace. This was the South—his South—and as the last sliver of sun slipped away, Joe thought about how he would spend the next thirty years tinkering, toiling, and trifling until his body could take no more.

He knew Wendy would be there for all of it, by his side every step of the way. She'd be the one to lighten the hard days with a smile, soften the blows with a joke, and steady him with her unwavering heart. She was the cornerstone, the one thing he could count on as sure as the sun rising over the vineyard each morning.

He knew his daughters would come and go, spreading their wings to build lives of their own. They'd leave for cities and careers, new opportunities pulling them away. But they would always come back. Back to the vineyard for Thanksgiving dinners and summer reunions, for birthdays and anniversaries, for the milestones that tied them to this land and to each other.

He knew the vineyard would bring seasons of triumph and disappointment. There would be years where the grapes came in perfectly, when their wine would earn accolades and praise. And there would be years when the storms were too strong or the sun too relentless, when the crops failed, and the profits dried up. They'd weather it all, just as they always had. Together, they'd care for the workers like family, rebuilding after droughts and devastating storms, after floods and fires. Because the vines always regrew. Life always found a way.

He knew he'd see his brother now and then. Their visits would be filled with laughter, the kind that only brothers who'd survived boyhood scrapes and Charleston streets could share.

Barry would visit, too, just as he always had, rolling in with a cooler of beer and stories too wild to be true, and they'd laugh like teenagers all over again. They would share a lifelong bond.

Jacinta would find time in her whirlwind life in the city to make several trips Upstate, where her family would be welcomed with open arms, with a table set for delicious meals, and a friendship that would last decades.

He knew his daughters would one day have families of their own—husbands, children, in-laws. The grandchildren would grow up here, running barefoot through the vines, learning to listen for the seasons and to respect the rhythm of the earth. He could already see them, tiny hands clutching baskets at harvest time, the same way his own children once did. Those grandchildren would carry forward the family's legacy.

But above all, he knew Wendy would be the constant. She'd be there through every up and down, through sickness and health, pain and joy, worry and success. They would grow old together, loving each other more with each passing year, weathering life's storms just as they did the storms that swept across the vineyard.

And one day, when the years had run their course, when his hands could no longer work the vines and his body had given all it could, he would wake for his last day on the land.

He'd stand beneath the wide sky, breathe in the scent of the earth, and smile.

He would feel the peace that only comes from a life well-lived, surrounded by the people he loved and who loved him in return.

And on that day, when his body could take no more, when he had lived his life to the fullest, he would look to the sky and be filled with happiness.

It would be time to see his son again.

THE END

AUTHOR'S NOTE:

As Joe and Wendy's adventure draws to a close, I wish to extend my deepest gratitude to the readers who have followed this journey. Writing these stories has been an incredible journey, and I'm truly humbled by the support and enthusiasm I've received along the way. Though Joe and Wendy's story has come to an end, these characters will always remain close to my heart. Thank you for allowing me to share this adventure with you and thank you for your support throughout the journey.

My new legal thriller series, set in Beaufort, South Carolina, launches in July 2025. The first book in this series is titled 'Reckoning Hour.' I hope you enjoy that series as well.

Best wishes,

Peter

RECKONING HOUR

Dean Lincoln Legal Thriller Book 1

Murder. Arson. Secrets. Justice is about to come home.

Big-city defense lawyer Dean Lincoln left his picturesque hometown of Beaufort years ago. But now, the lure of small-town life and a family matter have drawn him back.

Amidst the sultry heat and the Spanish moss, and beneath the facade of Southern small-town charm, Lincoln begins work again and is immediately thrown into two cases: a rich kid charged with murder and a poor kid accused of arson. Both swear they are innocent. Both feel the system is trying to crush them. And in this corner of the South, guilt is rarely decided in the courtroom…

Lincoln's return has stirred a long-standing grudge, and it could cost him everything—his career, his clients, even his life. As the clock runs out on the truth, trouble is closing in fast.

ALSO BY PETER O'MAHONEY

In the Joe Hennessy Legal Thriller series:

THE SOUTHERN LAWYER
THE SOUTHERN CRIMINAL
THE SOUTHERN KILLER
THE SOUTHERN TRIAL
THE SOUTHERN FRAUD

In the Dean Lincoln Series:

RECKONING HOUR
FATAL VERDICT

In the Tex Hunter Legal Thriller series:

POWER AND JUSTICE
FAITH AND JUSTICE
CORRUPT JUSTICE
DEADLY JUSTICE
SAVING JUSTICE
NATURAL JUSTICE
FREEDOM AND JUSTICE
LOSING JUSTICE
FAILING JUSTICE
FINAL JUSTICE

*****

In the Jack Valentine Series:

GATES OF POWER
THE HOSTAGE
THE SHOOTER
THE THIEF
THE WITNESS

Made in United States
Troutdale, OR
03/09/2025